THE ARMS OF DEATH

THE ARMS OF DEATH

MARK WAINWRIGHT

BLOOMSBURY

Many thanks to Joseph Goulden, whose book
The Death Merchants (Sidgwick and Jackson) provided
background material.

First published in Great Britain 1990

Copyright © Mark Wainwright 1990

Bloomsbury Publishing Ltd, 2 Soho Square, London W1V 5DE

A CIP catalogue record for this book is
available from the British Library.

ISBN 0 7475 0514 4

10 9 8 7 6 5 4 3 2 1

Filmset by Cambrian Typesetters,
Frimley, Surrey

Printed in Great Britain by Butler & Tanner Ltd,
Frome and London

Like any other explosives expert who has been released abruptly from the army and offered too much money to go and do something illegal in an unfriendly country, Halsey has his doubts. On the other hand it shouldn't be too difficult. As far as Halsey can tell it's just a simple training job; a specialist in the boom boom is required, he'd be 'doing his country a favor' and, in any case, he needs the money. As soon as he lands in Tripoli he knows he's screwed up – even the Cubans wanted nothing to do with *this* deal – but by then it's too late.

Elsewhere, in Paris a bomb explodes outside a synagogue, senators and generals gossip in Washington, arms dealers do what they always do, while things get heavier in Libya: the connection soon narrows down to one Jack O'Brien, the tin god with the golden wallet. But O'Brien, ex-marine and ex-CIA, has increasing problems of his own . . . As Halsey watches the crazies get crazier, and struggles to stay clear of the political and sexual intrigue seething around him, all he wants is out. But suddenly it's safer to stay in, especially with the ruthless but sexually inventive Marielle Bayer around . . .

Sharp, exciting and cynical, The Arms of Death is an explosive first thriller from a writer of huge promise.

FOR RICHARD NIXON, ALWAYS AN INSPIRATION

'Senseless terrorism is not as senseless as it may seem'
R M Nixon

Geneva

The way Ortega was telling it he was in the back of the Seville parked outside a motel somewhere in Arlington. The two of them were in the front and the fat one leaned back over the seat, thrust a pile of photos at him, and said, 'I want somebody killed.'

'Who is the fat one?' Martinez interrupted.

'I told you,' said Ortega.

'I just want to get it straight.'

'Katz.'

'Okay. Now go on and don't miss anything out.'

'The fat one, Katz, handed over the photos and said he wanted somebody killed. Or maybe it was the other way round with the photos. I don't remember. Then he talks about the money.'

'A million dollars.'

'A million dollars.'

'That is too much.' Martinez looked out towards the lake. A gray mist was rising, obscuring the mountains beyond.

'We've been over this I don't know how many times. You always say the same thing.' Ortega poured himself more coffee from a silver pot on the breakfast cart. 'This is good coffee. You should have some.'

'It's bad for my stomach. What did he say about the hit?'

'No details. Just the bag with the money and the expenses.'

'That was the second time you saw them. What about the first time?'

Ortega put his cup down and watched a lake steamer disappear. The smoke and the mist blending to become a cloak of invisibility. He was getting bored going over this. With a degree of impatience creeping into his voice he said, 'This person is not liked by a number of governments.'

'And you checked them out?'

I

'Mason told me they were kosher.' Ortega tried to make the statement final.

'What's kosher?'

'It's a Jewish word. Means clean.'

'Does that mean they are still working for the Agency?'

'Ask them yourself. You are going to meet them in – ' Ortega looked at his watch ' – fifteen minutes.' He got up from the table and put on the jacket to his beige summer-weight suit, lying on the bed. 'Listen,' said Ortega, emphasizing the word. 'If you don't like the proposition, why did you come?'

Martinez smiled, stood up and put his arm round his friend's shoulder. Standing together, the same build, they could have been brothers. 'I've never been to Switzerland and I wanted to learn to yodel.'

The two Cubans walked along the Quai du Mont Blanc at a leisurely pace in the direction of the station and the Hôtel Strasbourg-Univers. Turning away from the lake they stopped at a *tabac*. Ortega wanted Havana cigars. Martinez waited outside while Ortega went in and bought a box of Upmann Coronas and a copy of the *Herald Tribune*. When he left the shop he handed the paper to Martinez and briefly held the box open for him to take in the subtle blend of cedarwood and leaf before slipping it under his arm.

They arrived in the Rue Pradier early for their appointment. Ortega spoke with the man Katz on the internal phone and reported the conversation to Martinez.

'He says to get our asses up there.'

'I have not met this man and already I don't like him.'

Katz was there at the open door wearing a bathrobe. 'You want breakfast?'

The room was a mess. Food trays strewn around. Half-finished plates used as ashtrays. Clothes left lying over chairs. Martinez cleared a space at the table by the window and drew up a dining chair.

'I'm gonna order,' said Katz, picking up the phone. 'Yeah. Let me have lightly scrambled eggs, ham, english muffins – okay, croissants, and a coupla pots of coffee.' He put the phone down and started in the direction of the bathroom. 'I've got to take a crap.' He went into the bathroom and closed the door. 'You got the tools?'

Ortega wasn't sure if he'd heard. 'Tools? What tools?'

'For the job. You know the hit.'

Ortega looked at Martinez, raising his voice, he said, 'We don't have the tools.'

There was a pause. 'Well, no problem. We'll have breakfast, go over to the Libyan Consulate, pick out what you need.'

Martinez got up from the table and motioned to Ortega to come away from the door. They heard the sound of the cistern flush.

Martinez spoke softly. 'This does not sound kosher to me.'

Katz came out of the bathroom wearing only a pair of shorts with flying pink pigs printed on them, scratching at his white belly hanging over the waistband.

The breakfast cart arrived. Katz was looking for something to wear. He found a blue safari suit on the floor, took a dollar from the coat pocket and gave it to the waiter laying out the food on the table and stacking dirty dishes.

'That's okay, do that later.' He put on the blue pants, took a shirt from the back of a chair, sniffed the underarm and pulled it on over his head. 'Let's eat,' Katz said, clapping his hands in anticipation. He sat down at the table. 'Have some coffee.'

Martinez said, 'No coffee.'

Katz looked around. 'No fucking cups.' He got up and wandered round the room examining trays. He found what he wanted on top of the TV. There was a half-full cup of cold coffee, which he emptied over what remained of steak, beans and fries. He took the cup over to the table and poured fresh. 'Okay, let's take care of business.' Katz started putting away the food, talking and trying to keep his moustache out of his mouth. He pointed to an envelope lying on the table with his knife. 'Open it. You got an update on the photo and all the details there. This is a Libyan politician living down in Cairo. He's shooting his mouth off about the Libyan government. He's a trouble-maker and a revolutionary. The guy who runs Libya wants him shut up.'

Martinez looked at Ortega. He didn't need to say a word, Ortega understood perfectly.

Katz kept on going, taking their silence to mean approval. 'We have to do it right away.' He looked up from his breakfast. 'Go south right away.' Waving the knife.

'What do you mean?' said Martinez.

'You got to go south and do the hit.'

'Well, we are not prepared to go any place.' Martinez took the photograph together with the information sheet and put them back in the envelope.

'Are you jerking me around or what?' Katz got up from the table. Two hundred and forty pounds but not above average height. 'You have to go.' He was a good three inches shorter than Martinez, and Martinez was in good shape.

'I am not going any place.'

Martinez and Ortega sat at the bar of the Beau Rivage watching the lights coming on over Lake Geneva.

Katz came into the bar. He was wearing a white dinner jacket with a lace-front shirt and a purple velvet bow-tie. 'Let me buy you guys a drink,' said Katz. 'Just a sociable drink.' The Cubans ordered white wine and Katz a Jack Daniels. 'Make it a double. Ice.' Katz was in a good mood. He'd already put away a couple of cocktails and a bottle of wine with an early dinner.

' "Big Boy" is gonna be here tomorrow morning. I just got through talking with him on the phone. He'll iron out all your problems.'

'Who is big boy?' asked Martinez.

'It's code,' said Katz. 'It's his code name. You know "Big Boy", "Little Boy", va boom.' He laughed. The waiter brought the drinks. 'Are you drinking men?' They were drinking white wine so Katz figured they weren't. Too busy watching their weight. 'That's maybe a good thing.' He lifted the Jack Daniels and looked through the swirling ice. 'For a hundred a year . . .' He let the words hang and took a sip from the glass, savoring it. 'Those Chinks. I bet they could booby-trap the rocks in this glass. I seen a coathanger so like if you take a coat off it, it's the last coat you'll ever try on.' Katz finished the bourbon, slugging it down and ordered another. 'The Russians are good. You're gonna have to keep on your toes down there.'

'What Russians?' asked Martinez.

'The Russians and the Chinese. You're going to be working with.'

'Fucking Russians. I'm not working with no fucking communists.' Martinez standing up, spilling wine.

'There's no big problem. I've been invited to Russia,' said Katz.

'You got to be crazy – ' Martinez grabbed Katz's lapel ' – I got a

4

brother in jail by Castro. I don't go anyplace there are communists or Russians. They shoot my ass or I get killed trying to shoot them. I won't work with any son of a bitch communists. And I don't work with you because you are also a son of a bitch.' Martinez let go of an open-mouthed Katz and walked out of the bar, followed by Ortega. The audience of early evening drinkers returned to their Swiss insularity.

Katz said, 'Who needs those dumb spicks anyway?'

As they walked along the edge of the lake Martinez said, 'They're using the Cubans again.'

The next morning as Ortega and Martinez packed their bags the phone rang. Ortega took the call.

'Xavier, it's not as bad as Mr Katz is explaining. I'm really disappointed that you people don't want to be a part of this. There's a lot of money to be made.'

Ortega took a deep breath and exhaled slowly. 'There are more things in the world than money.' He put the phone down.

They finished packing. Martinez went over to the window. 'Maybe we could take a trip on the steamer around the lake.'

Ortega smiled. 'I want to call Washington.' He looked at his watch. 'I'll call Mason after lunch.'

Yodellehiho.

Washington DC

'We'll swing by the office and check on the cable traffic,' Schultz said. 'I'll introduce you all around. Then we can head on out to the farm. Someone wants to meet you.

'What do they call you? Nate?' Schultz made an effort to turn to the man sitting beside him as he nosed the blue BMW through the mid-morning traffic on Constitution Avenue. His fleshy neck appeared to be caught on the collar of a new gray Brooks Brothers suit.

Gray for sincerity.

He took his hand off the wheel and eased the collar with his index finger.

'Nathaniel?' said Schultz.

'They?'

'Whoever.'

'Halsey.'

'Okay. Halsey. Where are you from?'

'All over. I've never spent more than five years in any one place.'

'In that case you qualify. You won't expect a home from home.' Schultz eased the BMW into a vacant lot between two office buildings and pulled up outside a wood-plank hut set against a half-demolished wall. A kid came out aged no more than sixteen. Schultz leaned out the window. 'Where's Stevie?'

'The fuck knows,' said the kid.

Schultz got out of the car, taking the keys out of the ignition. He held them out in the palm of his hand. When the kid reached for them he clenched his fist. 'This is a new BMW 735i. I just had it waxed. Stevie usually parks it over by the wall away from the debris.' Having delivered this speech Schultz unclenched his fist, confident he'd made the point. The kid took the keys, no expression on his face.

Schultz and Halsey walked back to the street. Behind them they heard the sound of the car's engine being gunned. They turned in time to see the BMW going into a spin, slewing sideways, sending up a cloud of dust and stones. It disappeared down an incline into the pit beyond.

'Fuck it,' said Schultz, half to himself. And then to Halsey, 'You have to be a made man to get a parking space in this town.'

They had walked only a couple of blocks and Schultz was already sweating. He took out a blue and red silk handkerchief and wiped his forehead. 'I could lose a coupla pounds.' Halsey would have said if a couple was forty, he was about right. 'Executive lunches,' said Schultz, patting his stomach.

They turned on to K Street. 'Office is right around the corner.' Looking up at Halsey he winked. 'Handy for the White House.'

Behind a glass façade the lobby of the office building was lined with white, gray-veined Carrara marble. Schultz walked ahead towards a bank of elevators. He was striding purposefully, carrying his attaché case. Black and white suede, with his initials embossed in gold across the corner. He raised a hand in salute to a security guard standing behind a high desk off to the side.

They stood in silence waiting for the elevator. Halsey listened to the echoes of heavy leather shoes on marble. He had Schultz in the

6

corner of his eye. The door opened and two earnest-looking young men in matching blue suits marched out. They were having a conversation about IMF ballgrabbers. One of them pointing to a chart in the *Wall Street Journal*. They didn't look up as they crossed the floor still talking.

In the elevator Schultz pressed for eleven, looking at Halsey and smiling. Halsey examined the list of names of companies on the board above the floor buttons. They all had 'ology' in their title, as in technology and inter-technology, except International Commodities Inc on eleven. Schultz's smile was turning into a grin, creasing the small features of his face. Sixteen years in the army had taught Halsey not to figure a sense of humor.

They reached the eleventh floor and stepped out into a blue-carpeted hall. The walls white with blond oak doors at intervals. On the door opposite the elevator in bronzed metal lettering was the name 'International Commodities Inc'. Schultz walked ahead through the door into a small reception area. A young skinny woman wearing a mauve skirt and white blouse was bending, tearing off a telex from one of two machines in an alcove to the right.

Schultz said, 'Shit Crystal, if I catch you doing that again, I'm going to jump right in your panties.'

Crystal straightened up and without turning around started through the door to the inner office. 'Erwin,' she said in a bored tone, 'there's one asshole in there already.'

The line was delivered to an audience on the other side of the frosted glass partition that formed an enclosing wall to the reception area. There was a loud guffaw and a ripple of masculine laughter. Schultz reached out and put his hand on Halsey's arm. He lifted his eyes heavenwards. Halsey took that to mean Crystal loved to kid around and he took it all in good part. There was a brief pause, pressure to Halsey's elbow and they were through the door after Crystal.

She was handing the telex to a stocky man in his fifties. He looked at it and then up at Halsey. There were six desks in the office, which made it a little crowded. Only four of them were occupied, all by men in their mid-fifties but not in business suits. They wore casual clothes – sports shirts, slacks, and draped over chairs or hanging on the bentwood coat rack by the door were various plaid jackets.

'This is Nate Halsey,' said Schultz to no one in particular. 'Rear Admiral Gordon.' Indicating the man holding the telex with a nod of the head.

The admiral stood up without getting much taller. 'Welcome aboard.'

Halsey wasn't sure whether to offer his hand. The admiral reached behind him. He came back round with his jacket, slipping it on and moving out from the desk. He patted Halsey on the arm as he stepped past. 'Catch you on the back nine, Vince.' The admiral threw the remark over a plaid shoulder.

A thin silver-haired man over by the window looked up from his desk where he was applying tape to an old wooden putter. There was a three-day growth on his jowly jaw. Vince followed Halsey with his eyes as Schultz introduced him to Generals Kirby and Wolfsteen. Watching the mixed emotions. Resentment.

'This is General Bianali,' said Schultz.

'Call me Vince,' said Bianali, getting up to shake Halsey by the hand. 'What's your speciality, sergeant.'

'The boom boom,' said Halsey. 'And the name is Halsey.'

'At ease, Halsey.' Bianali sat down and picked up an unlit cigar lying beside a box of golf balls.

Schultz said, 'The admiral putting together another deal?'

'The little fucker is laying some piece of ass,' said Bianali. 'Probably my wife.' He held up the cigar to subdue the laughter. 'I would appreciate he'd do that for me.' Bianali smiled and chewed on the cigar as the laughter erupted.

Halsey was thinking he'd walked into a summer camp for generals.

'At 11.30 in the a.m.' said Bianali. 'Where does he get the energy?' The generals were laughing again.

Schultz steered Halsey into an adjoining office almost as large as the first. He put his attaché case down on a heavy mahogany double desk in the center of the room. 'They're a barrel of laughs.' There was contempt in Schultz's voice, as though he thought generals should behave in a more seemly manner.

Halsey realized that Schultz was never in the army; generals behaved how they pleased. He looked around. The style reminded him of the Oval office. There were Audubon bird prints in silver gilt frames hanging on the white-painted panelled walls, a photograph of the President taking the oath of allegiance squarely behind the desk, by the window a dark oak rocker and standing in the corner the Stars and Stripes.

Schultz was leaning on the desk making a call. There were two phones, a red and a white. He had the red receiver close to his ear. When Halsey tried to say something to him he held up his hand for silence and circled round to face the windows.

'Jack.' A pause. 'Yeah. I'm calling from the office.'

Halsey was beginning to get pissed off with Schultz. What was this game he was playing? He acted as though he was running this show. His office, his generals there.

'I'll check with Crystal. She would have told me though.' Schultz listened for a while, coming back to face Halsey. 'No. No news from the sandbox.' He smiled. There it was again, that damn smile.

'Okay. Okay.' That was final. Schultz put the phone down and stood up straight, opening up his body, indicating that he was now giving his full attention to Halsey. 'Let's hit the road.' He picked up his case, making for the door. Halsey followed him into an empty office. 'Three hours is a heavy day around here. They're off for a shot before lunch at the Army and Navy on Faragut Square.'

They walked through to the reception area where Crystal sat at her desk reading *Newsweek*. She looked up and smiled at Halsey.

'Is there anything happening that I should know about?' said Schultz.

'The Russians want to get back to the arms talks and I have a heavy period.'

Schultz clutched the attaché case to his side and took hold of the door handle.

'Out to lunch?'

Schultz opened the door. 'I'm out to the farm. Keep me in touch.'

'There isn't much to this job. I know how to operate a telex machine and use a phone. I also know how to take a joke.' Crystal shook her head slowly. Schultz was across the hall without turning around, pressing the button to call the elevator. The door closed automatically. Crystal and Halsey said their goodbyes. 'Take care now,' she said.

Schultz was holding the elevator, drumming impatiently on the console with his fingers. They descended four floors before Schultz felt the need to speak again. 'After lunch they're down to the golf course at Burning Tree or wherever.'

Halsey realized he was talking about the generals. That Schultz got a kick out of talking about the generals.

Stevie came out of the hut when he saw Halsey and Schultz walk on to the lot. 'Mr Schultz. I'll get your car.'

Halsey noticed the left sleeve of his combat jacket rolled back. There was no forearm. His hand seemed to be attached at the elbow.

The BMW came up the slope towards them at a funereal pace, braking gently level with the hut and stopping alongside Schultz. Stevie reached over and opened the door with his right hand, rolling out of the seat.

Schultz walked around the car checking for dents and chipped paintwork. 'Who was the kid here earlier?'

Stevie looked embarrassed. 'Yeah. See, he's married to my sister.'

Schultz understood the problem. 'It's tough being in business.' He slipped him a ten and a five. Stevie held the door open and Schultz got behind the wheel. Halsey went round to the other side. He got in and closed the door. The car took off and Halsey was thrown forward, hitting his head on the windshield as Schultz braked at the sidewalk.

'The pedal is a little sticky sometimes. I have to get it fixed.' The lunchtime traffic was moving slowly. Schultz directed the car west on New York Avenue. 'This your first time in the capital?' This was the second time Schultz had asked this same question. Before, on the way in from Dulles International. Halsey looked out the window. He came back with another question.

'So what kind of deals are they putting together?' Halsey made it sound casual.

'Little of this, little of that. You see they can't go into business for themselves. Against government regulations. They're restricted.'

'First you got to understand how this town works. There's no graft here, no peddling. What there is is you scratch my back and then there's a long line of people scratching until you get to the fella who is going to do your a favor. What the generals do is operate an influence brokerage. They pass on information and if that gets turned into cash, they get their percentage.'

'And that's Commodities Inc?' Halsey hoped Schultz would carry it from there now that he was up and running.

'We've got the international trading arm. Exporting manufactured goods. Then we have the exportation of services.'

The car crossed Roosevelt Bridge and turned north along the Memorial Parkway, shadowing the Potomac. Halsey, glancing across Schultz, had a sight of the Marine Memorial. He thought about his brother in the cemetery beyond.

'Communications technology. We're big in technology and information.'

'You don't have technology in the name.' Halsey remembered the list of companies in the elevator.

'That's because our business has a broad base and we wouldn't want to limit our horizons.'

This guy was an asshole. It made Halsey nervous thinking that he might be going to work for Schultz.

The car changed direction, leaving the river west again on Dolley Madison. Halsey stopped listening to Schultz. He watched the road, noticing the signpost for Vienna. The only thing Halsey knew was he'd been told by his commanding officer to call a certain number, and that earning a dollar might also be in the interests of his country. Good money. EOD. His line of work, the boom boom. Training, nothing dangerous. He needed the money for Eva and his kid. He had to have money for the divorce. If this worked out, make a cash settlement. If it didn't . . . If he didn't like the offer he could walk away.

These people had approached him. 'What's your job?' said Halsey, keeping the conversation going. He listened to Schultz but not for meaning.

'I'm an expediter. I iron things out, try and make sure the business runs smoothly.' Schultz slipped a Dolly Parton tape in the stereo. 'You like Country and Western?' Halsey said he did just to be amenable. 'When I play this tape I can see those big titties jumping up and down. Right in front of me.'

They were now in suburban Virginia, green and leafy. 'Hey, headquarters,' said Schultz jerking his head sideways.

Halsey looked. He thought he could see a sign that showed an emblem of some kind and words saying Central Intelligence Agency. So far Schultz had shown Halsey a Masonic ring. No, Schultz'd asked if Halsey knew about the Freemasons. Then the ring. When Halsey had asked why the questions, Schultz had said he wanted to see how Halsey would react to interrogation. On the phone speaking to Schultz they had talked about money. That was easy to understand. At the airport Schultz had given him a coin with an Arab inscription and said, 'Every one of our people carries one of these so he can establish trust with another operative.'

Now this was all mumbo jumbo. What added up was his discharge going right through. And the idea that Schultz was a front for an intelligence operation.

Beyond Vienna, past Fairfax, out across country on the Interstate 66 going towards the Shenandoah Valley. The car cruising at sixty, Schultz's mouth faster and Dolly Parton trying to compete.

The car turned down a back road lined with trees, hickory, cottonwoods and oaks, mostly. Set on the road a big white gate and over the gate in black gothic lettering, Mount Angus Farm. As they rode up the winding driveway Halsey begain adding up the acreage.

'Who does this farm belong to?'

'A good friend of mine,' said Schultz.

The farmhouse itself stood on a rise overlooking an artificial lake. The farmhouse didn't look real either. There were no farm buildings, but an International Harvester tractor was parked on the gravel in front. Schultz pulled up alongside the tractor. A pickup was approaching them along a track from buildings in the lee of two spreading oak trees. It was a new Suzuki in vomit yellow. Schultz walked towards the oncoming truck as it slowed, stopping where the track met the drive. A tall well-built man in his forties got out. He was wearing a workshirt, Levis and cowboy boots. Taking a twelve-gauge shotgun from the cab he broke the barrel, picked up an ammunition belt and came over to where Halsey stood by the car. Schultz tailed behind.

'Jack O'Brien.' O'Brien reached out his hand, fixing Halsey with pale blue eyes. The handshake was firm. 'I only hear good things.'

Halsey saw Schultz out of the corner of his eye. There was a dog-like expression on his face. Heavy, with a mournful look about the eyes. O'Brien, the object of devotion, led the way into the house around by the back.

'We have to go in this way or my wife gives me hell.' Halsey liked the easy way of the remark.

They entered a large kitchen dominated by a big refectory table with an old stove down one end under a brick chimney and new cherrywood glass-fronted cabinets lining the walls. O'Brien rested the gun on the table, kicked off his boots and carried the gun through into the hall. There was a curving staircase leading to the upper floors and at the base of the stairs a long case clock.

'Get Mr Halsey a drink, I'll be right with you.' O'Brien left Halsey and Schultz standing in front of double doors slightly ajar, and disappeared through a doorway off to the left. Halsey followed Schultz into what had to be the main room of the house. It was tasteful, he could see that. Dove gray walls, oriental rugs, two sofas with a Chinese bird design facing each other at right angles to the marble fireplace.

Schultz asked Halsey if he wanted a drink, 'It's got to be bourbon or beer. I don't know how to fix anything else.' He was standing by a side table with crystal decanters, three of them in an inlaid box, silver tags round the necks. 'Bourbon, scotch, gin.'

'Bourbon is fine.'

Schultz poured generous measures into heavy lead crystal tumblers and handed one to Halsey. He stood there with a smile creasing his face, the bounds of his generosity limitless with someone else's bourbon. They moved over to the marble fireplace. Standing, listening to the French ormolu clock on the mantel shelf. Halsey sipped his drink. Very smooth. He made a point of refusing a refill and carried his glass around the room as he examined the paintings. Gilt frames, subdued colors, illuminated. The only comment he felt confident in making was that they were early American. Schultz was helping himself to another large bourbon. He started telling Halsey about the hunting. Deer hunting at night with a pickup and a spotlight, catching them in the beam. Hitting a buck from seven hundred yards the other night. Halsey thought it was odds the guy couldn't hit a barn door from seven feet with a scatter gun. As he listened he began to wonder whether O'Brien would reappear. He'd have to endure Schultz. Sure that Schultz could keep this up.

'One time we had a senator out here. Fat little fella.'

Senators and generals, the farm. This was money and influence.

Halsey had the feeling that O'Brien must be a shaker and a mover in Washington.

'In the pickup being pursued by the law.'

'The law?' Halsey interrupted.

'Game warden. I beat him over the hill, killed the lights and skidded the pickup into the ditch.' Schultz looked to Halsey for approval. 'I had to drag the senator out. He just sat there shitting himself. Pushed the fella over a wall and dragged him back to the house. The warden came by. Jack was here. He opens the door, "What's that? Never heard of the truck," and gets heavy, "Fucking poachers on my land. You go out and nail those bastards." Like that. Yeah.' Remembering, almost crying, Schultz thought it was so funny. He had a drink.

'Can you believe it? You can't even shoot on your own goddamn land.' He snorted, indignant, and emptied his glass.

'When are we going to get down to business?'

Schultz went over to the drinks' table and picked up the decanter, before turning and saying he thought it was all settled. He didn't see the look on Halsey's face as he poured the scotch.

'This is a single malt. Not blended. Made on the Isle of Jura in Scotland.' It seemed to Halsey that Schultz had a way of getting to him – or maybe it was just being on edge. This was important. He needed the job, which meant being polite to Schultz. If he had to go to work for Schultz, then fuck it. He didn't need the job that badly.

O'Brien came through the door, apologizing for neglecting Halsey.

'I had some calls to make.' O'Brien poured himself a gin and lifted the lid off the ice bucket. The fact that there was no ice didn't seem to bother him. 'This is a habit I picked up in the navy.' And then, not pausing, as though it was the same thought, 'Now, you've had a preliminary briefing.' Halsey didn't think he had unless what Schultz had said was a briefing. He let it go. O'Brien said, 'What we have is an operating proprietary in the Middle East handling demolition and the sale of explosives. It's a simple cover company.'

O'Brien began talking about what he called 'the operation', keeping it low key, not referring to government, government agencies, but the implication was there. It sounded more and more like CIA.

Halsey thought about what his commanding officer had said about 'national interest'. Earning a dollar and serving your country.

'You'll get a ticket.' O'Brien didn't talk about a destination.

'A return ticket?' Halsey asked. O'Brien ignored the question. Halsey didn't want to make an issue of the ticket. He was getting an advance of five thousand. O'Brien's manner was tough. What he said had authority. But he didn't pull rank.

'Who am I working for?'

'Me,' said O'Brien, looking right at Halsey. 'You're working for me. We don't have a contract. Nothing on paper. This is the deal.' He took a long pull at the gin. 'The deal is if I welsh you'll come looking for me.' He paused and straightened up. 'Looking to kill me. If you welsh I'll be coming after you. That's our contract.'

When O'Brien had finished speaking he waited to make sure he'd been understood, not encouraging questions, before going over to the table with the bar.

'Let's have a drink.' O'Brien took each of the decanters in turn, filling two clean glasses and refilling his own. He handed them round and offered a toast. 'Here's to a good and profitable relationship.' Raising his glass. 'If things work out there'll be big bonuses.' He turned to Schultz. 'Am I right?' Slapping him on the back, O'Brien upended the glass and put it down on a low granite table, the only obviously new piece in the room. He turned to leave, saying to Schultz that Halsey should have anything he wanted and to Halsey that he was sorry he had an important business meeting that couldn't be rescheduled.

'You take good care of him,' said O'Brien, 'show him around the farm.' Facing them as he closed the double doors.

Schultz had the decanter in his hand. 'Get it while you can.' The last of the bourbon. 'How about a beer?'

That seemed like a good idea. Halsey was feeling very sober thinking about his next move. He followed Schultz out towards the kitchen and down the back stairs to a low-ceilinged cellar. There was a heavy steel door at the foot of the stairs, standing open, and steel panelling around the walls and lining the ceiling. The cellar appeared to stretch the whole length and width of the house but there wasn't much floor space. A row of bunks took up one wall. K rations and tinned goods covered a large area. A small Honda generator flanked by drums of gasoline stood beneath some kind of ducting. Schultz opened a big old Westinghouse refrigerator. It was stacked with Schlitz.

'In case of emergencies.' Schultz passed Halsey a beer and put his glass in the space left by the can while he pulled the tab on another. 'Hey. Why don't we do a little hunting? We have all the equipment. Guns.'

In a subdivided section about twelve feet square there was the armory, every kind of small arms, handguns, sporting rifles, right the way through to a grenade launcher. Halsey picked up a side-by-side shotgun. It was hand-made, he could tell. Running his palm along the walnut stock, over the engraving of two pheasants. On the side of the locks the name of the gunmaker, Jas Purdey & Sons.

'You're not going to believe how much that cost.'

Schultz was taking the opportunity to give Halsey the benefit of his knowledge of guns. The gun looked like one of those Japanese imports or the other way round. This was the original, unique. Each piece of the gun numbered. How they used to make guns, before Colt came along.

Schultz sucking on his beer and slapping his gut. 'Made to order. They make maybe thirty a year.' Waiting to deliver the next line, giving it space, waiting for Halsey to make some half-assed guess. 'Forty thousand dollars American.'

Halsey put the gun back in the rack. He noticed a Sharps-Borchardt rifle, very rare, tempting him to pick it up. Instead he took a Mauser machine pistol and pointed it at Schultz.

'Hey take it easy. That thing may be loaded.' Schultz stepped back a pace, lifting his hand to protect himself.

Halsey gave him his mean killer steely-eyed stare. 'Where is it I'm flying to?'

Schultz, nervous. 'Shit. I can't tell you that.'

It was very quiet. The only sound the whine from the refrigerator. In the silence came the click of the Mauser on an empty chamber. Halsey smiled. Schultz smiled, seeing it was a joke. Halsey put the gun in the rack and went back into the main cellar over to the Westinghouse.

'You had me worried for a moment there.' Schultz was trying to recover. 'Let's go eat something. Ham'n eggs? I'm a damn good cook. Then we can take a look round the farm.' He gave Halsey a moment. 'I could use another beer myself.'

Halsey came away from the wall of Schlitz carrying two cans and gave one to Schultz, kicking the door shut behind him. Schultz started looking in the cardboard cartons on the floor. He found what he was looking for, a bottle of Wild Turkey.

'We have all we need right here,' said Schultz. He reached into another carton and came up with a packet. 'Ham'n eggs.' He tossed the packet at Halsey, laughing as Halsey caught it.

Halsey followed Schultz up the stairs seeing a sign, a plaque above the doorway, 'See you in Armageddon'. He stopped at the head of the staircase hearing voices. A woman saying something about you never give me any consideration, you invite anyone you damn well please. As they reached the hall the clock was striking three. The voices seemed to be coming from the upper floors. Schultz stood beside Halsey, listening. They heard O'Brien getting loud.

'Who the fuck owns this house, goddamn it?'

'Elaine,' said Schultz. He offered no further explanation and drifted off towards the kitchen. The shouting faded away.

In the kitchen Schultz had taken off his suit jacket, now hanging over the back of a chair. He had on an apron with a woman's body wearing a black brassiere and black lacy panties. Halsey could see that Schultz was unsteady on his feet.

Halsey leaned on the door jamb. 'You have the number of a cab?'

'You don't like ham'n eggs?' Schultz swung around, his eyes small and bloodshot.

'I'm Jewish. Where's the phone?'

Schultz tried hard to make the connection, forgetting the question. 'I'm sorry.'

'Where's the phone?' Halsey was becoming impatient, bored. He wanted to get out. Get away from Schultz and his bullshit.

'Phone's in the office.' Schultz pointed in the direction of the front of the house.

The office looked empty. Wooden panelling, a leather-topped writing table with two telephones, one red, one black. Halsey sat down at the table and tried the drawers. Both locked. He looked up at the wall facing. There was a photograph in a carved frame. It showed O'Brien standing beside a tractor. O'Brien smiling at the tractor. Schultz came through the door holding his wallet in one hand and a glass in the other. He put the glass on the table, oh so carefully. Not spilling a drop. From the wallet he took a business card with gold edging and handed it to Halsey. 'Clark's Limousines' printed in bold type and 'Travel in Style' in italics.

'My brother-in-law,' said Schultz. He picked up the drink. 'I have a piece of the company.' Smiling inanely.

Halsey dialled the number on the card and waited for someone to pick up the phone. He glanced over at the tractor and realized it was the same one parked out in front. 'Nice tractor.'

Schultz said, 'Jack's a farm boy. Hell, he loves that tractor.'

Halsey ordered the limo and then went back to the kitchen where Schultz was standing at the stove cracking eggs into a big pan.

'You wanna change your mind?'

'About what?' asked Halsey.

'Eating. What did you think? About the deal?'

Hasley wasn't paying attention. 'Why would I do that?'

'It happens,' Schultz said.

'Once I decide to go through with something . . .'

'I'll come by in the morning with the ticket and the money.'

'Do that.' Halsey heard the sound of a car on the gravel.

'That'll be the limo.'

'And we were having such a good time.' Something Halsey didn't say.

'Ten o'clock,' said Schultz.

'Fine.'

Schultz's brother-in-law said call me George and gave Halsey a tour of the farm in the black Lincoln Town Car, all the time giving a running commentary on points of interest and the history of the car's mechanical defects.

'I bought this off a guy who runs a funeral home in Manassas. Been on the graveside and back. Where can I go wrong?'

'They got a heated pool there and a tennis court that lights up at night. Though why the fuck you'd wanna play tennis at night beats me.

'Where can I go wrong? Buying this heap of shit I can go wrong. The transmission is shot. The suspension is fucked. This car has been to hell and back. That's got to be around the clock and a rough ride.

'How many acres you figure this is? Five hundred, a thousand?' George turned and looked over his shoulder, then back in time to avoid a tree stump. 'Close.' Straightening the car out. 'Lemme tell you. Over two thousand acres, two thousand three hundred, something like that. Corn, grain, pastures, horses, prize herd. Over there, sports complex. Sauna, jacuzzi, handball court. You name it. The guy has money. Throws it around like he's got no arms. You get my meaning. Lives like he's on welfare.' The suspension grated as the car hit the ramp at the gate. George swore under his breath. 'Did he tell you he owns a piece of the company?' George looked in the mirror.

'Schultz?'

'Yeah, my brother-in-law.'

'He said that.'

'Gave me the money for this. Now he's squeezing me for a return on his investment.' Then with some venom, 'I'd like to return his fucking investment.'

George lapsed into silence and Halsey asked a question. 'Are you going around the Parkway?'

'What, the Washington Memorial? Sure, if you wanna go the scenic route.'

'No I don't. We came out that way.'

'Who with? Some cab. You were ripped off. That's thirty miles outta your way.'

So why had Schultz gone thirty miles out of his way? It was difficult to figure out. Halsey had to assume it was so he could say 'Headquarters'. Maybe Schultz just couldn't resist bragging. Probably telling his dumb girlfriends, 'I have these generals working for me.' What Halsey should do was check it out.

George said, 'Jack O'Brien's wife is a real bitch. Thinks she's the First Lady. Can't blame Jack for screwing around.' He was in his stride again, running stories together as though they were one seamless narrative.

They were crossing the Rochambeau bridge and going up Fourteenth Street past the Washington Monument. The White House disappearing behind the Commerce building. On up Fourteenth Street making a left on to K.

The Capital Hilton, a big canopy in front. A white stretch Mercedes was leaving. The Lincoln came to a halt with some dignity and style. George turned and delivered a little speech,

'I hope you had a pleasant ride. If you need a car while you're here in Washington . . .' Handing over one of his gold-edged cards.

Halsey checked in. The girl at the desk, whose name-tag introduced her as Ms Annabelle Wright, gave him her best if-there's-anything-else look. Halsey narrowed his eyes and took the offered key.

The man in the cane chair, reading the *Post*, kept glancing at the reception desk. He waited until Halsey was on his way to the elevator before folding the paper carefully and pushing up on the arms of the chair, taking his weight on his left leg as he pivoted round to bring himself upright. He started towards the elevator, then changed his mind and went over to the desk.

'Did Mr Halsey check in?'

Ms Wright could smell stale whisky. She looked up from the desk seeing a red-haired man with red blotchy skin wearing a slept-in worsted suit.

'Mr Halsey. Yes. He just checked in.'

The man nodded, rocking back, holding on to the counter. Ms Wright was slightly embarrassed. He thanked her and left in the direction of the bar, limping.

Halsey sat on the bed in his room, resting his arms on his knees and staring at the floor. He had the number of the CIA at Langley from enquiries written on the pad by the phone. He looked around at the green walls, the black oriental furniture, and listened to the traffic on 16th Street, trying to make a decision to pick up the phone and dial the number. In the army you didn't have to think for yourself. It was easy, made life easy.

The phone was answered by a woman who wanted to know why he was calling. He started to feel foolish, trying to explain. Before he managed to make sense of what he was saying the line clicked and a man's voice said, 'My name is Smith. How can I help you?'

Halsey began again. This time with more conviction. 'I'm on active duty military. I don't know what this is. It's possible I could be working for a foreign government. I don't know if I'm talking about subversion but I would appreciate some guidance.'

Smith listened carefully, not interrupting. When Halsey had finished he said, 'Just let me take down a few details, Mr Halsey, starting with your name, rank and so on.'

Halsey began with what he knew, explaining everything in a time-order sequence. It didn't add up to much. He concluded with a question. 'Is this a CIA operation?'

Smith said. 'You're at the Hilton now. Look why don't I do some checking and call you back.'

'Yeah. Okay.'

'There's just one more thing Mr Halsey. You say you've known about this for some weeks now. Why haven't you contacted us before?' Smith paused but, without giving Halsey time to reply he said, 'Expect my call,' and hung up.

Fuck him, who did this guy think he was, turning it around? Halsey walked over to the window and back to the writing table, caught sight of the headed paper and sat down to write a letter. Halsey didn't get beyond 'Dear Willi' before he stopped and screwed up the sheet. It was his son's birthday coming up next month and if he caught the plane in the morning there wouldn't be time to mail him a present. He took out his wallet, found a hundred dollar bill and slipped it in an envelope which he then addressed to Santa Barbara. Halsey hoped his mother would let the boy spend the money. He held the wallet open looking at a photo. Willi with Eva leaning over his shoulder and straightening the Yankees baseball cap. William was named for Eva's father Wilhelm Ganz. Maybe he'd write Eva, send her a postcard from wherever. What he had to do was get her address from his mother. If he couldn't think of what to write Willi he'd just say happy birthday and send the money. Even call him on his birthday. Willi would say, 'Where are you?'

Halsey took a shower. Showers always made him feel good. As soon as the hot water hit his body, the jet stimulating his skin.

He walked out of the bathroom wearing a towel around the waist and went over to the window. Now was the time he needed a cigarette. A pack of Luckies. Breaking the seal and getting that aroma of fresh tobacco. The traffic on 16th Street was getting heavy. Halsey could see all the way down to Lincoln Park, cars with their taillights in the semi-darkness.

Whatever happened, whatever he decided, he was going to have a good meal on Jack O'Brien. Halsey put on his Levis, a blue sports shirt and black tasselled loafers. He took out of the closet a dark blue blazer, double breasted with gold buttons. He slipped it on, looking in the mirror. The blue of the outfit made his eyes look bluer. Running his hand around his face and feeling the stubble he wondered if there would be any gray in his beard. Halsey thought about Jack O'Brien, shaking hands. He reached out as though to shake his own hand in the mirror and then looked down at the real hand in front of him, turning it over, suntanned.

The phone rang. He picked it up on the second ring. 'Halsey.'

'This is John Smith. May I come up, Mr Halsey?'

Halsey went over to the desk, picked up his wallet and straightened out the papers. There was a quiet knock at the door. Halsey stepped over and opened it. John Smith stood, legs apart, hands clasped.

'Mr Halsey.' Smith smiled. 'I was on my way to a meeting.'

Halsey leant forward and gave the offered hand a brief pressure. 'Come in.' Waving his arm in a slack gesture.

Smith had on a dark chalk-stripe business suit, a white button-down shirt with a green paisley tie. The impression of a young executive was completed with black wing-tips.

'Is your name really Smith?'

'Really,' said Smith, producing his ID card. He was in his late twenties, possibly younger, Halsey thought. His manner made him seem older.

'What did you find out?'

'Let me ask you a question first.'

'Go ahead.'

'Who was your contact?'

'Contact?'

'The first person to talk to you about this.'

'My commanding officer.'

Smith nodded sagely. He walked away from Halsey towards the window. 'The computer drew a blank.'

'What does that mean?'

Smith turned around. 'The fact is the computer blocked.'

Halsey thought about that and came to the only possible conclusion. 'This is a CIA operation?'

'I didn't say that.' Smith looked defensive.

'What did you say?' Halsey was getting annoyed, realizing he wasn't going to get a straight answer.

After a pause Smith said, 'My advice to you is to pursue this as you see fit.'

'Tell me this. Is O'Brien CIA?'

'He's no longer with the Agency.' Trying to say it without any inflexion. Smith caught sight of the envelope on the table. 'Your son's birthday.' He picked the letter up by the corner and dropped it back on the table. 'It's a shame you won't be there.'

Halsey assumed that the statement was some sort of affirmation but said nothing.

'Tell me,' Smith wandered over to the window again, his back to the room. 'Do you still communicate with your wife?'

'I haven't seen her in two, three years. She calls our son mostly or writes him letters. I had a card, Christmas.' Halsey thought about it. 'Why'd you ask?'

'Seeing your son's letter.' Smith walked towards Halsey, reaching out his hand. 'Pleased to meet you, Mr Halsey.'

'Is that what they teach you out at Langley,' remembering O'Brien's easy manner.

'Pardon?' said Smith.

'Nothing.'

When Halsey called Eddie Kozinski and told him that he was at the Capital Hilton, in town for one night, Eddie said he'd be right over. They arranged to meet in Trader Vic's. Halsey was sitting there with a Mai Tai in front of him when Kozinski walked in. He stood up and the two men embraced. Kozinski shorter, heavier, with black hair and beard.

'Hey, what are you drinking?' said Halsey.

'What do you drink in a Hawaiian paradise?'

'Mai Tai,' said Halsey, and attracted the attention of the waiter. 'Two of these.'

'How's your ass, fella?'

'I'm getting my ass on out of the army and over to Africa.'

'Africa?'

The last time Halsey had seen Kozinski was at China Lake down in the Mojave desert. Kozinski was working for the CIA in the weapons division. Halsey was down there on a detached duty assignment discussing secondary timers.

'Yeah, Africa,' said Halsey.

'Sounds interesting. Pay good?'

'Ninety thousand and a bonus.'

'You're shitting me?'

Halsey finished his first drink.

'You ain't,' said Kozinski. He began searching his pockets for a pack of cigarettes. Found some Pall Malls in the right hand pocket of his tweed sports coat. 'You want one of these? No, I forgot, you quit.' He took one out and tapped the end on his thumb and put it in his mouth. Only then did he begin to look for a light.

'It seems to me that for a guy who is pulling down seventeen hundred bucks a week you don't look too happy. What's the drawback? It's in a harem and you have to have your balls off first?'

Halsey thought about what was worrying him. 'You know Ashby?' Kozinski nodded. 'Had me in his office one day, says, "How'd you like to go to work in Africa. I don't know what they're doin' but it pays heavy dust," says, "Call this number," gives me a piece of paper, says, "Also be doin' your patriotic duty." So I call the number. Talk to a guy. Guy calls me, tells me his name is Schultz and he's willing to pay ninety thousand. I fly into Washington, meet this jerk Schultz, who takes me out to this two-thousand-acre spread in Loudon county owned by a guy, name of O'Brien, who might be the head of this organization. He tells me there are things he can't tell me. All I need to know is training. They'll let me know where. I get a five thousand advance and a ticket. And I forgot to mention O'Brien is ex-CIA.'

'If you want my opinion,' said Mason, talking at the phone from the other side of the room.

He was interrupted by the voice distorting through the speaker, 'I'm getting advice.'

Mason was pacing up and down past a wall of leather-bound books. Meticulously brushing the black dinner jacket he was wearing, talking to the phone on the desk. 'You fucked up. Am I right?' Mason waited for a reply but the voice didn't answer. 'I'm the one who has to clean up the shit.'

The voice conciliatory, 'Look, I didn't fuck up.' Then angry, 'It was that jerk Katz.'

'Which is where I come to the advice: dump the fucker.' Mason listened for another voice off.

'The car's here, Bill.'

Mason went over to the fireplace and looked in the gilt mirror. He straightened his black silk bow-tie.

The voice said, 'He's in solid with the number two man.'

'That's your problem. I'm offering my advice.' Mason turned away from the mirror. 'Just remember your problems are not my problems. I hope I make myself clear.'

'Listen, I'll call you tomorrow.'

'In the meantime,' said Mason, 'talk to Ortega.' The connection went dead. Mason looked in the mirror thinking how young he looked. He looked boyish, if a forty-two-year-old man can look boyish. Blond curly hair, a broad open face and a seraphic smile.

Halsey and Kozinski had dinner at the hotel in the continental ambience of Twigs where they had steaks and imported Guinness in an urban woodland glade – tree trunk tables, a twig cloth and a carpet of leaves. The waiter, in a black vest and white apron, wondered if they would like coffee. Kozinski wanted to know if they could finish up the meal with nuts and berries. The waiter said he didn't think they had any but he'd ask in the kitchen.

When the waiter had gone, Kozinski said, 'You never leave the CIA. It's like a brotherhood. The Elks and the Masons.'

Halsey thought about Schultz showing him the ring and talking about Masonic rites. Thinking what the fuck do the Masons have to do with the CIA?

'You know,' said Kozinski in measured tones, 'someone here has been using their imagination. Some faggot has been co-ordinating the delicate shades of the forest to achieve this subtle statement in green and brown.'

They moved to the bar and switched to bourbon.

'Take the fucking money. Take the money and if it's not kosher, get on the next flight out,' Kozinski said. 'Order us a couple more. And a couple of beers. I have to take a piss.'

Halsey looked over towards the baby grand-piano. A woman in a black cocktail dress was leaning over the keyboard, picking out a few notes of 'Blues in the Night'. There was something about the way she held her head on one side, the curve of her neck, that reminded him of Eva. Why was he thinking about Eva? He leant back in the chair and a blotchy face came into his line of vision.

'I've been waiting for you.'

'And you had a few drinks while you were waiting.'

'Your name's Halsey.' Reaching out his hand, he said, 'I'm, I'm Michael Lynch.'

Halsey shook his clammy limp hand, trying to be sociable.

Lynch said, 'You don't know me.'

'Let's keep it that way.'

'Listen,' getting insistent, 'listen, I have to tell you – ' rephrasing it ' – I've got to tell you about International Commodities . . . International Commodities. Katz. You know Katz. Fat, big moustache.'

'I haven't met Katz. I never heard of the guy. I have no idea what you're talking about. Now I'm trying to have a quiet drink.'

One of the cocktail waiters came over and said directly to Halsey, 'Is everything all right?' Lynch made an attempt to brush the waiter aside, stepping in front of him to regain Halsey's attention.

'Jack O'Brien. You know Jack O'Brien.'

Halsey was puzzled. Who was this guy?

The waiter had a pissed-off expression on his face. 'I'm going to have to ask you to leave, sir.' He put his hand on Lynch's arm, trying to lead him away. Lynch took a swing at the waiter and fell on his ass. Halsey made a move to get up and help Lynch back to his feet. The waiter was there already, apologizing for bumping into him. 'Let me call you a cab, sir. The hotel will pay.'

It was then that Halsey noticed the wooden leg.

Lynch was adjusting the prosthesis, shouting, 'Too damn right, the hotel's gonna pay.' Lynch stood up helped by the waiter. I'm going to sue the ass off Conrad Hilton.' Lynch leant on the waiter, turned and looked over his shoulder. He laughed.

'Who was that guy?' said Kozinski.

'Never seen him before in my life. But he seems to know me.'

Kozinski sat down. 'Where are those drinks?' Another waiter came over and took their order. He apologized, looking solemn, saying this kind of incident shouldn't happen in the bar of the Capital Hilton Hotel.

When the waiter slid away, Kozinski said, 'You don't look outraged.'

'Maybe he had something to say.'

'You got time to listen to every drunk comes along and wants to give you a piece of advice?'

'He knows who I am. Said he knew Jack O'Brien, the guy I met today.'

The drinks arrived, compliments of the management. Kozinski lifted his glass. 'I was gonna tell you about this job I got but on reflection I don't think I will. I might get to thinking about seventeen hundred a week and the asshole I work for. So I'll give you a toast.'

Halsey lifted his glass of bourbon, getting ready.

'Fuck 'em. Take the money. Fuck 'em.' The two men emptied their glasses, the ice rattling around. 'And,' said Kozinski, 'if there's another opening for a fat — ' he belched ' — balding guy who can't stand to look at his old lady, you have my number.'

Halsey was up at seven a.m. A matter of habit. He took a shower, shaved and packed his bag, leaving out a pair of chinos, his old Weejuns and a pale blue Penneys featherweight jacket laid out on the bed. He took his passport from a side pocket and tossed it on top of the jacket then zippered up the bag. He dressed slowly, standing by the window looking out at cars, pedestrians, the regular masses of buildings. There was a feeling that Halsey couldn't shake off. A feeling of darkness. He told himself it was just apprehension, starting a new job in a new country.

He picked up the passport and slipped it in his inside pocket, put the bag by the door and checked to see if he'd left anything. Satisfied, he took the room key and headed for the elevator.

Ms Wright at the reception desk remembered Halsey's name and called him by it when she said good morning. Halsey wanted to know where breakfast was served. She directed him to the Colonial Coffee Shop. Halsey thanked her with a crooked smile.

Eating a solitary breakfast he began to wonder if he should have listened to Lynch. But there was no point letting that kind of thing prey on your mind. He sipped coffee, considering how he might kill time until Schultz showed at ten. Take a walk down to the White House. Sit a spell there in the Oval Office with the President, chewing the fat. Or take a ride down to Arlington, the cemetery.

Halsey left the hotel, striking out east along K Street thronging with the men and women who worked in the offices — secretaries, businessmen, lobbyists. People he had nothing in common with. They all seemed to be walking in the opposite direction. Occasionally he caught sight of someone going the same way, a figure in the crowd.

The people seemed to be looking down at the sidewalk or off at some fixed point in the distance. Halsey changed direction, going back towards the Hilton, going with the crowd. He was taking the money. Take the money and fuck the consequences. He wasn't so different from the people on the street.

Schultz said, 'Here's your ticket and the money,' handing over a manila envelope. He was very businesslike in his gray business suit, carefully wiping the surface of the table with a napkin before putting the suede attaché case down. The waitress started over towards their table. Schultz sent her away with an imperious wave.

'If you look at your ticket, it's only as far as London.' Schultz put his elbows on the table and leant forward clasping his hands. He glanced in both directions, checking to make sure they weren't overheard. 'Someone will meet you there in the international zone and give you a ticket for your forward destination.' Halsey wondered if he was reading from a card, the way he rattled it off.

'The man who will meet you is easily recognizable. He's about two-forty pounds, five eight with a moustache.'

Halsey restrained himself from asking Schultz if this was Agent X, instead saying, 'Does he have a name?'

'His name is Katz.' Leaning closer he said, 'He will show you his wristwatch, a gold Rolex Oyster.' Schultz closed the case and signalled to the waitress. She ignored him.

The limo was waiting in front of the hotel. George had his feet up on the seat, picking his teeth with a cocktail stick. He saw Halsey and brought his feet round, tossing the pick out the window. He began whistling through his teeth as the car sprang to life and he put it in drive, swinging out under the canopy above the entrance. His black cap with the shiny peak was beside him on the seat. Reluctantly he put it on and without bothering to check in the mirror to see if it was straight he got out.

'George,' said Halsey. George touched the peak of his cap and opened the rear door of the Lincoln. He closed the door after Halsey and went round to the trunk to supervise the loading of the baggage.

'You want to go out to the National Girl Scout Camp.' George slid behind the wheel.

'Dulles.'

'Dulles it is.' George started whistling again as the car pulled out into a line of vehicles on 16th Street going south. Halsey couldn't make out the tune. What was it?

The White House against a deep blue sky with cotton clouds looked like a three-dimensional pressing of some holy shrine.

'Off We Go Into the Wild Blue Yonder'. That was the tune.

Halsey asked George if he'd heard of Michael Lynch.

'Mikey. Got a wooden leg?'

'That's him.'

'Yeah. I know Mikey. A real soak. I haven't seen him for some time. Is he okay? I heard he was hiding out.'

'Hiding out?'

'Jack O'Brien's really pissed at him for some reason.' George looked over his shoulder. 'Used to work for Jack. Got canned so I heard. How d'you know Mikey?'

'I met him in the bar last night. Said he knew Jack O'Brien.'

'What did he have to say for himself?'

'He was drunk.'

'That's Mikey. Alcoholic. Worst kind of drunk.'

Airborne

On the plane over the Atlantic Halsey had a dream.

Eva was running up a long winding open staircase. He remembered the staircase but couldn't think where it was. Eva had on a black dress. A cocktail dress with a diamond brooch. He chased her up the staircase. She was carrying something in her hand. A letter. He saw his name on the envelope in spidery writing as it fell through the void. He had to decide whether he should go back down the staircase and get the letter. If he did that he'd lose Eva. So he ran on up the stairs. Finally catching her, tearing her dress. She turned away. He pulled her down. Heavy. His weight on her, ripping the crêpe de Chine. Pressing his prick against her thigh.

Halsey woke up with the steward bending over in front of him to pick up a plastic cup. As the steward swivelled round on his haunches and came upright for a moment his eyes were level with Halsey's crotch. He gave Halsey a simpering smile before walking back down the aisle in the direction of the galley. Halsey found a flight magazine in the rack to cover his erection. He got up from the seat holding the magazine and staggered forward as the plane hit a patch of turbulence. By grabbing on to an occasional head-rest he made it to the restroom, went in and bolted the door. Halsey ran cold water and splashed his face with a cupped hand. He dried his hands and reached down with his left to pull his balls up. He thought about masturbating.

Strolling back to his seat the chimes sounded and the seatbelt light came on together with the No Smoking sign. Halsey looked out the window. They were coming in to land at London Gatwick in the rain. The lights of the terminal were fractured in the darkness. Halsey hated landing. The sudden jolt, the screeching tires.

London Gatwick

Katz looked very real. Two hundred and forty pounds wet. The rain dripping from his heavy moustache, darkening the shoulders of the brown leather jacket. He showed Halsey the watch.

'Let's get a drink and talk.'

They found an empty table by a glass wall looking out over the runways and the rain. Planes landing, taxiing, spray being thrown up by the tires.

'That's London. They don't have fogs here any more.' Katz wiped his face with his hand and looked at Halsey. 'Where you're going the sun shines.'

'Where's that?'

'Libya.'

Halsey took in a deep breath feeling a tightening in his chest.

'Now I want you to get in solid with the people you're gonna be working with. Whatever you need to do, short of letting them bend you over and fuck you in the ass.' Katz laughed, lightening it up. 'I don't know what you heard about Arabs.' Katz reached inside his safari-style jacket and took out an envelope, almost the same brown as the leather. 'Here's your ticket. You'll be met at the airport in Tripoli.'

'I need a visa?'

'The man'll walk you right through, no problem.'

Their business concluded, Katz went over to the bar and brought back two beers and two scotches. 'Cheers old chap.' Katz gave the moustache a twirl. 'Old boy.' He had a playful manner laughing at his own jokes.

'Last guy doing your job came through here carrying enough binary explosive to blow London off the map. He was so drunk he walked right through customs with these fucking cans. I nearly shit myself. Had to contact our man at British Intelligence, get him back through.'

They finished their drinks. Katz said he had some other business to take care of, winking. He stood up, punched Halsey on the arm. 'Don't worry. You're gonna be working for me.'

The flight out didn't leave until the following morning. Halsey had to try and get some sleep on one of the benches in the lounge, holding on to his luggage. He was woken at four a.m. when an Indian or Pakistani in some kind of uniform tried to walk away with one of his bags. After that he couldn't sleep, although his body clock told him he should.

Paris

The woman known as Anna Brecht descended the staircase of the apartment building in the Rue Henri Regnault, said good morning to Madame Thiery, the concierge sweeping the step, and turned right towards the Metro Porte d'Orléans. She stopped at the boulangerie on Rue Père Corentin as always and bought two croissants. She asked Natalie, the young woman behind the counter, to keep a baguette for her. Brecht had arrived earlier than usual, avoiding Madame Laurent, the baker's wife – at that hour having breakfast with her husband. Madame Laurent would have noticed the new attaché case.

Brecht was well dressed but not ostentatiously so, in a gray skirt, cream blouse and a dark-blue topcoat. All her clothes had been bought at the same time from Galleries Lafayette. She was tall and shapely with her hair dyed a rich auburn color. It was the outward appearance of a businesswoman. She wore large pale-pink-rimmed glasses that covered her face, making it look smaller, and flat court shoes to keep her height to a minimum. The glasses had plain lenses.

She took the train to Réaumur Sébastopol and began walking in the direction of the Bourse but turned north into the maze of streets behind the Boulevard de Bonne Nouvelle and then doubled back along the Rue d'Aboukir, coming out by the arch of the Porte de St Denis. Satisfied that she wasn't being followed, she went west again, pausing to observe the reflections in a shop window.

The doors of Nôtre Dame de Bonne Nouvelle stood open. It was ten years since Brecht had entered a church and then a Protestant church – austere, plain. She found the expression of Catholicism awesome and obscene. The fetor of the votive candles, the idolatry of the religious images. Brecht slid into a pew to the side in the dark shadow of a pillar, glancing around. Carefully she placed the attaché case on her lap and bent her head as though in prayer.

A priest at the altar made the sign of the cross and moved off along the side aisle towards the sacristy. There were few people in the church, some praying, some waiting for their confessions to be heard. A man in a pale raincoat walked down the center aisle to the altar, bent his knee, crossed himself and came back down the aisle. Brecht looked up. As the man drew level he caught her eye.

Brecht brought the case towards her and held it steady. She examined the tumbler beside the hasp, trying to concentrate. She knew she shouldn't have taken the valium. All she had to do was line up the left hand numbers. No chance involved. Somehow it seemed hard to do. The numbers clicked into alignment, arming the device – six six six.

After the darkness of the church the sunlight hurt her eyes. Brecht walked past the man in the pale raincoat standing on the corner of the Boulevard de Bonne Nouvelle and crossed the street to the synagogue.

She slid the attaché case into the pannier of the Mobylette motor-cycle parked outside and taking a small padlock out of her pocket, locked the flap. The man across the street watched Brecht leave before turning in the opposite direction towards the Rue St Denis.

At five after nine Brecht arrived at the Banque de Commerce building in the Rue de la Chausée d'Antin and rode the elevator to the fourth floor. Marie Claude Carrière was coming out of her office when the elevator doors opened. Brecht said good morning and apologized for being late. There was no need to arrive on time. Her first class was at nine fifteen.

On the two days a week, Tuesday and Wednesday, that Brecht had classes, she and Marie Claude drank coffee together in the office overlooking the Opéra. On that Tuesday morning, sipping the black bitter Italian coffee, Carrière asked Brecht if she had reconsidered the offer to work full-time at the bank. Brecht gave the same reply she had given before – that her private clients paid well and she had an obligation to them. This was a lie, since she had no other clients, no other work.

The men in their conservative business suits stood up when Brecht entered, saying '*Guten Tag*'. They sat down when she sat at her desk. She was in no mood to teach a class, listening for the explosion. As she glanced at her watch she heard the distant sound of sirens.

The later editions of *Paris Soir* carried the story with a photograph of the synagogue on an inside page. No one was killed, no one injured. It didn't make the TV news. The *Herald Tribune* had a four-inch column on page two with a headline 'Senseless Terrorism?' The headline was part of the quotation carried in the second paragraph. A phone call after the blast from a woman had ended what was clearly a prepared statement with a quotation, 'Senseless terrorism is often not as senseless as it may seem.'

One of the copy-editors recognized the quote and commented, 'I wonder how Richard Nixon got into a terrorist manifesto alongside Marx and Maringella.'

London Gatwick

When they called the flight at nine thirty a.m. Halsey was feeling lost in time. He had an overwhelming sense of unreality.

It was a British Caledonian flight, the stewardesses wearing kilts. A redhead with a slight Scottish burr in her voice asked Halsey if he wanted a drink. He said he thought it was a little early but since he'd had some bad news a scotch might calm his nerves.

'Make it a double.' When she came back with the drink he said, 'I like your kilt.'

'It's no really a kilt. And this isn't my tartan. I'm a Campbell. Like the soup. Did you want any water?'

Tripoli

Halsey looked out the cabin window. The plane was making a turn, banking left, the Mediterranean below. The pilot announced that in Tarabulus the temperature was an even 82° Fahrenheit, 28° Celsius. The engines were roaring with reverse thrust. They were landing. Halsey had a sick feeling in the pit of his stomach.

The plane hit the tarmac and bounced a couple of times. Even before reaching the end of the runway Halsey was up out of his seat pulling his flight bag down from the overhead stow locker. The redhead was coming by.

Halsey said, 'Are you stopping over? Maybe we could have a drink?'

'Not this trip.' She walked by and turned around, the kilt swirling. 'I hope you enjoy your stay.'

Halsey wasn't sure if there was a hint of mockery in her voice. He asked a pale man standing beside him what Tarabulus was.

'It's where we are. Arabic for lavatory I shouldn't wonder.' He introduced himself. 'Les Shah from Yorkshire. Pleased to meet you.' They shook hands standing in the aisle. Passengers were getting up all around them. The plane taxiing to a standstill.

'Here we go,' said Shah. They walked out into bright sunlight, the sky a deep, deep blue and the airport buildings a vivid white. Shah explained that all this was new. 'Used to be an aircraft hangar. Left over from the war. Still had the bullet holes in the walls.'

'*Representation is Fraud.*'

'*Democracy is the Supervision of the People by the People.*'

The interior of the Libyan Arab People's terminal building was hung with quotations from *The Green Book* and photographs of Colonel Gadafi. The color scheme predominantly green and white. Staccato hammering came from green booths, the sound of passports being pounded.

Shah moved off to join a line. 'Seventeen hours is my own personal record. It can take days. Or if they don't like the look of you they put you on the first flight out.'

A small Arab in a heavy brown serge suit came up to Halsey. He had a telex in his hand and bowed slightly as he read the name in front of him. He then took out a silver cigarette case and offered a cigarette. Halsey shook his head. The Arab took a business card from the case and handed it to him. The card read 'Omar Bakkush, Director of Marketing, Tarlex International Corp, Washington DC'. Bakkush smiled showing a lot of gold teeth and asked for Halsey's passport. They walked straight through customs and immigration. Bakkush handed over the passport to a uniformed Arab at a green desk who seemed to have no function and sat there morosely. The official didn't look at the document and tossed it in a drawer. When Halsey tried to ask for it back he was waved away with an impatient sweep of the arm. Bakkush pulled at Halsey's coat.

Out of earshot of the official, Halsey said, 'How about getting my passport back?'

Bakkush began explaining politely that he wouldn't need the passport until he left the country. Halsey cut in saying that since he hadn't gone through immigration there was no record of his entering the country. He didn't have a passport. Technically he didn't exist. Bakkush made placatory noises.

'Please, Mr Jack will fix tomorrow.' Bakkush was steering Halsey towards the exit.

Leaving the terminal building they were confronted by two dark-skinned Arabs, stylishly dressed, leaning against a black Peugeot 404. Bakkush seemed to know them. Halsey knew what they were, or at least assumed he did. A discussion with Bakkush in Arabic turned into an argument that ended abruptly, leaving him standing there looking foolish. Halsey was invited, in halting English, to take a ride in the car. He looked over at Bakkush who stared back blankly.

From the back of the Peugeot Halsey could see a landscape of olive trees in rows, and a line of Russian T-55 tanks parked, Libyan soldiers standing idly by. The car was doing maybe eighty down a four-lane highway passing old VWs and new Toyotas. Along the side of the road at regular intervals there were wrecks. Burnt out, gutted or just abandoned. Off in the distance to the left beyond partially cultivated land was a small corrugated shack painted green. Apart from the soldiers Halsey hadn't seen anyone. He was looking out the window trying to figure out why an overturned Fiat truck had been left there to rust, when the car swerved and he was thrown across the back seat. The horn was going and Halsey didn't need a translation to know what the driver was saying. Behind them on the wrong side of the road doing thirty was a Peugeot pickup, a young camel weighing down the back.

With all the shouting and arm waving the driver didn't see the old man. The car braked a hundred yards on and reversed to where the body lay motionless in the dirt. The two Arabs got out and wandered back to what looked like a bundle of clothing lying beside the road. Halsey watched out the rear window. There was a lot of head-shaking and talking. The driver took out his cigarettes, offered the package, lit both with a lighter and came back to the car. He made Halsey the same offer. Halsey took the cigarette. He didn't feel in any position to refuse. Inhaling deeply, filling his lungs, he smiled at the driver.

By the time the cigarettes were down to stubs a decision had been made. The bent body of the old man went in the trunk alongside Halsey's bags.

Halsey thought that there might be some kind of festival going on. They had reached the outskirts of Tripoli and the road was decked with banners. There were photographs of Gadafi on the lamp-posts – army colonel, statesman, spiritual leader, Bedouin tribesman. More quotations from *The Green Book*. Behind the banners, new Soviet-style apartment blocks.

'*Ash hadu an la ilaha illa.*' Allah! The minarets of mosques rising above the skyline. A city of towers. The car was moving towards the call to prayer. They were in an older part of the city looking more like southern Italy than North Africa. Halsey caught sight of the harbor before the car turned into a side street and parked.

The driver held open the rear door. Halsey got out and was led into a new building guarded by two uniformed soldiers with semi-automatic rifles, although no one seemed interested in checking IDs. Halsey was taken in the elevator to the top floor where he was met as the doors opened by an elderly Arab wearing a traditional *howli*. Halsey stepped out and the doors closed silently. Without a word passing between them Halsey followed the old man down a short blind corridor and found himself in a dimly-lit empty office. As he looked around he was briefly aware of a movement behind him and then was alone. The light came from a wall of electronically operated blinds, even and shadowless. The furniture, glass, steel and leather, very modern. The only thing Arabic in the room a Misrātah carpet.

A door off to the side opened and a small gray-haired Arab in his fifties with a bristly military moustache came in carrying a stack of files, which he placed with great precision on the glass desk. He didn't look at Halsey. Unnerving. He picked up a file from the top of the stack and examined the contents, occasionally glancing in Halsey's direction while fingering the moustache. Without warning he slapped the papers down and left the way he had come.

Halsey stood there staring at the desk, wondering if that was his file. He thought about taking a look. There was bound to be electronic surveillance. The door behind him opened and a gnarled hand beckoned. The Arab in the *howli* was there again with a gap-toothed smile. They walked to the elevator. It stood open, the driver of the Peugeot waiting.

The car was still parked outside. A young kid was dragging a sheep along the sidewalk on a long rope. They waited for it to go by. The driver chauffeured Halsey into the back and went round to take up his position behind the wheel. There seemed to be an atmosphere in the car that was reflected in a more violent driving style. It could have been to do with the body or a question of whose turn it was to drive.

They were going west towards the setting sun. A red sky like nothing Halsey had ever seen. The sea off to the right, crossing the mouth of a wadi, riding in silence. Halsey tried asking where he was being taken but didn't get an answer.

Not more than ten minutes on the coast road the car left the highway and swung on to a rutted dirt track leading to a construction site. They stopped outside a four-storey villa looking like a white blockhouse and smelling like a garbage dump. The car door was held open and Halsey stepped out. He saw a pack of lean hungry cats scavenging a mountain of debris near a chain-link fence. The trunk was open and his bags were dumped in the scrub to the side. The body was gone.

As the Peugeot pulled away down the track the door to the villa opened a crack. Halsey heard an American voice from inside.

'It's okay. They've gone.' The door opened fully. A grinning face welcomed Halsey. 'You must be Halsey. I'm Doug Chasen.'

Chasen had on an orange Hawaiian shirt and red Bermuda shorts, no shoes. Standing stoop-shouldered in the narrow entrance.

Halsey picked up the bags and went towards the door. 'What the fuck is going on?'

'Hell, I just work here.' Chasen came off the wall, giving himself the impetus to make the flight of stone steps leading up.

Halsey followed on.

They stopped climbing two flights up, going through a beaded curtain into a primitive kitchen.

'This here is Mister Charlie Crow.' Chasen indicated the man sitting behind a small table covered with a yellow gingham oilcloth.

Crow stood up. Six four and wide, dark, slow moving. Halsey felt the grip of a massive hand. Crow said, 'Everyone around here is called Mister.'

'It's usually "Mister John" because the Ayrabs can't remember your name.' Chasen handed Halsey a cup. 'Have a drink.'

Crow sat back down and picked up the glass in front of him, waving it in the general direction of a bottle of clear liquid standing on the table.

'I believe I need it,' said Halsey. He poured a measure.

Crow reached over and prevented Halsey from taking a drink. 'Have some juice in it.'

'What is this?' said Halsey.

'Flash,' said Crow.

'Is that the local Arab drink?'

'Arabs don't drink, mostly. Against their religion.' Crow poured grapefruit juice into Halsey's cup. 'I think it's made from orange pulp, the flash.' Halsey tasted it. He screwed up his face. It was mean. 'You'll get used to it,' said Crow. 'If you like, it comes colored to look like bourbon. But it tastes about the same.'

Halsey found a stool and sat down. Tentatively sipping at the drink he began relating the events of the last two days. When Halsey mentioned Lynch, Chasen said two things. Firstly, Mikey's fallen in the bottle again, and then that they heard he was talking all kinds of crap. The guy's a fucking nut.

Halsey asked what kind of crap.

'Who knows? We just heard. What did he say?'

Halsey told them that Lynch hadn't said anything. Chasen seemed relieved.

Chasen grinned. 'I had a tough day myself. Here.' He lifted the bottle, 'Have another drink. It's tough all over.' Helping himself and then Halsey. 'At the end of a long day I'm glad the goons didn't come in. We'd have to flush the flash . . . Flush the flash.'

'Are we prisoners here or what?'

'They got closed-circuit TV outside. They let us know we're being kept under surveillance,' said Crow.

'You free to leave the country?'

'Listen,' said Chasen, 'if you're planning on leaving you got to talk to Jack O'Brien. He's off somewhere. He'll be back coupla days. See what he says.'

Halsey wondered what O'Brien would say and do if he decided to quit. Did he feel justified in wanting to get out? He'd been in worse situations in Vietnam. But even in Vietnam living conditions outside the combat zone were more civilized than this shit-hole.

'Is there anything to eat?' said Chasen.

'You're the chef,' said Crow.

Chasen got up from the table and went over to the wall cupboards beside the sink. He rummaged around and came out with a can that had no label. 'Beans. I think it's beans.' He shook the can. 'Sounds like beans to me.'

'Why don't you open the fucker and put us all out of our agony?' Crow poured another shot of flash. 'That's it. You forget to shop today?'

Chasen started looking for a can opener and couldn't find one. He picked up a bread knife and began to attack the lid, gouging holes but making no significant impression.

'Is this franks and beans?' said Halsey.

'Just beans,' said Crow. 'Franks is pork. You can't get pork. Not clean. Against the law.'

'We have some crackers.' Chasen stopped stabbing the can, leaving the blade in an open wound and took down a packet from the cupboard. He offered one to Halsey.

'Jesus fucking Christ. The thing moved.' Halsey took the cracker and dropped it on the floor.

When Halsey woke up he couldn't work out what time of day it was. His watch had eastern time and he didn't remember the time difference. He looked around. The sun was slanting in the shutters, casting a striped shadow across the bodies of Crow and Chasen in their sleeping bags. Chasen was snoring, the pillow of his inflatable bed going up and down. Halsey made a move and there was a rasping sound. Carefully he eased himself out of bed and went over to the window. Through the slats of the blind the sky was the same deep blue. On the balcony of a villa less than ten yards away there was a woman in a white bathrobe, standing facing the sea, her back to Halsey.

'What time is it?' said Crow, getting up on one elbow.

'Two o'clock,' Halsey said. 'What's the time difference?'

'It's too early for difficult questions like that. My watch is over there on that pile of clothes.'

Halsey glanced out the window. The woman on the balcony had disappeared. He collected the watch. 'Eight o'clock.'

'Shit. Time to go to work.' Crow shook Chasen.

Halsey took a shower in tepid brown water. He shaved and dressed in fatigues, boots shining. He stepped through the curtains dividing the sleeping quarters and the kitchen. Crow and Chasen were sitting there at the table with plates of beans in front of them, looking sick. They were dressed much the same as Halsey but unshaven and looking as though they'd slept in their fatigues. He made himself a cup of instant coffee. It didn't taste much like coffee.

At eight forty-five they went to work in a beaten up old Eagle, Crow driving.

'Where are we going?' asked Halsey.

'People's Palace,' said Crow.

The People's Palace was a mixture of styles – Italian and Arabic – to the south of the city, surrounded by orange groves.

Crow said, 'Used to belong to King Idris. Now it's the people's. You see we live in a democracy.' He parked the Eagle at the rear of the palace.

Soldiers carrying Skorpion sub-machine-guns were wandering through the date palms.

They were met by a smartly-dressed army officer, a lieutenant, who seemed pleased to see them and said good morning.

'Now, what's good about it?' said Crow. The officer thought

that was funny. Crow said to Halsey, 'This here is Benny. We call him Benny because we can't say his name.'

The officer saluted. 'Seyed Majid Ben Sa'oud,' and offered his hand.

'Nate Halsey.' He reached out and shook Ben Sa'oud's hand.

'Well, Mister John,' Ben Sa'oud addressed Crow, 'what is the lesson for today?'

'Now, you know my name, Benny.' Crow looked over at Halsey. 'It's Benny's little game. Because I'm stupid, Benny here pretends to be stupid.' Ben Sa'oud laughed. They started walking towards what were the servants' quarters.

'You know how Benny learned such good English.' Crow had a smirk on his face. 'Watching *Robin Hood* on TV. Doesn't know how to fire a gun but he's good with a bow and arrow.'

They went through a door into a large workshop that might once have been stables. Lying around the place on benches were various household items – clocks, radios, vases. Halsey moved over to the nearest bench and picked up an ashtray. It had been made out of data-sheet – thin explosive – useful if you want to make a letter bomb. There were tins of Triex and Quadrex, binary explosive, stacked over by the wall. Halsey swore under his breath, thinking fuck, this is a bomb-making factory.

The students were filing into the workshop.

'The élite,' Chasen chortled behind his hand. They were behaving like seven-year-old kids.

Crow said, 'It's tough staying alive round here.' He shook his head.

Chasen took the lesson with Ben Sa'oud translating, although the students seemed to follow the English. Halsey sat to one side and listened as Chasen tried to deal with the complexities of electricity, circuit diagrams, explaining in simplistic terms. High-school physics. Chasen started getting frustrated, losing their attention. The abstract left them in the dark. It was even funny.

Halsey stopped listening. Here he was involved in teaching bomb-making to Arabs. He hadn't signed up for this. He was a render safe man. Sure, that involved knowing how to go about putting together devices like these. They were crude, wouldn't fool anyone. He tried to remember what Jack O'Brien had said. All O'Brien said was training. Talk to the man. In the meantime, if it meant he'd stay alive, he'd better teach these Libyans a lesson to remember.

Coffee was served on a beaten copper tray. Arab coffee which Halsey liked. He told Ben Sa'oud that he had an idea for the next class. Sipping from the demitasse he explained that he needed some meat. Any kind. Rotten meat would do. Ben Sa'oud wanted to know what it was for.

'It's a little joke I want to play on your students,' Halsey said. Ben Sa'oud went away chuckling to himself.

'Ayrabs love a good joke,' said Crow.

Chasen said, 'They're so busy playing tricks on each other and grab-assing around they don't have time to learn anything.'

'Have you tried coming at it from a different direction?' Halsey asked.

'You've seen them. Seen how they act. They're as thick as shit,' said Chasen.

'Do they know what a blasting cap is? You think you can find me one.'

Crow thought he could. 'If they never heard of one I reckon maybe they're going to.'

There was a lot of chattering going on. Halsey had found an old army boot lying around and was packing it with the putrefying carcass of a lamb. When he had crammed in as much as he could he began the lesson, starting with generalities. Handling explosives was dangerous. Like pointing a gun at someone. You take the clip out, think it isn't loaded but there's one in the chamber. They weren't taking him seriously.

The whole class had gathered around the boot hanging from a rope in the middle of the workshop. The cap went off, echoing in the enclosed space. Blood and mincemeat spattered them. Chasen, Crow and Ben Sa'oud standing back laughing. Halsey thinking this isn't funny.

'There are no games here.' Halsey narrowed his eyes, glaring at the students. 'Games lead to the graveyard.'

Paris

In her head Brecht called him *ombre* or *ombrage*, a faceless shadow. She hadn't seen him get on at Chatelet but she knew he was there in the next car. At six p.m. the Métro was crowded. Carl

Krupps got off at Alesia, the second last stop on the line. Brecht saw him as the train moved out. She rode on to Porte d'Orléans and caught the next train back. At Alesia Krupps got in the same car.

They changed trains for direction Étoile at Montparnasse-Bienvenue, keeping twenty yards apart through the long tunnels. Brecht felt claustrophobic. And tense.

The doors of the train slid back. Brecht hadn't been aware of time passing. The horn sounded and she stepped on to the platform at La Défense. The train pulled out. She became aware of the piped accordion muzac. The moving staircase carried her towards the shopping precinct. With the time coming up to six forty-five, there were minutes to kill. Enough time for Brecht to buy a bottle of aspirin.

On the escalator back down to the parking level Krupps stood right behind her. A shadow you could reach out and touch. He placed the zip-top case that he carried on her step. It was large enough to take an office folder or a Browning GP .35 automatic with a short silencer and a clip of thirteen low-velocity bullets. Brecht collected the case before the end of the ride and walked down the last ten steps.

Chantal Monceau sat behind the wheel of a silver Renault Five, the engine running. Brecht and Krupps took up their positions near the Renault. At six fifty-eight a black Cadillac Seville with diplomatic plates entered the garage. Monceau gunned the engine. The driver of the Cadillac looked over and pulled up, allowing the Renault room to move out.

The space, reserved forty-eight hours earlier, had been chosen to provide maximum cover. They had had a dry run two weeks before with another car. The man in the Cadillac was punctual and alert to the available space.

As the Renault took off, the Cadillac went forward to reverse up. A red Citroen coming along made a move to swing into the opening. Both cars had to brake to avoid collision. The Cadillac driver got out and started shouting, 'Get outta there, you motherfucker.'

Brecht glanced at Krupps. She started looking around, seeing if the argument was attracting any attention. The seconds passed. She could feel the sweat running down her arm. Then the Citroen was gone in a pall of burning rubber.

Colonel Clyde Rand got back in his car and maneuvered into his space. Brecht had the case open and her hand on the gun as she came round the front of the Cadillac.

Rand was getting out the door when something made him change his mind. It could have been the expression on the woman's face. He remembered that he wasn't carrying, that he'd left his army Colt in the glove compartment.

Two bullets hit Rand in the side through the window as he leant forward trying to reach across.

Brecht squeezed the trigger to get off two head shots but the gun jammed. She kicked the car door, catching Rand's open body as he slumped forward. He was still moving, crawling along the seat. Then Krupps was there using the door as a blunt instrument. He grabbed Brecht's gun, ejecting the jammed shell and firing two shots into Rand's back and, as his head came up, two more into the neck, aiming at the base of the skull. Krupps tossed the gun into the car, dragged the body to the ground and closed the door. The interior light went out.

Le Vingt Heures News had a TV crew at the scene. The bullets that had passed through the window left two perfect holes less than an inch apart. From the shattered glass a zoom-out revealed a blood-soaked blanket covering the body and blood staining the blackened concrete.

At seven fifteen a woman with a poodle had discovered the body and called the police. That was the substance of the story. It was worth ninety seconds of airtime.

The next day the *Herald Tribune* ran a front-page story with a photograph of Colonel Clyde Rand in his uniform. It ran under the headline 'US Attaché Slain in Paris':

Colonel Clyde Rand, forty-three, the assistant military attaché in Paris, was gunned down last night in a parking garage at La Défense. The assassination occurred at around seven p.m. as Colonel Rand got out of his car. The attacker fired six shots at close range.

A statement was received by this newspaper at seven-fifty, claiming responsibility for the execution of Colonel Rand. The caller, a young woman, spoke in French and heavily-accented English for less than a minute, ending her call, "We've got to have more of this assassination."

The quotation went unattributed in the early editions, but later the connection with the synagogue bombing was made – identified as Richard Nixon's reaction facing proposed budget cuts to assassination squads operating in Vietnam. Nixon had been angry about reports in the *New York Times* about the My Lai massacre.

Tripoli

'It's the will of Allah,' said O'Brien. 'Is that what you're saying? Kismet.' He shook his head. 'Kiss my ass.'

Katz sat there at the green metal desk listening, waiting. He rocked back on the wooden chair. O'Brien pacing at his back, occasionally glancing out the window at the deepening sky over the sea.

'You fucked up.' O'Brien was almost shouting.

Katz said in a level tone, 'You lined these spics up. They don't wanna do it.'

Through the door a woman's voice said, 'Can I use the phone?'

O'Brien stopped at the desk. His mouth hanging open as he pivoted around. 'Two minutes, Francine.'

They heard footsteps moving away. O'Brien started pacing again, saying that he'd talked to Langley. Katz decided there was no point in arguing or even listening to this putz.

Francine listened at the door. All she could hear was O'Brien shouting, making no sense. She'd given it two minutes, so knocked. 'Can I come in now, boys?' Her voice was husky. Francine opened the door. A woman in her early thirties. The two men gazed at her as she walked over to the phone. Francine was ignoring them.

Katz said, 'Who wants a drink?'

Katz and O'Brien drifted off towards the bathroom. There was a little bar set up on the cistern. Flash and some guava juice. O'Brien poured two generous measures.

'Cheers, old boy,' said Katz.

'What's this old boy shit. Hanging round the Admiral Codrington pub too long. You're getting a beer belly there.'

They took their drinks out on to the first floor balcony. The sea partially obscured behind the construction site, rusting steel and gray slab.

'Where's Fredo with the scotch?' said Katz.

O'Brien looked at his cloudy drink. 'The price is up to a hundred and fifty a bottle.'

'You can afford one fifty.' Katz waving a cigarette. 'You don't wanna pay that little faggot Fredo. I know a guy works for one of the oil companies.' Katz leant over the balcony. His blue safari suit darker than the sky. 'I was in Jalloud's office this after. Jalloud wasn't around. I was talking to Musa. Musa says to me very seriously that it is a shame Islamic law won't let him take a drink. Says he thinks it's important on social occasions. Says when he's in the States there's an ad on TV, Paul Masson de-alcoholized wine. He wants to know is that right or some bullshit. I say it's another miracle of science. Wine into water.' He belched.

Less than fifty feet away in the adjacent villa Halsey, Crow and Chasen were standing around the kitchen table sipping beer.

'It's alcohol,' said Chasen.

'On the scale of things,' said Crow.

Halsey dipped his index finger in the beer, stirring up what looked like long threads of algae.

'Home brew.' Chasen shrugged. 'When they bring the cans through customs they take the labels off which is smart because you don't want a label says beer. The only problem is that now no one knows what's in the cans. So you got a drink in front of you looks like there oughta be fish swimming around in it.'

Halsey said, 'What do you do round here for amusement?'

'Well, Doug here beats his meat,' Crow said.

'Charlie,' said Chasen, giving Crow a sideways look, 'no one knows what Charlie has going. A mystery. Could be he's seeing a camel.'

Crow walked away out on to the balcony.

Jack O'Brien saw Crow and shouted across. 'Come on over and have a drink.'

O'Brien met his EOD detachment at the front door of the villa in full view of the TV camera high up on the steel pole.

'How's your ass, fella?' O'Brien clapped Crow on the back, putting his arm around his shoulder and leading him over to the staircase. He waited for Halsey and Chasen, following them up to the second floor.

Francine was typing a letter at the desk. She glanced up as Crow came through the door and back to the Adler. 'Help yourself to a drink.' The typewriter clattering rhythmically.

Katz was leaning on the file cabinet with a bag of potato chips. He nodded to Halsey, Crow and Chasen. 'Have a chip. Sheep flavor.'

Francine finished the letter, whipped the page out of the roller and put it in the desk drawer. As she got up Chasen introduced Halsey. They said hello and Francine moved over to the tray on the other desk with a stack of plastic imitation cut-glass tumblers and an unmarked can.

'Have some guava juice.' She lined up three tumblers and poured.

Chasen carried his over to where Katz was standing and collected a handful of chips.

Francine handed Halsey a juice. 'So how do you like it at Shangri-La? Our little villa by the sea.'

'If you don't send us equipment we can use, we're gonna end up in the shit,' said Crow.

'Timers,' said O'Brien. 'Thirty thousand timers.'

'What the fuck are we going to do with thirty thousand timers?'

'This is state of the art,' said O'Brien.

'Thirty thousand?'

'That's just the first order.' O'Brien lifted his tumbler. He needed a refill. Started for the bathroom.

Crow collected a juice from the desk and followed O'Brien across the lobby.

O'Brien had a bottle. 'You want a drink?' He held out the bottle.

Crow brushed by the blue, flaking wall, picking up white dust on his fatigues.

O'Brien poured. 'Thirty thousand is just the first order. The Libyans are buying five hundred thousand.'

'Half a million timers?' Crow wondered what the Libyans wanted with half a million timers.

'What did the guy have? He didn't have shit. He had sand. Born in the desert,' said Katz.

'So fucking what?' said Chasen.

'All I'm saying, it's like Lee Trevino.'

'Yeah. All he had was sand.'

'I'm making a point. Trevino was a poor spic kid; now he's US Open champion.'

'So what's the point?'

'I knew the guy when he had nothing is what I'm saying.'

'When I was working as a courier outta Malta for the CIA, I used to be in and out of Libya. I spent time in his tent there in the desert listening to him talking. Talking about his plans. How things were gonna change when the king was outta the way.'

Chasen looked unconvinced.

'The guy paid his dues.'

Chasen said, 'I hear he goes round in high heels and make up. Now I don't know what you were doing in Gadafi's tent. But I hope it didn't involve swapping dress patterns, because the guy is a fucking transvestite.'

They sat around the kitchen table eating a dinner of burgers, rice and peas. With six people it was crowded. Crow was laying out some of the problems he was having. Being put under pressure.

Halsey interrupted. 'We should be teaching the Libyans basics. Electricity, chemistry.'

'They are dangerous,' said Crow. 'How are we supposed to teach a bunch of sand Ayrabs?' He held up a slice of burger. 'Most of them are right out of the desert. Some of them haven't even seen a truck or heard of electricity.

'It's hard to get their attention. They're nomads. They don't stay in one place and their minds don't stay in one place.'

O'Brien said, 'I don't care what you teach the little fuckers, as long as you keep Musa and Jalloud happy.'

'We can't teach any damn thing if we don't have the equipment.'

'You made your point,' said O'Brien. Katz sat picking his teeth with a matchstick.

'Great meal, Francine,' said O'Brien. He exhaled, patting his stomach. 'Wanna watch the Bond movie?'

There was a low murmur of dissent.

Katz picked up a *Marvel* comic lying on a pile in the corner. He thumbed the page. 'The Hulk. This guy looks like you, Charlie.' He glanced at Crow. 'Green and ugly.'

'Where did that pile of shit come from?' said O'Brien.

Francine said, 'Some Green Berets came through'.

'Those guys must have a mental age of nine,' said O'Brien.

Katz was laughing at a Japanese magazine he found. A man in a kimono buggering another man. 'Take a look at this Jack.'

O'Brien saw the cover. 'Get rid of that filth.'

Gadafi was on TV shaking hands with a long line of Syrian diplomats standing under a green awning. Halsey was watching with some interest. Gadafi in his army uniform. Colonel or general. A statesman, Nasser. A Bedouin living in a tent.

O'Brien went straight to the TV as he came into the office. It stood on a green metal cart against the wall. O'Brien angled it around. 'Libyan TV.' The screen was distorted with noise. Gadafi came back, still shaking hands. 'They show the whole thing. Right along the line. Haven't figured out how to turn the camera off.'

The screen cut to the news anchorman in full Arab robes.

O'Brien was plugging in the video machine. He slid in a tape and pressed play. *Robin Hood* titles with a song, 'Robin Hood, Robin Hood, riding through the glen. Robin Hood, Robin Hood, with his merry men.' There was a sequence of an arrow being fired. 'Feared by the bad, loved by the good, Robin Hood.' The image was overtaken by a noise, zig-zag lines. Then James Bond and Goldfinger were playing golf. Oddjob, the Korean, carrying a golf bag.

'How far are we into the movie?' Halsey asked.

'Not long,' said O'Brien. 'Bond's screwed Shirley Eaton, caught Goldfinger cheating at cards. Now he's after the secret of where the gold is.' O'Brien had seen the tape ten times. He didn't get bored.

'This is the scene where Bond loses the golf game but he wins on a technicality because he switches balls on Goldfinger. Goldfinger has the wrong ball. Against the rules of the game.'

O'Brien was half turned, facing Halsey. Halsey sat in the heavy gray metal chair with green upholstered arms.

O'Brien continued the commentary. 'Oddjob there, the Korean in the black suit, can take your head off with his hat. Steel piece around the brim. Bond has this Aston Martin with machine guns behind the lights, revolving licence plates, oil slick, smoke screen. And an ejector seat.'

Katz had come in the office while O'Brien was talking, and was standing listening to O'Brien and glancing over at the screen. 'Thing I wanna know,' he said, 'he gets to play with these tinker toys and screw all these women. He never takes a crap and he never gets a social disease.'

In the fading light from the window and the glare from the TV O'Brien sat stony-faced watching 007.

Katz said, 'We're getting a game together.'

Katz rejoined the poker game around the kitchen table. 'He's probably giving Halsey that shit about how James Bond is fantasy but when he was in South East Asia . . .'

Laughter echoed down the staircase.

O'Brien said, 'I still have nightmares about Nam.' He put his hand on Halsey's knee.

'I can't tell you the whole story here. You're just gonna have to trust me. Respect my position. Go along with things for a while.' O'Brien looked over at the TV, smiling. 'This. This is Pussy Galore.' He gave Halsey's knee a squeeze. Halsey looked down. O'Brien kept watching the movie.

Francine was washing the dishes. The card game was in progress. Halsey saw the hands. Chasen was betting with a pair of tens. Katz had a pile of dirhams in front of him and a few dinars. He had two fours showing. Halsey figured he didn't have the third four.

Halsey offered to help Francine. 'I'll dry. Is this the cloth?' Halsey picked up what was once a brown shirt. 'Are they playing for real money?'

'A few dollars.' Francine handed him a plate. 'I'll take you shopping. You can learn the meaning of money and how to spend it.' She scrubbed at the rice pan.

Chasen called with two tens. Katz had the other four.

'You have to see the supermarkets,' said Francine.

'Do they have a souk here?'

'Everything is being taken over by the state. They're closing down private enterprise. Closing down the souk and the taxi drivers. The place is falling apart.'

'What about the black market?'

'Whisky, pork and flash.' Francine dried her hands on the shirt Halsey was holding. 'Take my advice. Don't drink the water or the flash.

'Now I have to go send some telexes. Why don't you come

along? You're gonna have to learn how to use the machine some time.'

Halsey followed Francine down to the ground floor. The telex machine was set up in an alcove under the concrete staircase. A spider crawled out and scuttled across the floor. Francine sat down on a wooden crate.

'You need a number. Just like a regular phone. You dial in the number for the company and the country and get an answer-back. That tells you you're through. Then you type in the message, "Send more cookies." At the end of the message you say who you are by pressing this key. If you want to send a long message you have a paper tape here that you type on to. You dial up, put the tape in and when you get the answer-back press the send key.'

While she demonstrated the whole procedure so that Halsey could follow, she started talking about marriage. And found out that Halsey was separated. And told Halsey that she was married. She also said that a lot of marriages were marriages in name only.

'Have you met Jack's wife?'

Halsey said he hadn't.

'In fact he has two. The legal one in Washington and the other one in London. There's "fuck her" in Washington – "Fuck her. She isn't screwing another cent out of me." – the real Mrs O'Brien, Elaine. And "She" in London. "She" runs the office and comes here on conjugal visits. We all have to get out of the villa for a couple of days. "She", otherwise known as Jacqueline.'

'Jack and Jackie. Cute.'

Abruptly Francine's expression soured. 'A bitch. Jack is also shtupping some woman works for one of the oil companies. And Gadafi.' The telex started to clatter. 'I don't think it's sexual with Gadafi. I think it's the money.'

Crow and Chasen were coming down the stairs. They said their goodnights. Halsey followed on, stopping at the front door looking back at Francine. She smiled.

'Goodnight Abdul,' said Chasen. He waved at the camera angled down, covering the front of the villa.

Halsey stared into the lens.

'When we first arrived, Abdul there,' Chasen pointed to the camera. 'He used to follow us everywhere we went. Now he sits on his ass all day watching TV. It's better all round because Abdul had a personal problem. If you couldn't see him you could smell him. I would have thought body odor was a distinct disadvantage in his line of work.

'A Libyan's idea of work is sitting behind a desk doing squat all day. Having a TV to watch is probably a bonus.'

Halsey lay in bed with his hands behind his head, watching a fly cross the ceiling, listening to the waves breaking on the beach. Sleep came to him easily but he slept badly, troubled with dreams of death. Death from fragmentation. Being torn limb from limb, flesh from flesh. Ripped apart by a blast. Being aware of what was happening for that split second that lasted forever in the nightmare.

Halsey woke at four a.m. It must have been the sound of the engine that woke him. He got up from the bed, taking his shirt to dry the sweat running down his back, and looked through the shutters. Charlie Crow was parking the Eagle.

Halsey was lying awake on his bed when Crow tiptoed in with his boots in his hand, cursing silently at Chasen's sprawled body.

Crow's eyes became accustomed to the light and he saw Halsey. 'I couldn't sleep. I just stepped out for some air.'

Halsey didn't reply, half nodded, closed his eyes, drifting, hoping not to dream.

At the People's Palace the next day Crow and Chasen were put to work on silencers. Ben Sa'oud led them to a small room that had once been used as a cold store. It had been fitted out with machine tools and benches.

'It's a little cool in here,' said Chasen. 'How about getting us a stove?'

'Where are the pieces you want silent devices for?'

Ben Sa'oud indicated a small crate on one of the benches. Chasen was close enough to throw the lid back. The crate was full of every kind of handgun thrown in haphazardly.

Pulling them out one at a time, Chasen said, 'You want a silencer for every one of these?' He held a Webley revolver in his hand. It was loaded. Chasen snapped the gun open and took the shells out, leaving one chambered, spinning the cylinder as he brought the barrel up.

Handing the gun to Ben Sa'oud, 'You wanna play Russian Roulette?'

Ben Sa'oud had no idea what Chasen was saying. He smiled nervously.

'One bullet and a one in six chance of blowing your brains out,' said Chasen. He laughed. 'Just having a joke there, Benny.'

Crow said, 'You can't silence a revolver. The gas escapes through the chambers.' He picked up a Walther PPK from the crate. 'The bigger the caliber, the more silencing it needs. We can make silencers for the automatics. But if you want to keep them manageable they won't be very silent.'

'We'll make one for the Walther and you can try it out,' said Chasen. 'Pretend you're James Bond.' He jumped into a crouch using his fingers as a gun, imitating the heavy guitars playing the theme music.

Halsey was giving a lecture on basic physics. Drawing circuit diagrams on the blackboard. When Ben Sa'oud joined him on the rostrum built of old beer cases, he started again with a translation, making sure he was understood. But the interest wasn't there.

Over coffee Halsey began questioning Ben Sa'oud about what motivated the men he was teaching. From the reply Halsey decided it was fear. The fear of failure. After the break he told Ben Sa'oud to tell everyone that he was going to hold weekly exams, that if they failed their commanding officer would be informed and they'd be removed from the course. The right thing to say because the reaction he got was immediate, rapt attention. As it turned out the timing of this warning was perfect. An army major appeared at the back of the workshop about a half hour after the lecture began. Halsey figured he was being checked out.

Ben Sa'oud introduced the major at the end of the lecture. He was very complimentary about Halsey's teaching.

'I have learnt a lot from this class.' The major spoke with an American accent. But he had the stilted speech of an Arab.

Halsey bowed his head politely.

'Perhaps one day we could have a demonstration. Something impressive. Perhaps a car bomb.' The major seemed excited by the idea.

Halsey said, 'We don't have the explosives or the timers.'

'I understand Mister Jack will be providing us with the right equipment.'

This was the first Halsey had heard about it. And why a car bomb?

That afternoon, five minutes after Halsey started teaching the class, a man and a woman appeared in the shadows. They must have come in some side door because he didn't see them arrive. About the same height. The man was wearing dark tinted glasses and the woman Ray-Bans, although the room was dark, lit only by shafts of sunlight from high narrow windows. They stayed in the shadows. He couldn't see them clearly but it was obvious they weren't Arabs.

The next day they returned, for the whole day this time. Slipping away before the lecture ended and he said, 'Any questions?' They became a permanent addition to the class. Halsey gave them names. Claus and Carlotta. Claus, because the tinted glasses made the man look German, and Carlotta because the woman had black hair drawn back from her forehead and a deep tan. Spanish or South American, he wasn't sure. Ben Sa'oud didn't know anything about them. Told only to accommodate two foreign students who wished to observe and not participate. One day Halsey asked Claus and Carlotta a direct question.

Although he gave it nearly a minute there was no answer forthcoming.

The woman obsessed him. Halsey started getting up every morning in the certain knowledge that she would be there in the shadows. He wanted to see her eyes behind the Ray-Bans. He walked up to her and without saying a word . . . in his mind.

Arab women covered their faces. But you could still see their eyes. He looked at them on the street, trying to catch their gaze. As soon as they saw him they'd look away.

Cowboy boots in Levis. Black, hand-tooled and a black shirt. Halsey was describing conductivity and he glanced in her direction. For a moment there he was sure their eyes met.

She had eyes like stars.

'Musa showed up today.' Crow was breathing heavily, running and talking. 'Looked at the suppressors, says they're too big. Tried them out, says they're too loud. So I said — you want them a coupla inches long and go phutt like they do in the movies? Jumps up and down, says, yes that's what he wants. I say it ain't possible. The guy goes crazy.'

Crow slowed, watching Halsey leave him. After three miles Crow had had enough and sat down on the edge of the cinder track. Halsey did another four laps without any apparent effort, sprinting the last fifty. He pulled up opposite Crow, his hands on hips, back bent, breathing deeply.

'I don't have the stamina,' said Crow, pushing up, dusting cinders and dirt from his tracksuit. 'One hundred, two. Anything over that, no stamina.'

They could hear distant shouting as they walked towards the tunnel that led out of the stadium. A black African was trying sprint starts. Powering off his blocks.

'This guy is good. He has the right build,' Halsey said.

The African cleared three hurdles. He slowed after the third hurdle, lifted his head smiling, showing very white teeth.

Crow said, 'Arabs running. Never seen an Arab out on the track.'

They came through the tunnel into the parking lot. Halsey saw crowds of students gathering over by a building at the other end of the University complex, near the Sidi al Marsri road. Then he saw the soldiers. The access to the road was blocked with trucks.

'You wanna find out what's going on?'

Halsey shook his head.

'I don't see any other way out of here. Without running the risk of getting shot at.'

Halsey looked over his shoulder at the perimeter. Three soldiers with Kalashnikovs, bayonets fixed, were heading in their direction. Two broke away, moving off towards the stadium.

'*Yalla.*' The soldier held the rifle level with Halsey's stomach.

Crow said, 'Listen, you wanna see some papers?' The soldier was shouting now.

Halsey held up his hands and started walking. 'He wants us to move.'

Crow followed. 'What's this about?'

The Kalashnikov swung on to his back.

Across open ground, from the faculty buildings either side of the central circulation road, small groups of students were being herded together. They got so far and could go no further, because the crowd stretched out and surrounded them as others came at the back. Halsey was aware that no one knew what was going on. He noticed that everyone seemed apprehensive.

Off in the distance Halsey heard chanting. Someone revved a heavy diesel engine. A yellow crane jib with a small platform rose above the line of heads. Halsey could see three figures. One wearing a black uniform, the other two tied to the outside of the metal barrier around the platform.

The crane reached a height of twenty feet and stopped. Somebody started shouting through a loud hailer. Halsey watched the people around him trying to gauge what was being said by the reaction. The agitation in the crowd died. The disembodied voice fell silent. Up above, the man in the black uniform held up two nooses. A woman screamed.

Halsey looked at Crow. Crow said, 'My God.' All around faces were turned away.

When the body fell the rope snapped against the platform, rocking the jib arm. Halsey felt his throat constrict. A man beside him vomited in the gutter. The second body dropped into the void and the crane lurched. On the gantry the executioner stood alone, gripping the rail, calling down. The crane started rising and then descended slowly to the point where the bodies could no longer be seen. The executioner climbed over the barrier and jumped down. The bodies reappeared, dangling, dancing over the crowd. Halsey felt a wave of nausea.

Crow said, 'Christ. They must have been drugged.'

It was all over in minutes. The soldiers were allowing the students to leave. Trucks were pulling out on to the road. Everyone drifting away, too stunned to speak. As the crowd thinned out, Halsey was sure he saw the woman he called Carlotta. He saw her standing with her arm against a VW Beetle, head bent, dry retching.

'Let's get the fuck outta here,' Crow said.

The woman straightened up, she got in the car. Halsey wanted to go over and say, what, great hanging, let's have a drink. He turned away, following Crow as the VW rattled into life.

The Eagle cruised slowly by the two corpses, carefully skirting the crane. Someone had tied signs in Arabic to the legs. A reminder of their crimes. Sacrifices to Al Fatah.

Washington DC

'I like to see the blood flow,' said the senator.

O'Brien tossed the T-bone on the barbecue. There was a deep red stain on his white shirt.

'That's why I went into politics.' Ash fell from the senator's nicotine-stained fingers on to the jacket of his English-tailored Prince of Wales pattern suit. He brushed the ash away with the same hand. 'Satisfy my bloodlust.'

O'Brien stabbed the steak with a fork. Blood oozed from the wound and dripped in the fire as the uncooked side fell on to the griddle.

The senator checked his fly buttons. 'I hear you're screwing my secretary, Jack.' He looked up. 'I rather frown on this liaison. My fatherly concern for Arlene . . .'

O'Brien interrupted. 'You are fucking that piece of ass when you can get it up.'

'Damned if I'll be cuckolded or become a procurer.'

O'Brien said, 'Procuring Inspector Generals is more your line of work.' He laughed. 'And you stand to make half a million which is more than any pimp ever made from a whore.'

The senator held up his cigarette to make a point.

O'Brien said, 'You're sitting on your ass while this whore is out feeding back pricing information. You're sitting on your ass toying with Arlene's tits, trying to get it up so you can fuck her. And figure out at the same time how you can fuck me.'

He slapped the bleeding meat on a plate and twisted the fork.

Bill Mason, in jodhpurs, brown leather riding boots and a white Lacoste sports shirt, crossed the lawn, walking away from the lake up towards the charbroil set up under an oak tree.

Mason held out his hand. 'Senator Farnsworth. Bill Mason. We met on the Intelligence Select Committee last month.'

The senator didn't hesitate. 'Bill. Good to see you again. I didn't know you were a friend of Jack's.'

They shook hands.

'How about a steak? Anyone need a drink?' Mason moved over to the cane bar-cart less than ten feet away.

'Fix me another one of these,' O'Brien said.

Mason said, 'Gin, ice?'

'Generous with the gin.'

The senator had his steak. He collected his highball from the slatted wooden garden table behind O'Brien and made his way over to the larger garden table laid out with salads and a choice of desserts. Mason followed with his eyes the erect bearing, the well-tailored elder statesman.

'When I look at Senator Henry Farnsworth of Illinois,' said O'Brien, 'the distinguished senator, I think of all the baksheesh he's had over the years. He can't afford a new suit. Does he have a vice I don't know about?'

Mason wandered back to the barbecue with a gin in one hand and a beer in the other. 'The suit's probably twenty years old, part of the poor but honest backwoods lawyer carrying the voice of Illinois to the Capitol.'

'How you want the steak?'

'Medium rare and on a plate.' Mason tried his beer. 'Where is our hostess?'

'That bitch.' O'Brien finished the drink in his glass and collected the fresh one from Mason. 'Probably tormenting those other bitches in the county set, showing them what my money buys.' He speared the steak, turned it over and waved the fork. 'This place and Elaine. Breaking my back.'

'Sell the farm. Get a divorce.'

O'Brien rolled the ice around his glass. 'I'm thinking of going into politics.'

Mason had a mouthful of beer. He coughed, almost choked, but recovered well. 'Run for Congress?'

'I'm giving it some serious thought.'

'I have a feeling you might have one or two problems on foreign policy issues.'

'I see my experience in the Middle East as an asset.'

Mason nodded and walked over to the bar-cart to pour himself a stiff drink. 'How're things in Tripoli?' He wondered if it wasn't time to start distancing himself from O'Brien.

San Bernardino

Leo Schine at seventy was proud to be asked to play a part. He was a patriot. Born in the Warsaw Ghetto, he emigrated with his parents after the First World War. Fighting in the Second World War with the 34th Infantry, he had a battlefield commission in the desert and was heroically wounded, receiving the Silver Star for gallantry in action. Leo Schine had been honored by his adopted country, and when he saw the camps at Buchenwald and Auschwitz he got down on his knees and cried for the dead and dying, for his family back home in the States and for himself. He cried for America.

Now he was a semi-retired lawyer with a practice that was winding down. He still had some good clients. Some had started in business at the same time he had in the early fifties, getting his law degree on the GI Bill and hanging up his shingle.

Harry Morgan had been with him less than ten years and Schine hadn't done more than routine legal paperwork. Morgan called him one day saying he needed a pro forma contract for a Liechtenstein company selling chemicals. Schine drafted the contract and thought no more about it. A few days later Morgan called asking him if he'd go to Geneva to arrange payments and then on to a supplier in Canada.

In Montreal Schine had found out that the chemicals were plastic explosives, C4. He wasn't surprised. Back in California, one or two things started to bother him.

'Leo. Good to see you. How was your trip?'

Morgan had old brick warehouses on the outskirts of San Bernardino and a shack that he called headquarters.

'At my age, you come back, it's a good trip.' Schine in his suit jacket two sizes too large, the pants bagging.

'You're three years older than I am. I'm not ready for Sun City.'

Morgan was sitting at a scarred wooden desk. Schine standing, looking down at the iron-gray crewcut. The bulk of the man overflowing the wooden chair.

Morgan took off his half-rim glasses and returned a sheaf of papers to the desktop. 'Take a seat, Leo. What's on your mind?'

'Why didn't you tell me it was C4?' Schine glanced out the window. A yellow forklift roared by with a stack of pallets.

'Christ, Leo, you know I'm an old army man. I operate on a need to know basis.' Morgan rocked back. There were dark rings of sweat under the armpits of his shirt. 'I'm a licensed dealer.'

'You're planning on shipping that C4 out of the country. You need a permit.' Schine saw labels on the desk. 'Drilling mud. Since when are you in the oil business?'

The forklift came by again carrying oildrums.

'What's going on?'

Morgan had a grave expression on his face. He cleared his throat, 'Leo, we've been lawyer and client now for what, ten years? Friends for a good many of those years. I could ask you to forget what you've seen. But I respect you and hope we have a relationship of trust.' He steepled his fingers. 'What I'm about to tell you I don't have to tell you. In fact I may even be breaking the law. But I figure it's lawyer/client privilege. I know you're a patriot. Wounded in action. Silver Star. I know you'd want to serve your country again, given the chance.' Morgan swivelled around in the chair to face the window and back to face Schine. 'I'm working for the National Security Council.'

'Jesus wept,' said Schine.

Morgan waited, staring at him. Finally he eased himself out of the chair in a deliberate manner and moved over to the small safe and dialled the combination, taking out a large manila envelope, tossing it on the desk. 'I want you to do your job and serve your country at the same time.' Morgan looked for the right response.

'Tell me what you want me to do.'

'I want you to take the money in the envelope to a freight-forwarding company in Miami. Fly to Houston and supervise the loading of a charter. Make sure everything runs without a hitch.'

'Where is the shipment going?'

Morgan came round the desk, checking to make sure they weren't overheard. Leaning forward he said, 'Libya.'

Schine reflected on the knowledge. 'Ours is not to reason why. Ours is but to do or die. Right?'

Morgan took a small silver disc from his back pocket. 'This is a National Security identification piece. I want you to carry it at all times throughout this operation.' He pressed the medallion into Schine's hand.

Schine looked at it. Inscribed on the face were the words GOD, MAN AND COUNTRY.

Tripoli

'Did you shop with your wife?' asked Francine.

'Yeah,' said Halsey.

They walked down an aisle lined on either side, four shelves high, with Fairy Snow. Halsey stopped pushing the cart and examined a pack. Detergent. Stretching into the distance.

Halsey said, 'Detergent,' not believing that there was that much detergent in Africa. Turning the cart, halfway down into the next aisle, empty shelves. He stopped and looked both ways. Nothing. Francine was going on. She came back.

'Sometimes they forget to re-order. Or they can't get the goods. Olive oil, cooking oil. The Italians planted enough olive trees here to produce all the Libyans need.' Francine stepped in front of Halsey, grabbing the bar of the cart. 'They import American corn oil.'

They arrived at shelves stacked with Bulgarian evaporated milk. Francine began throwing cans in the cart.

'Get it while you can.' Moving on she said, 'Dietary law. No pig. No frankfurters, salami. Same as Jewish dietary laws.' Looking at Halsey. 'People try and sneak ham or baloney through the customs.

'You heard the one about the priest and the rabbi? On a train.'

Halsey could see she wanted to tell the joke, or make a point.

'They're discussing sin. The priest says, "Have you tried pork?" ' making the priest Irish, 'and the rabbi says, "Have you tried screwing?" The priest doesn't want to say anything. Then he confesses. Rabbi says, "Better than pork?" ' '

Halsey laughed.

'We need rice,' said Francine, trying to remember where the rice was. 'I think it's over by the checkout.'

'Are you from a strict family?'

'Strict?'

'Orthodox. You're Jewish.'

Halsey stopped the cart. 'Yes, I'm Jewish.' He narrowed his eyes turning the statement into a question.

Francine said, 'I'm Irish and Polack at the same time. Two racial stereotypes for the same money. My grandmother died in Treblinka alongside the Jews and the homosexuals.'

Halsey was sorry.

Francine continued on towards the checkout. 'Jack doesn't like Jews. He doesn't like blacks or Arabs. In fact there are very few people Jack has a good word for. The Irish. The Kennedys. He sees himself in the same rough-hewn mould as Jack Kennedy. Buccaneer, political mover. Ambassador O'Brien. Jews are too smart. Calls himself a democrat.' They reached the rice. 'And Nixon. Nixon is Irish.'

Halsey picked up a fifty kilo bag.

'Eva. Is that a German name?'
Halsey said, 'I don't know. But yes she is German.'
'How long were you married?'
Halsey couldn't remember. Willi was five. 'Two, three years.'
'You still in touch?'
'I send her a cheque once in a while. She lives in Germany. The kid is with his grandmother in California.'
'A supermarket in Libya is a long way from California.'

Halsey was driving on the coast road out of Tripoli, the Uqban Bin Nafia Highway going east. Fredo in the front of the Eagle, Chasen and Crow in back.

Fredo in a sharp Italian suit, wrap-around dark glasses, heavy rings and a Beretta 9mm automatic. A made man. A member of the Honored Society. From Corleone, he said. Fredo liked to talk.

'Gambling and loan-sharking. I'm in this bar near Walpole with Raymond Iacoretti, who's a good friend of Papa Doc Duvalier down in Haiti. I had this thing going where I would get these guys and make them an offer to put their money to work on the streets. Return a point a week, two points off the top. Greed. I'm talking about greed. You can reach out . . .'

'How far is this place?' said Chasen.

Fredo looked over his shoulder. 'Two hundred kilometers.'

'What's that in miles?' Chasen was unhappy.

'Hundred and twenty.' Fredo hadn't said where they were going. He liked to keep things mysterious. 'I'm talking about insurance salesmen, doctors. They go for it because they got money, hidden money they don't want to tell Uncle Sam. It's psychological. You talk, see what they're interested in. Women, introduce the guy to a woman. Find out if maybe they're homosexual. Faggots. There's a place, a gay club. I'm talking about the fifties. People were moral. The guy gets a blow job, never been blown in his life. He's grateful. And I'm picking up the check.

'The guy really goes for the idea. He's around the environment and he's gonna have his money out on the streets. Reluctantly, you take his money because you're doing the guy a favor. A couple weeks you let the bozo have a point. He likes it so much he wants to increase his investment. You got maybe a hundred, you kiss the guy off.'

Fredo had been in Libya since the sixties when the king was in power and the Italians ran the place. Now the Italians were just another group of foreign workers.

Fredo said, 'You go along the coast and you say, "This must be a nice place, Libya. I think I'll build a hotel here. Start a casino. Beaches are good. The sun shines. Camels, palm trees, olive trees, a few Libyans standing around their old tunny boats. Miami in north Africa. Make a lot of money, real estate." Then you take a look around. Whadda ya see? You see ruins. Castles, towns, farms. And you begin to wonder what happened. Where are the Romans, the Spanish, the Turks, the French, the Italians? They didn't hang around. And you have to ask yourself why.' Fredo staring out towards the shore.

'And what's the answer?' asked Chasen.

'Fucked if I know.'

The road stretched out ahead, shimmering. Driving across parched pre-desert, the sea a deep blue edged with gold, olive groves, lush green cultivated landscape, a tree-lined oasis. In the distance, not far from Al Khums, a camel train.

Fredo said, 'A coupla kilometers up the road. There's a town, Zlitan.'

Crow spoke for the first time since Tripoli. 'This the place?'

'Have to take care of a little business,' said Fredo.

'See a guy about a camel,' said Chasen.

Halsey parked the Eagle in the shade of a palm near the square. Fredo said to hang round, count the palm trees. They have a lot of palm trees. He was going to be gone ten, fifteen mintues. After about thirty seconds Halsey said he wanted to take a look around.

Chasen said, 'I could use a cold beer.'

Crow and Chasen went in search of a beer. A mirage.

Fredo was leaving the square. Halsey decided to go in the same direction towards the round white tower reaching above the town. Fredo had disappeared down an alley.

Halsey found himself on a broad dirt street with one tall palm snaking high above the low white buildings. Taller than the tree, the minaret of a mosque with arrow-slit windows in line up to the blue balcony.

A group of men in white howlis, sitting on a stone bench, or standing, stared at Halsey. Halsey looked around. Everything was white, the buildings, the Arabs on the white step. The roof of the mosque was a white egg-box construction. He took a pair of dark glasses from the neck of his white polo shirt and started retracing his steps. Not sure where the square was, not hurrying back.

Down an alley in shadow, following a kid in a black jacket holding a white box up high with his right hand. Pastries in a cardboard box. The alley was dark and cool. Coming into the sunlight, crossing a street with vine-covered shops and into another alley in the same shadow. Halsey remembered that the kid carried on walking, turning into a street. Looking over to the left and seeing a shape, something he recognized, or someone. Then nothing. Seeing a vivid blue sky. Then nothing. Remembered a fragrance. A faint fragrance that somehow didn't belong to the street. Perfume. A woman's perfume.

Halsey came round a few minutes later in the alley, throwing up. He had been dragged out of sight of the street. Standing up he checked his wallet. Still there in the back pocket. The dark glasses lay in the dirt, the lenses shattered.

'Where the fuck have you been?' said Crow. 'Looks like you just had the shit kicked out of you.'

Halsey got in the four-wheeler. Fredo was sitting in the front with a cold drink in his hand. He offered the plastic cup to Halsey.

'Orange juice.'

Halsey grabbed and emptied the cup in one movement.

'You lose much money?' Fredo said.

'Not a cent.'

The wheels of the Eagle spun in the dust.

In Misrātah Fredo directed them to a tract of land that had the makings of a construction site. A group of mobile homes and offices lay alongside the road forming an open-sided triangle.

'Pull over here,' said Fredo.

Chasen drove on to the track made by the heavy plant, over to a red trailer.

'Hold it right here.' Fredo got out and went into the trailer. Five mintues later he came to the door and waved to come in.

There was a muscular Italian wearing shorts and a blue-and-white striped soccer shirt sat at a small table. Fredo introduced him as Franco. They all squeezed round the table. Franco brought out a bottle of Johnny Walker Black Label and poured shots into various cups, jars and glasses from a shelf.

Fredo said, 'This one's on the house. The rest we gotta pay for. Salute.'

On the drive back to Tripoli with four cases of scotch Fredo started singing Sicilian folk songs. With Fredo singing and the pounding from the road, Halsey began to feel his head.

Fredo said, 'You don't look so good.'

They stopped between Zlitan and Al Khums near the ruins of a Roman city so Halsey could get some air. Halsey walked in the twilight among the pillars of classical stone. A crumbling former civilization. His head was still hurting. He was trying to remember something just beyond his reach, something that happened in the alley.

Fredo appeared from behind an arch. 'Whadda ya think?'

'If you like columns it's not bad,' said Halsey. The silence defined by the distant breaking waves on the shore and the cicadas. The broken stones taking on shapes in the half light.

'This used to be a great civilization. Look at it now. *Che sera sera.*'

O'Brien stood in the office in front of the large glass desk, alternately staring out through the blinds at the castle and down at the unique pattern of the Misrātah carpet.

The man behind the desk fingered his stubbly moustache and said nothing.

O'Brien made a rasping sound in his throat. 'Brother Jalloud.'

Jalloud held up his hand for silence.

Lying on the desk, caught in a shaft of light, was Tuareg dagger. Jalloud ran his finger along the etched blade. A curving edge. Deep red blood trickled and dripped on the glass. He watched a pool of blood form, before standing and taking a white linen handkerchief from the breast pocket of his charcoal gray suit. Jalloud stanched the flow of blood, balling up the handkerchief in his fist.

'Jalloud thinks he's a fucking Shiite martyr.'

Francine was making a sandwich. Putting cheese on the bread. 'He's a Sunni,' she said.

'Quoting the fucking Koran at me. The heaven on high. The balance. That I might not fucking transgress.'

*   *   *

65

O'Brien examined the carpet, not listening to Jalloud. The abstract design a woven garden. The Garden of Allah. Breeze from the fan rattling the blind. He couldn't figure Jalloud.

'Velveeta cheese,' said Francine.
    O'Brien said, 'Christ, that fucking Arab ate my lunch.'
    'Velveeta. Your favorite, Jack.'

O'Brien stood alone in the office. He tried looking round for the hidden cameras. Jalloud was probably in the next room with a line of monitors watching him on TV. Or running a tape of the interview. See how it went.
    O'Brien had been there five minutes. The old Arab was at the door. He turned his back and went down the corridor. O'Brien followed. The elevator was waiting. As the doors closed, the old Arab creased his face in a smile.

'You want a cheese sandwich?' Francine held up a can of aerosol cheese.
    Halsey seemed hesitant.
    'American cheese. Imported.' Francine set about making the sandwiches and Halsey filled the kettle. The faucet gushed air before the water came.
    A hammer started up on the nearby construction site.
    Halsey said, 'Where's Jack?'
    The hammer stopped.
    'He's gone to a meeting with Jalloud.'
    Halsey found two mugs.
    'There's a jar of Maxwell House.' Francine sliced bread. 'Are you still married to your wife?'
    'So who else's wife should I be married to.'
    'A question with a question.'
    'Have you seen your old man?' Halsey spread margarine on the cut slices.
    'He's back from Benghazi next week. On his way out to Geneva. Bringing back more Green Berets.'
    'What do they do?'
    'Teach advanced basic training.'
    'You don't see much of him.'
    'He's screwing around.' Cheese oozed out of the canister. 'Is that how your marriage ended?'

'Eva just walked out. She said she couldn't live in America.'
Halsey poured water over the coffee granules, dissolving them. He
poured canned milk into both mugs. 'Why don't you go back to
the States? Get out?'

Francine shook her head, turning away. There was a tear in her
eye. Halsey put his arm round her shoulder.

The hammer started again.

'What the fuck's going on here?' O'Brien walked in the kitchen.

Halsey said, 'We're having lunch.'

'Lunch.'

Francine moved away from Halsey. 'So how'd the meeting go?'

'That chickenshit cocksucker.'

'Have a cheese sandwich,' said Francine.

'Screwing all my deals. He's fucking me both ways.'

Francine said, 'I always knew you were versatile Jack.'

O'Brien ignored her. 'No one wants to do business with me
because they figure I'm working for Jalloud. They won't do
business without being on the take. They figure I'm gonna tell
Jalloud. So they won't do business. Jalloud has got me by the balls
and he's squeezing.'

'Have a cheese sandwich, Jack,' said Francine.

O'Brien said, 'Velveeta?'

'The Velveeta's all gone. We've got cheddar and chive.'

'Jesus fucking Christ. Who had the Velveeta?'

Francine said, 'Jalloud.'

Houston

Leo Schine was on the tarmac at Houston Intercontinental
watching the flatbed truck with the drums labelled 'drilling mud'
pull up alongside the DC8 charter. A tug pulling the conveyor belt
was approaching in the other direction. The temperature was in
the nineties and Schine was sweating in his seersucker suit. He
looked uncomfortable.

Willie Dougan took the tug under the body of the plane, lining
up the conveyor belt with the cargo door, parked and strolled over
to where Schine was standing near the truck. He had a pissed off
expression on his face.

'Mr Schine,' said Dougan. 'We don't have no forklift truck.' He shook his head wearily. 'We're gonna have to load these fuckers by hand. It's gonna take a long time and it's hot as hell out here. What I'm sayin', go have a cold one, sit in that air-conditioned bar. Have one for me.'

Schine took off his straw hat and mopped his head. 'Mr Dougan, I'd like to do that but I have to watch you load the drums.'

Dougan spat a mouthful of tobacco juice. 'No offence, Mr Schine. I don't figure any of my boys gonna steal your drillin' mud.'

'No offence, Mr Dougan. I have my duty to do.'

Dougan looked away over to where the loading crew were walking towards them. They were singing. Singing 'You Are My Sunshine'. Dougan stood there with his hands on his hips and watched them for a while. Then said, 'Hell, I'm glad you boys are havin' such a good time while I'm doin' all the work. I think I'm gonna shit-can the lot of you and hire me a bunch of niggers. Sing better.'

A head taller than the other crewmen, John McCall broke away, went over to Dougan and picked him up in a bear hug, shaking him around.

'Quit that and put me down, motherfucker.'

Dougan almost swallowed the quid of tobacco, choking, his face red.

McCall put him down. 'Yeah. Bunch of niggers, huh,' he said. Dougan trying to regain his authority. The crew laughing.

'You ain't gonna be laughing like jackasses when I tell you the forklift is on the fritz again.' Dougan grinned as general discontent spread.

After fifteen minutes McCall climbed down from the cargo hold and went to stand beside Dougan. He took a few deep breaths. 'You callin' a time out?' said Dougan.

'Hot and it stinks of cattle in there. Who's the little guy in the Frank Sinatra hat?'

'Jew boy checkin' we don't misappropriate his drillin' mud.'

'How do I apply for his job?'

Dougan spat juice. 'First you go to college four years. And you don't screw around playin' football. Then you go to law school three years. Then you get some dumb-assed clients gonna pay you a thousand bucks a day countin' fuckin' drums of drillin' mud. But before you do all this you gotta get yourself chosen. You know what I'm sayin'.' He glanced over at Schine. 'You gotta get yourself picked by God. An' you know how you can recognize God's chosen people,' Dougan paused and smiled, 'cos they're the ones sittin' on their ass countin', you're doin' all the fuckin' work.'

An hour went by in the blistering heat. Schine sat on his attaché case in the shade of the truck with his jacket off and his tie loose round his neck. He got up and stretched his legs, walking in Dougan's direction with his jacket over his shoulder, carrying the attaché case. He tipped the hat back, looking more like Sinatra.

'Mr Dougan,' said Schine. 'Ah. I think I will get that cold drink.'

Dougan spat tobacco and smiled. He directed him to the rest room. 'You'll find a Coke machine.'

Schine disappeared round a corner. Dougan told the men to take a break. McCall wandered over to Dougan. 'I knew the little fucker wouldn't stay the distance.'

Sweat was running down McCall's face. He ran his shoulder across his eyebrows and tasted salt on his lips. 'I don't see you bustin' your ass.'

Dougan stepped forward and shouted to the crew stretched out in various shady corners. 'John here is sayin' he don't need no help to get the rest of these loaded. So I guess you got the day off.'

There was general cheering.

'Okay, back to work.'

'Hey, we only just quit workin'.'

'I enjoy kickin' ass. Until I retire from this job in five years I'm gonna kick ass. Savvy?'

The crew in the hold switched with the men working the truck. McCall got up on the back of the flatbed. The job was to work the drums along on their rims over to the belt. It took two men to get the drums up and keep them moving along. McCall figured he could swing one of them on his own. He got a hold and started rolling. Dougan looked over, thinking dumb fucking ox, shaking his head.

McCall's knee gave out. He screamed out, 'Ah shit. My leg.'

The drum fell down the side of the truck and hit the ground, spilling viscous mud. Dougan went over to the site of the accident. The container was right out of shape. Very little of the contents seemed to be spilled. But the lid would never go back.

'Get the tug. Somebody get some sand, cover this up.' Dougan looked up at McCall. 'How's the leg?'

'Okay I guess.' McCall held his thigh, letting the knee move without any weight on it.

They had the drum upright.

McCall said, 'That's the weirdest drillin' mud I ever saw.'

'All right, get rid of this thing before the jew boy comes back.'

They loaded the drum on to the back of the tug.

'Take it to the nearest dumpster. I want the truck moved to cover this mess.'

The truck was in place and the crew working again when Schine came under the wing of the plane with his attaché case held out. Coke cans were piled on top. He walked over to Dougan and said he thought that the men might like a drink.

McCall standing there said, 'That's mighty nice of you.' Hobbling over on his injured knee.

Dougan reluctantly took a can.

Schine said, 'What happened to your leg?'

'Old football injury. I had a coupla seasons as a line backer with the Oilers.' McCall showed pain. 'Then my knee gave out.'

The tug was coming across the shimmering strip, burning black smoke.

'That's too bad,' said Schine.

Tripoli

'Fucker is top of my shit list. O'Brien was putting the phone down.

Katz said, 'What fucker's that?'

'Fucking Lynch.'

Katz was sitting in front of the Adler, typing a proposal on electronic surveillance equipment. He carried on punishing the machine with two fingers.

O'Brien, pacing, said, 'When I get my hands on that shit, I'm gonna take his wooden leg away from him and use it to beat his fucking brains in.' He stopped to fill his glass with more flash from the bottle on the desk. Not diluting it with juice.

'You oughta cut down,' said Katz.

O'Brien grunted and took a pull at the drink. He grimaced as it went down. Poured some orange from a carton and stirred with his finger.

Katz decided that staying in business with O'Brien was playing with a loaded gun. He stopped typing, nodding to himself, his analysis.

O'Brien sat down in a new yellow lounge-chair. He racked it to an upright position and slumped back. Extreme tiredness swept over him. Mesmerized by the clatter of the machine, he dozed.

A car was coming along the track. O'Brien's body jerked in spasm. In a half second he came awake, swung his legs over and stood up, looking down through the window.

'Holy shit. It's Musa's Merc.'

Katz grabbed the bottle of flash and stashed it in the file cabinet. He took his glass and followed O'Brien into the bathroom. They flushed the drinks down the pan. O'Brien found the mouthwash, spun the cup, took a swig from the bottle and gave it to Katz. Heavy blows echoed through the villa. O'Brien nearly gagged, swallowing some of the mouthwash. The rest he sent in the general direction of the washbasin.

O'Brien hit the stairs running, flattening his hair with the palm of his hand. He checked his appearance in a wrought-iron frame mirror in the lobby.

Katz carefully wiped the neck of the bottle with a towel before pouring mouthwash into his glass. 'Cheers old boy.'

O'Brien opened the front door. Captain Ibrahim Musa was standing there in a white silk suit next to a uniformed soldier. 'Mr Jack,' Musa took off metal rim sunglasses. His eyes were dark. 'I would be pleased to introduce Lieutenant Omar el Bishari.'

'Well gentlemen,' O'Brien oozing charm, 'this is a great honor. My house is your house.'

He led the way up the stairs to the office, saying that any friend of Captain Musa . . .

'How about a glass of mint tea?' said O'Brien.

Musa nodded.

'And some of those . . . chocolate chip cookies?'

Musa cracked a smile. Thin lips, a gaunt face.

'Frank. Could you get some tea for our guests? And cookies.'

Katz said, 'Yeah, sure.' He went off to the kitchen. It would be obscene. O'Brien in there. Jerking off with a few notes round his dick. Christ, O'Brien would do anything for money, reach in his own pocket steal some money.

'Let me get this straight,' said O'Brien. 'You want fifty handguns.

And you're willing to pay five thousand a piece. They have to be American handguns, bought and registered in the States.' O'Brien couldn't believe it. A quarter of a million for fifty guns. 'I'm not going to ask you why you want these guns.'

Musa interrupted. 'We want these weapons for assassination.'

O'Brien laughed involuntarily. 'Why don't you go to the local store?'

'We want American guns.'

O'Brien, standing by the desk in front of Musa, raised his eyebrows and pursed his lips. He would have licked them.

'Quarter of a million.' O'Brien turned away and then back. 'I don't think we should mention this to Mr Frank.'

Musa smiled.

O'Brien thought about writing a contract. Keep it simple. 'Cash on the nail. We don't want to put this through the books.'

Musa said. 'There is currency in my office. Dollars. Francs. Marks.'

O'Brien had an impression of a room, the walls stacked with notes. Millions.

'I will tell you next week where to deliver the first consignment,' said Musa.

'We didn't talk about delivery.' O'Brien heard Katz on the stairs and looked over at Musa's stony face. 'What the hell. Free delivery for such a good customer.'

Katz came in with a tray.

'Ah, tea,' said Musa.

'And cookies?' O'Brien asked Katz.

'Sorry. No cookies. You must have eaten the last one, Jack.'

Airborne

Schine couldn't get comfortable on the crate in the cargo hold of the DC8. He was bent and aching, trying to keep his legs from going to sleep. He rested his head and shoulders against the bulkhead, looking out over a sea of black drums. By the time the plane was loaded it had been impossible to count them. But then as the redneck said, who was going to steal drilling mud?

An old man perched on a box in the cargo hold of a DC8 over the Mediterranean. Schine felt ridiculous. He had had plenty of time to think about the situation. Consider the irony. The stench of cattle was overwhelming. A cattle plane carrying eleven tons of C4 to Libya. Someone in government planned this, approved the shipment.

Tripoli

Morgan had gone on ahead. He wanted to be there and collect his money from O'Brien. Three hundred thousand on one deal. He was there to meet the flight when it landed.

'Leo, you don't look too good. You okay?' Morgan was sympathetic.

'I feel sick Harry.' Schine unsteady on his feet. Morgan took his arm and helped him to the airport building. He sat down on a green molded plastic seat and looked up at Morgan. 'That's better. Stink of cattle.' Schine saw beyond Morgan Muammar al Gadafi. His face staring down.

'When you're feeling up to it, we have a car waiting outside.'

Schine said, 'I'll be all right when I take a shower, get out of these clothes.' The suit was crumpled and smeared with drilling mud and cowshit.

'Maybe something to eat,' said Morgan.

Schine shook his head, feeling his stomach churn.

'Listen, did you get my bag?'

Morgan said, 'How many?'

'Just the one.'

Morgan went off, leaving Schine to try and recover. Schine looked around, wondering why he ever wanted to get involved in this. His knee was hurting where he'd scraped it on the hatch leaving the plane. There was grazes on the palms of his hands where he'd tried to stop himelf from kissing the tarmac as he fell. A headache from the flight lingered.

When Morgan found Schine thirty minutes later he was standing naked facing the wall in a small windowless room. Schine turned, covering his genitals.

'Here.' Morgan handed over a stinking bundle of clothes. 'Get dressed, Leo, and let's get outta here.'

'What's going on, Harry?'

'I don't know. They made a mistake. Happens all the time apparently.'

Schine put his clothes on facing the wall. He followed Morgan back out on to the concourse. Morgan was making for the exit. Schine put his hand on Morgan's arm.

'I'll take the next available flight. I don't care where it's going.'

Morgan stopped. 'They have our passports, Leo. The consignment has to be verified before we're allowed to leave.' He continued on.

Schine had no strength to argue.

'Nine or ten million in a number of deals. There's a deal to equip the forces with uniforms could gross three, four millions.'

Morgan sat there in O'Brien's office, listening to O'Brien counting in millions.

'How much are you making on this deal?' said O'Brien.

'Eighty thousand.'

O'Brien slid his hand into the pocket of his pants. 'Why don't I tell the Libyans there's another twelve pounds in those drums. All you do is change the figures on the consignment note. I'll cut you in twenty percent on the new price.

'Twenty-five.'

O'Brien removed his right hand from his pants and the two men shook hands. Morgan set about changing the figures.

'Won't the Libyans weigh the drums?' said Morgan.

'Whadda ya think,' said O'Brien. 'The Arabs may have invented mathematics but I haven't met one smart enough to count his fingers after he shakes hands.' He laughed. 'You've got to understand the psychology of these people. When I tell them about the extra twelve pounds, right before I tell them I'm going to ask them, "Where do you figure this came from?" They'll look dumb and say, "I don't know, tell us Mr Jack." Then I'll look serious and say, "Stolen from the US Arsenal in Washington DC." And they'll burst out laughing and jump up and down. Wet their pants it's so funny.

'I tell them about the extra twelve pounds. They say "Mr Jack, Mr Jack, that's even funnier. Here's another two hundred thousand.' " O'Brien held out his palm. ' "And here's fifty for you. Buy yourself something." '

74

Washington DC

'Mikey. I heard you were hanging out here.' Katz sat down at the table near the bar.

The bar was dark and warm. And up until that moment Lynch had been feeling safe. Sitting there in a corner with a seltzer in front of him untouched.

Katz caught the waiter's attention and ordered a gin and tonic. 'What'll you have Mikey?'

'I have a drink.'

'You'll change your mind. And a scotch rocks.'

The waiter drifted off to another table.

Katz took out a pack of Camels and his Zippo. He offered Lynch a cigarette, took one and threw the pack on the table.

The waiter brought the drinks, putting them on little paper coasters with an embossed sun and lion design.

Katz was serious. 'Mikey, Jack is very upset you doing this to him. He's been like a father to you.'

Lynch looked at the glass on the tabletop. The ice melting.

'It can all be straightened out. You had one or two drinks and you talked to some people. All you do is call them up and say it was a mistake.' Katz patted Lynch on the leg.

'Okay, who'd you talk to. You talked to the family. Who else?'

'FBI.'

'Whadda they say?'

'I don't think they believed me.'

'Then we don't have a problem. Jack is gonna be very happy.' Katz picked up the gin and tonic, took the slice of lemon and ate the flesh. 'He talked about having someone take care of you.'

Lynch turned pale.

'Jack gets upset, doesn't know what he's saying.' Katz stubbed the cigarette into a black ceramic ashtray.

'I have a meeting tomorrow,' said Lynch.

Katz held the Camels and Zippo in his hand, pulling them towards him. He flipped the Zippo with his thumb and took another Camel, taking his own time.

'Drink up, Mikey. We're having a celebration here. Sheep back to the fold. The prodigal son returns.' Katz waved to the waiter, drawing a circle in the air. 'Watch this.' He spun the wheel of the

75

lighter. There were sparks and no flame. Spun the wheel again and it caught. 'Magic.' Katz lit the cigarette.

The waiter was there placing the glasses on fresh coasters.

'Let me have some of those nuts,' said Katz. 'Whadda ya say we finish these and go have a drink?'

Lynch looked at the two glasses of whisky on the table. The ice had melted in the first. The second had droplets of condensation forming. He reached out and put the back of his hand to the surface, feeling the chill of the ice.

Katz toyed with his glass, rolling the ice around, making a rattling sound.

'I was out in the desert down to Sabhah and it was hot, over a hundred. Could have been up to a hundred and twenty. The sand gets so hot they bake the bread, burying it. You know when it's cooked because the loaves send up little jets of sand. So I'm on the road going south. I stop, get out, stretch my legs, have a drink. There's this sea of sand stretching out either side of the road. A jackal is watching me about a coupla hundred yards off. The sand eddying, rolling. I get the water canister and whadda ya think? It's empty. The fucking thing is empty. My neck is so dry I can hardly swallow. You know how it is when you get that dry throat seizes up. Hard to breathe. And I look round the jackal has gone. Out of nowhere comes this tower of sand ninety feet high, more. There I am in the middle of the desert. The sky is so full of sand you can't see the sun. I have to get down in the sand and crawl along the ground with my jacket over my head, crawl across to the car. I'm under the car and the sand is piling up. I think I'm gonna be buried alive. Just another sand dune.' Katz made sucking sounds with the ice, watching Lynch with the whisky in front of him.

'There's a story about a holy man in the desert near Sabhah looking for water. His mouth all dried up, blisters on his face, can hardly move his lips. He can't hardly walk. This sheep appears. First off he thinks it's in his mind, he's going crazy with the heat. That happens. The sheep gets closer, he knows its for real. So he throws himself flat and gets out his knife. When the sheep gets close enough he slits the belly and drinks the blood. Then he finds a date in the stomach. So he figures where there's a date there's a palm tree and where there's a palm tree there's an oasis. He follows the sheep tracks and finds the water.' Katz touched Lynch's glass with his own. 'You're not drinking.' He held his glass up to show the waiter that he needed a refill. 'Cheers, chin-chin.'

Lynch had the whisky in his hand for five seconds, then chugged it down like a man dying of thirst.

Shock waves reverberated through the mountain. Rocks were falling, breaking away from the mountainside. A big crack opened up in a wall. The dwarves were at work again and they were using hammer drills.

'Mr Lynch. This is agent Hogg and agent Bratner. Open the door.' Hogg carried on hammering.

Lynch dragged himself off the bed and across the floor. Somehow he managed to reach out and slip the latch but then slumped down behind the door. Hogg heard the body fall. The door was open. Through the crack he could see the torso. He leant against the door, moving the dead weight over far enough to slide through.

Lynch lay on the floor fully dressed, wrapped in the bed cover. There was an overwhelming stench of alcohol and a half-empty fifth of Jim Beam on the bed.

'He's drunk as a skunk and smells worse.' Bratner took a step backwards. He glanced down the forecourt to where the manager and a group of the motel's residents were discussing the fate of the man in chalet five.

'We're wasting our time. Let's go back down the road and get a cuppa Java at that coffee shop.'

Hogg hunkered down by the inert body. 'Mr Lynch, wake up. Mike, come on, wake up.'

'He can't hear you. You got more chance waking the dead.'

The covers started to move. Without any warning Lynch screamed, 'My leg, my leg. Where's my leg?'

Bratner stepped into the room and closed the door. Hogg knelt down trying to examine Lynch under the covers. He felt down one side, reaching round. There was an empty pant leg. Bratner saw an expression of disbelief spread across Hogg's face.

'Leg's gone.'

'What do you mean, gone?' said Bratner.

Hogg waved the cuff. Lynch moaned and rolled around.

'Any blood?' Bratner looked around for signs of a struggle.

Hogg helped Lynch on to the bed. Bratner went into the

bathroom expecting to find blood in the tub. Out of the corner of his eye he saw a shadow behind the shower curtain. Something in there. Slowly he drew the curtain aside. Standing in the corner wearing a black sock and a black Oxford shoe was the leg.

'Okay, I found it.' Bratner went back in the bedroom, carrying the artificial leg and sat down on the bed.

'Here's your leg, Mikey.'

Tripoli

Francine leaned on the balcony, her left leg crossed behind her right. Her hip thrust out in a curve.

'What time's everyone arriving?' Halsey watched the tunny boats going out to fish. Following the stars rising with the moon in the evening sky.

'Soon.'

A gentle breeze blowing off the sea ruffled Francine's hair. Halsey, tanned in a white polo shirt, faced her, his back to the balcony wall.

'You're looking hunky tonight.' Francine sipped the scotch. She heard the four wheeler driving down the track, the gears crunching. Fredo and Crow. Fredo behind the wheel. 'Woman driver.'

The Eagle was weighed down at the back, grounding on the suspension.

Halsey said, 'I'll give them a hand.' He finished his drink and put the glass down. 'How come Fredo and Charlie are always around together?'

'They're planning to assassinate Gadafi and take over Libya.'

'Charlie doesn't get back till three and four in the morning.'

Fredo came through the door.

'*Ciao*, Fredo,' said Francine.

'Ah, *che bella*.' Fredo went over to the balcony and took Francine's hand, kissing it with lascivious kisses.

'Fredo used to be a pimp,' said Francine. 'You can tell by the suit. Glows in the dark.'

Crow crashed into the room, a crate in either hand. 'Fredo can't carry a fucking crate on account of his nail varnish.'

Fredo offered his hands to Francine. 'I just spent twenty bucks getting this manicure.' He turned to Halsey. 'I started pimping when I was ten years old. In Rome. The end of the war. Making more money than a ten-year-old knows about spending. I had no family to support. The GIs get drunk, you take their wallet away from them.' Fredo pulled out a platinum cigarette case. He offered Francine a cigarette. 'Turkish on this side, Virginia on the other.'

Francine said no.

Halsey followed Crow down to get the beer.

Fredo felt in his pocket and came out with a matching lighter. 'Solid.' He showed her a heavy link ID bracelet, rolling his wrist. Then took a Turkish cigarette from the case. 'How about a drink?'

'Sure. We got scotch.'

'And?'

'And we got scotch.' Francine found a glass and poured Johnny Walker.

'Any ice?' Fredo held out the flame.

'Some.'

'We are gonna need ice. I got some vodka coming.' He peeled a piece of leaf from his lip.

'Who's bringing the vodka?'

'I invited a few Russian pilots. They use it to cool the Mig engines.'

Crow and Halsey dropped their crates on the kitchen floor.

'Take it easy with that stuff. Probably highly volatile. Like Francine here. Go right off in your hand.' Fredo winked at Halsey.

Crow said, 'Do we have the scotch in a safe place?'

Fredo put his ringed hand on Francine's thigh.

'Fredo,' Crow said.

'Yeah.' Fredo turned slowly.

A look passed between them.

Fredo moved away from Francine. '*Ciao*, baby. A little business to take care of.'

When Fredo and Crow had gone, Francine said, 'That suit. They can see that suit on Betelgeuse. They probably think it's intelligent life.'

Halsey said, 'Can I get you another drink?'

'Thanks hunk.' She handed over her glass. 'Did you catch what was going on with Charlie and Fredo?'

'What?'
'The little green-eyed devil.'

'I'm not talking about a deal,' said Fredo. 'There are certain business interests that would like to ask you a small favor. Naturally you could name your price. We're not asking you to get involved. Talk to a few people.' He filled his glass from the bottle on O'Brien's desk. 'Gadafi is a little flaky. A mad dog. Unstable.'

O'Brien sat at the desk, his hands clasped across his chest, leaning back in the chair with a glazed expression.

'These are honorable men. All honorable men. They want you should look favorably on them. We know you have the ear of powerful people.'

'I wouldn't say Gadafi was crazy,' said O'Brien.

Fredo glanced from O'Brien to Crow. Crow looked away. He was getting more morose as the alcohol went down.

'Jack,' said Fredo. 'I'm not wired. Search me.' He held out his arms. A supplicant. 'I'm not working for Musa.' Fredo relaxed. 'All I want you to do is talk to the Agency. That's all I'm asking. Christ, it's not water into wine.'

'O'Brien stared at Fredo, not moving. Anesthetized. He opened his mouth and the words came out slurred. 'Maybe I should have a word with my good friend Seif el Islam Jalloud and tell him some fucking wop is planning to take out Gadafi.'

The color drained from Fredo's face, his jaw slackened. 'You're kidding us around Jack.'

O'Brien threw himself forward and pointed at Crow. 'You in on this?' He didn't wait for an answer. 'I've been away ten days. I come back and I hear people are bad mouthing me around the Libyans. Trying to make out I'm ripping them off and how, if they get the contracts, it's all gonna change.'

Crow interrupted O'Brien. 'I'm the one taking all the shit, the equipment fails, the timers don't work. I'm the one taking the shit.'

'Who gave you a job?' asked O'Brien. 'You were a renta cop. A fucking five dollar an hour and bring your own gun renta cop. 'You've been listening to this asshole – ' O'Brien pointed to Fredo ' – Works for the local mafia. Thinks he's Don Corleone. The only thing dangerous about this cocksucker is the suit.' O'Brien laughed hard, nearly choking.

*　　*　　*

'What's Jack laughing about?' said Halsey.

'Must have been something funny Fredo said.'

Francine and Halsey were shapes in the fading light. The party was getting crowded and loud. Two Russian pilots were going round with bottles of pure spirit making friends, especially among the women. Halsey heard shouting from outside. The sound of cars.

Katz said, 'Probably Jalloud, Musa and his crowd. I told them to drop by.'

Halsey moved away, through a group of oil workers discussing chilli recipes, over to the staircase.

Katz said to Francine, 'Doesn't he know I was bullshitting about Jalloud?'

Francine didn't reply. She gazed out searching for the line joining the sea and sky.

Eddie Kozinski, his head down and breathing heavily, was climbing the stairs. He reached the top.

Halsey said, 'You are out of shape.'

'I need a cigarette.' Getting his breath. 'Hey.' Kozinski grabbed Halsey.

Halsey took a handful of flesh. 'Putting on a few pounds here.'

'The high life in Benghazi.'

'I'll get you a drink.' Halsey looked around and found a Kraft Cheese glass under the sink. There was a little scotch left in the bottle on the kitchen table. He emptied it into the glass. Beer and a case of scotch remained under the table. The cloth was strewn with styrofoam cups, some filled, some with floating butts.

Kozinski lifted the glass. 'Fuck 'em.'

'Fuck 'em.'

'I didn't hear from you. I thought maybe you'd ended up on a lunch menu.' Kozinski tried the scotch. 'I had this phone call. Mysterious phone call. Go to a certain street address. The old lady thinks it's some piece of ass.'

Chasen searched the room and found Halsey. He went over to the two men. Halsey with his arm round Kozinski's neck. Chasen said something in his other ear, something about Fredo and Crow getting out of hand.

Halsey detached himself from Kozinski and drew an arc over the room with his hand. 'Anything you want. We have hot dogs, imported, and hotter women.'

Halsey followed Chasen down the stairs and out of the villa. Walking away into the darkness. The sky brilliant with stars.

Chasen went ahead towards the road, side stepping the potholes. 'These guys are drunk. And they're mad at Jack for some reason. Madder than hell. This is serious. Fredo's got a gun.'

Fredo and Crow were standing by the road talking. Every so often a car would come by, illuminating them for five seconds on the curve, then plunging them into semi-darkness.

'He's dangerous,' said Fredo. 'But I aint' scared of that putana. I'm gonna blow him the fuck away.'

Fredo saw Chasen and then Halsey coming along the track. He tapped Crow on the arm. And Crow turned.

Fredo said, 'We gotta get rid of Jack.'

'What are you planning on doing?' said Chasen.

To make it obvious Fredo reached in his jacket and brought out a 9mm Beretta. He slid the clip from the gun and slammed it back. Taking the safety off, jacking one in the chamber.

'He thinks I ain't a man of honor.' Fredo had a bottle of scotch by his feet. He picked it up and took a long drink, then handed it to Halsey. 'Drink. Have a drink.'

Fredo lurched forward holding the gun down. He tried bringing it up, steadying his arm with the other hand.

Halsey looked at Chasen.

Fredo put the Beretta down. 'I can't hold the gun straight.' He started to cry.

Crow stepped forward and put his arm round Fredo. 'Don't worry. Gimme the gun.' He wrestled the weapon from Fredo's hand, peeling back the knuckles.

'Charlie,' said Halsey. 'You're gonna end up inside a Libyan jail or worse.'

Crow pushed past, taking the bottle from him.

Halsey and Chasen left Fredo crying by the road and followed on behind Crow. The rutted track required all Crow's attention. He fixed the villa in his line of sight.

The villa seemed to be bending with sound and light. Off to the right, cats were gathered around a garbage can. He pointed the gun in their direction and fired off an imaginary shot. They ignored him. Crow threw the bottle. The cats yowled, scattering with the shards of glass. 'Shit. What the fuck did I do that for? Waste of good whisky.' Crow turned, walking backwards to talk to Halsey and Chasen. 'You cover my tail.' Almost falling over.

O'Brien was in the office with the door locked.

Crow stumbled around the villa asking people if they'd seen Jack. No one seemed to notice the gun. Someone said they'd seen him with a woman called Connie.

Connie was standing behind the desk. Her hands reaching for the corners. Her skirt rucked up and Jack O'Brien behind her, his face red. He was holding her hips. His thighs against hers. The sound of her shouting, 'Fuck me. Yes, fuck me,' could be heard on the stairs. O'Brien thrusting forward when Crow burst through the door.

'He is fucking you,' said Crow.

'Oh my God,' said Connie.

'If you're planning to use that,' said O'Brien, 'give me two minutes.' And carried on fucking.

'Let me go Jack! He's got a gun.' She started screaming, trying to break away.

O'Brien pinned her against the desk with one hand. Connie had the weight off her feet and couldn't move. Chasen and Halsey stood behind Crow, not believing what they were seeing. Connie's screams became low sobs.

Crow waved the gun. 'You may be screwing her but you're not screwing me. I want that fucking fifteen thousand.'

O'Brien grunted and withdrew his prick. He zipped the pale orange pants, leaving a stain in the crotch. Connie slid off the desk, hiding, rearranging her skirt and blouse. O'Brien moved around to within three feet of Crow.

'You fucking pervert.' The veins on O'Brien's neck stood out. 'Sit the fuck down and shut the fuck up.'

Crow backed away into a chair and sat down. The gun fell to his side.

'I've been carrying your ass since you got here. You're not worth the money I pay you now. Fifteen thousand is a performance bonus. I haven't even seen you get it up.'

Halsey got down and took the gun from Crow's limp hand. He didn't seem to notice. O'Brien paced and pointed at Crow, telling him he should have had his ass handed to him. Crow was visibly shrinking. 'Musa's gonna close the palace down unless you start to deliver.' O'Brien stopped and looked at Crow, his neck relaxing, the blood draining away. 'Hey, good buddy.' He punched Crow on the arm. 'There's a mountain of money out there. All we have to do is take it. Listen, we're all gonna make a lot of money. Why don't you go and sleep it off. We'll talk some more later.'

Crow got up, O'Brien's arm coming around his shoulder. O'Brien smiled a crooked smile. Crow left the office, his head down. He went down the staircase and left the villa by the open door.

O'Brien tested the broken doorlock. He said to Chasen. 'Get him the fuck outta Libya.' His mouth drawn out in a thin line, saying the words through his teeth.

Connie was on her hands and knees, searching for her panties.

O'Brien laughed, seeing the fat ass. 'I'm gonna remember you just the way you are.' He glanced at Chasen and Halsey. 'Let's get a drink.'

Katz was talking to Eddie Kozinski in the kitchen, telling him about Gadafi and the desert.

'He has a fortress out there at Bab al Azizia. Guarded by T-55 tanks, anti-aircraft guns, closed-circuit TV and electronic surveillance. Sam missiles, anti-missile missiles. Everything. The guy lives in a tent. Lives in a fucking tent. Somebody tried to kill him. They showed it on TV. The gutters running with blood. Bodies lying in the street dismembered. That's the TV station.'

O'Brien, Chasen and Halsey drifted over to the kitchen table. O'Brien made himself a flash cocktail, offering Chasen the bottle.

'I think I'll have scotch.'

'Have some vodka.' A Russian carrying a clear bottle poured Chasen a drink.

O'Brien moved away over to where Francine was talking to her husband.

Katz finished what he was saying about Gadafi and asked Chasen about what happened in the office. Halsey looked round the party, half listening to Chasen. He saw Francine and thought about wandering over. He decided against the idea. There beyond the doorway in the shadow was the woman Carlotta. She wasn't Spanish. She wore a white high-button collar blouse and black cossack pants. Raven black hair. Halsey started towards the door.

The woman glanced round the room without moving.

'Would you like a drink?' said Halsey.

'I'm trying to find someone.' The accent was heavy German.

'That's not an answer to the question. Do you like scotch?'

'Scotch?'

'Whisky.'

'Ah, whisky. Yes, I'll have some whisky.'

Halsey stole a glass from one of the oil workers and rinsed it at the sink. There was no scotch left under the table.

Halsey said, 'I have a bottle stashed on the roof.'

Stars, all they could see were stars. An eternity of stars. The distant oncoming waves breaking on the beach. Halsey was close enough to smell her perfume. They heard the sound of shouting and screaming together with laughter coming from the villa. A camera flash illuminated the landscape for a thousandth of a second, then faded. Halsey heard Francine's voice raised. O'Brien shouting, angry.

'I don't know your name.'

'Marielle.'

There was a crash followed by a thud and silence, briefly. A rumbling echo of thunder. Halsey turned towards the TV camera.

'Are you a friend of Jack's?' said Halsey.

Marielle shrugged. 'I don't know Jack. Someone told me I could get a drink here.'

Halsey nodded and offered the bottle. Marielle helped herself to scotch and poured some in Halsey's glass.

'This is my first drink in six months.' She sipped and crossed her arms.

Halsey saw the shape of her breasts. He felt his balls and prick stirring. And staring into dark eyes was drawn into her orbit. She opened her mouth as their lips met, their tongues touching. Halsey threw the whisky glass over the parapet. It sailed into space, leaving a trail. He put his hand on her breast. She moaned softly.

A jet of flame shot up in the sky. A garbage can in back had caught light. The fire was moving towards the villa. A figure appeared and disappeared in a second. People started out the front door, shouting. Some were going for their cars, others were running around to the fire. The car horns and revving engines drowned the shouts. Headlights criss-crossed the darkness below. A Peugeot station-wagon was trying to maneuver around a VW Beetle. Marielle said it was her car.

Halsey led the way down the steep steps. At the kitchen entrance he met Francine.

'What happened?' said Halsey.

'Some guy's been exposing himself. Jack beat the living shit out of him. You know what he's like about perversion.' Francine's eyes watched Marielle go on down the staircase. 'He must have set light to the villa.'

Halsey heard the Beetle start up. He ran down two flights. The car was pulling away along the track. With a burst of speed he caught up to the slow-moving car, rapping on the window. Marielle braked. Halsey got in and slumped in the seat.

'Why were you in such a hurry to leave?' Halsey said.

'It would have been a mistake to hang around. And besides, I got what I came for.' She stared at Halsey. Then reached down to the floor and came up with the bottle of scotch.

Marielle stopped outside an apartment building. Halsey saw the harbor and the Marcus Aurelius arch. They were in the old city, a maze of streets. Marielle tore the white blouse from her belt, lifting it up. Halsey saw her breasts in the light from the moon. He reached out and touched her.

'They'll stone us.' Halsey could feel her breath on his face. He bit her neck, touching soft breasts.

She broke away and covered herself. Halsey was rampant. Marielle ran her nails slowly over the bulge in his Levis and unbuttoned them. She massaged until he wanted to come. Without saying anything to Halsey she got out of the car.

They climbed stone steps, Halsey five paces back.

Marielle let them in and led the way across the lobby to the ancient cage elevator. Inside she closed the gates and pressed for four. Halsey unbuttoned the top two buttons of her pants as he stood behind her.

She turned and pushed him away. 'We forgot the whisky.'

'Fuck the whisky.'

The apartment was empty except for one chair and a king-size double bed. Out the window Halsey could see a mosque with an octagonal minaret. He wasn't thinking about religion, standing there. Her hand on his thigh, running across his flat stomach. That perfume, the heady sensation. Halsey swung round and brought their bodies together with his hands on her ass. She felt the heat of him burning her. Halsey moved his fingers, fumbling, slipping through folds of silk into folds of sticky flesh. She held his prick, bringing the end in contact with her cunt. Halsey forced her against the wall and lifted her up. Then he was fucking her, driving deep and taking the breath out of her. Their mouths came together. She was moaning soft, low. He could feel himself getting harder. Marielle bit his chest. There was a tautness in her body. The muscles tightened. He was spurting inside her.

They slept in the big double bed, sprawled across it where they had fallen. Before dawn he awoke with her mouth round his prick. Halsey raised himself up and brushed aside the hair concealing her face. She rose and fell on his glistening hardness, running her tongue around the glans. She smiled.

Halsey reached out and put his hand behind her thigh. His mouth along her. Plunging his tongue into sweetness. Then he was there behind her, pushing his prick into her. She had her hand under his balls. He moved in and around giving her gentle pleasure, holding hips, thrusting. His hand covered her belly and down, finding her cunt, fingers stroking. Balls and flanks slapping her ass. Bringing them to the edge.

The sun drawing a line across the rooftops.

When Halsey woke the light was streaming in the window and Marielle was gone. He lay there staring at the flaking ceiling, his head aching. The fan rotated slowly.

Halsey got up and went into the marble-tiled bathroom, the stucco walls unpainted. In the mirrored cabinet there was a bottle of spa water and a packet of headache tablets. Halsey swallowed two tablets washed down with water from the bottle. There was also a toothbrush in a cellophane wrapper but no toothpaste. He opened the wrapper and started brushing his teeth with the bottled water. He looked around the apartment. Other than the contents of the cabinet and a towel there was no evidence that anyone lived there. And no phone.

Halsey took a shower, the water spitting down from a height, stinging his flesh.

Francine said, 'So you got laid.' Halsey didn't reply. He was making coffee, filling a Bialetti espresso machine he'd bought in the souq.

'You want coffee?' He put the machine on the stove.

'Yes I want coffee,' said Francine. 'Okay, come on. Kiss and tell.'

'Coffee was discovered by the Arabs. The Yemenis. There's a story about this Arab screwing the king's daughter. He was banished to the mountains. Found the coffee berries and they made him a saint.'

'So you're not gonna tell me,' said Francine. 'Okay. Talking of getting laid, Jack told me his wife is arriving on one of her conjugal visits. "Elaine"? I said. That pissed him off.

'I'm gonna have to move out of the villa.' She got up from the table to look for cups. Francine opened the cupboard, her white towelling robe falling back. Halsey couldn't help seeing her small white breasts. She looked at Halsey. The folds falling back into place. The coffee pot hissed and ejaculated steam.

'The coffee's made.' Halsey said.

'I'll get the milk.'

'No milk for me.'

Halsey poured two cups of very black coffee. 'How is it Jack doesn't fly to London?'

'He says he's pulling out of London and Washington. Says he's saving money. Doesn't need the office space. All he needs is a telex.'

Halsey tried the coffee.

'A lot of what goes on here doesn't add up.' Francine sipped from the small white cup. 'My God, this is strong.' She went to the refrigerator for milk.

'It's Italian coffee. Not strong. Just a dark roast.'

The milk turned the coffee the color of mud.

'The accounts,' said Francine. 'Jack wasn't keeping any accounts. On one contract alone he lost a million dollars. He was making money on the deal, about eight hundred thousand dollars. But he should have been making nearer two million. Jack is working with margins so big he doesn't miss a million.' Francine shook her head, not convinced that anyone could lose that much money.

Halsey was thinking Jack could afford to lose the money. The US Treasury would make it good.

Francine said, 'Can I give you a little piece of advice?'

Halsey put down the cup.

'Charlie is in exile. He caught the plane out. Frank and Jack haven't been getting along. Jack has a couple of big contracts. One of them's for uniforms. The other one I don't know, he's keeping a close mouth. There aren't too many people around here that Jack will trust. I think he has an eye on you.

'Here's the advice. Whatever Jack says, however much money he offers, don't take it.'

Halsey drove round the old city looking for the apartment building. He saw the octagonal tower of the mosque and found a place to park. In the harsh daylight the building seemed more seedy than he remembered. He got out of the Eagle and went over to the entrance. The door was open. Halsey wandered in. There was a strong smell of cous-cous cooking. He waited for the elevator. The cage arrived and he rode up to the fourth floor.

The unnumbered door opened the second time Halsey knocked. A fat, bald man in an undershirt allowed only a narrow view of the apartment. Halsey asked if he knew Marielle. He wasn't sure if the Arab understood.

The sound of a baby crying came from inside the apartment. The man shook his head and closed the door. Halsey glanced up and down the corridor. It was the right door.

He headed the Eagle west and didn't make the turn for the villa, driving out along the coast towards Tunisia. For a moment with his foot down on the coastal highway Halsey thought about continuing on through Algeria and Morocco up into Spain.

On a beach near Ba Kammash Halsey drove the four-wheeler down to the soft sand, still wet from the ebbing tide. Tire tracks gouging a parallel path to the sea. The sea a shallow lagoon out to the island of Farwah. The Mediterranean sparkled with distant points of reflected sunlight.

He wanted a cigarette. Down the back of the front seat he found a crushed pack of Camel filters in a crushproof pack. But no matches. A sign from God not to start smoking again. Then he noticed the old man sitting in the shade of a tunny boat.

Halsey walked along the sand. The glare from the sea made him shade his eyes. He approached the boat holding out the cigarettes, offering the pack and asking for a light. The old man, squatting, took a cigarette, tore the filter off and put the other end in his mouth. He bent his head to a stove heating a blackened kettle, lit the cigarette and handed the smoldering tip to Halsey. A grizzled, gray face grinning. The old man gestured for him to sit down. Halsey leant against the boarding of the boat and watched the flames.

The old man heaped sugar in the kettle and poured viscous dark-brown tea into two glasses. He handed one to Halsey. They had another cigarette, sipping tea, listening to the waves breaking on the shore.

'Hey there, old buddy.'
'Jack.'
O'Brien put his arm around Halsey's shoulder. 'What's that?'
Halsey showed the two red mullet the old man had given him. O'Brien stared at the fish with glazed eyes. He guided Halsey into the office.
'Have a drink.'
Halsey found a Superman comic and wrapped the fish in the pages putting the bundle on the desk.
O'Brien had nothing on his mind apart from the need to talk. He started reminiscing about his boyhood down on the farm, getting up at five every morning to milk the cows. Walking four miles to school, four miles back. In winter so cold your piss freezes. Tripoli was a paradise by comparison. Food to eat and no winter to turn your balls to blocks of ice.
O'Brien helped himself to flash. Halsey didn't want a drink.
'The first time I didn't have to think about where the next meal was coming from was in Vietnam. That was no picnic.' O'Brien told Halsey about sleepless nights. Hearing men out in the darkness calling to him. Ordered into an ambush, he had lost half the men in his platoon. 'I stood this close to communism.' He dragged up his shirt tail, showing a jagged scar in his side.
The war in Vietnam. Vientam and stopping communism. Communism and the Bay of Pigs. 'Nixon wouldn't have fucked that up. That whole fucking eastern establishment couldn't organize a fuck in a brothel. The CIA made twenty-three attempts to assassinate Castro. Am I smoking Havana cigars? Nixon wanted me to organize a new intelligence agency. He didn't trust them, called them "cunts in aspic".

'If the CIA hadn't fucked up over Watergate I'd be heading up my own agency. Instead of in this shithouse.'

Halsey saw O'Brien sag into a chair. He looked at the fish, their heads sticking out of the comic, glazed eyes staring back.

'What are you planning on doing with those fish?' O'Brien said. 'Why don't you throw them out for the cats.' O'Brien reached for the desk drawer and pulled out a gun. 'Throw them close.'

Halsey tossed the two fish into the yard and immediately cats came running. The first shot struck the ground a foot from the nearest cat. The second shot hit the animal in the back. The cat flinched and carried on eating. O'Brien threw the BB automatic at the scrabbling hoard. And missed.

Francine called out from the balcony above. 'Hey. Picking this guy up at the airport?'

O'Brien looked at Halsey.

'What's his name?' said Halsey.

'Ed Gianni. Short.' O'Brien holding his hand three feet off the ground. 'Black curly hair, going bald. Getting a belly.'

'Italian?'

'American.' O'Brien put his arm around Halsey's shoulder again. 'We'll have lunch.'

Halsey arrived late at the airport. The flight was in. Taxis were leaving. He stayed near the exit waiting for one hour. There was no sign of Gianni. Halsey called the villa. Francine said they hadn't heard.

Another hour went by. He called again and Francine said she'd check the hotels.

Halsey saw Gianni crossing the concourse, told her to forget it and hung up. He intercepted him near the exit.

'Where the fuck have you been fella?' said Gianni.

'What happened?' said Halsey.

'What happened? Some fucking Arab thinks he's Gadafi been barking at me for two solid hours. I'm deaf in this ear.' He indicated his left ear.

Halsey took one of his cases and started towards the parking lot.

'I gave him a load of bullshit about being a personal friend of Jalloud.'

'What was it?'

'Israeli stamp in the passport.'

'You're lucky to be a free man.' Halsey thought that the guy didn't look that stupid. But you never could tell.

Gianni was following Halsey in the darkness, stumbling over the hard furrows between the cars. He was cursing under his breath, trying to keep his balance. Then he was grabbing air as he collided with a half-hidden concrete post.

'Hey.'

Halsey turned around.

'I lost my bag.'

Halsey was carrying a bag, Gianni another. 'Your bag?'

'Yeah. Small Gucci purse. Matches the other bags.'

Halsey kicked at a shape on the ground. 'Here.'

Gianni bent down to retrieve it.

'What do you carry in that?'

'My passport. I used to carry my passport.'

Gianni wasn't impressed with the four-wheeler. He had Halsey clear the back seat for the bags and placed a handkerchief on the passenger seat. In the confines of the interior Halsey found Gianni's aftershave overwhelming. He wound down the window.

'No air conditioning,' Gianni said.

Halsey shrugged.

The seams of Gianni's Vicuna suit were under pressure. There were fine white salt lines under the arms. His cream silk shirt had popped a button trying to cover an expanding stomach. Halsey watched him out the corner of his eye taking in the shadowy landscape. Watching him play with the large knot of his rep. tie. They journeyed in silence.

As Halsey made the turn off the coast road down the track, he spoke for the first time since the airport. 'Our luxury beachside villa.'

Gianni's jaw fell. 'You're kidding me.'

Halsey shook his head.

'Jack O'Brien lives here?'

The headlights swept across the garbage dump, catching the scavenging cats in the beam. One of the cats called out, a low wailing sound.

'Jack's out,' said Chasen. 'He's taking Connie out to dinner.'

Gianni was glancing around, his jaw lower. 'Where do I sleep? With the camels?'

A cockroach crawled out from under the stove. Gianni made a noise in his throat halfway between a repressed laugh and a rattle of disgust.

'What's that perfume you're wearing?' said Chasen.

'It's aftershave.'

'Very nice,' said Chasen. He winked at Halsey. 'Why don't I show you around?'

'Just tell me where I find my room.'

'You're bunking with Halsey,' said Chasen.

Gianni made it clear he didn't care for the idea.

Chasen said, 'Last week we had eighteen in one room. You couldn't move for bodies.'

'When is Jack getting back?' said Gianni.

'He won't be back till tomorrow.'

Halsey had the espresso machine in his hand. 'You want coffee?'

Gianni hesitated. 'I think I'll take a shower and have a shave. Turn in early.'

Halsey poured two cups of coffee, brought them over to the table and sat down. Gianni left the kitchen on his way to the bathroom.

'You think he's a fruit?' said Chasen.

Halsey shook his head.

'Carries a handbag, wears perfume . . .'

They could hear noises coming from the bathroom. Halsey finished his coffee and went over to the cupboard under the sink. He found what he wanted.

The water coming from the faucet was brown, sluggish and cold. There were green stains on the washbasin and a fungus over the wall behind, beneath the mirror. Gianni could see his beard in patches where the silver remained on the glass. The blade in the razor wasn't sharp. He'd forgotten to pack blades. A rattling door handle made him start. Blood trickled down his chin.

'The door's locked.' Gianni checked that the bolt was in place. He heard Halsey's voice.

'I have to take a piss.'

Gianni cleared his throat. 'Can't it wait?'

'Open the door. I have to piss.' Halsey started knocking.

The door opened. Halsey pushed past Gianni unbuttoning his jeans. He stood there in front of the pan. Gianni carried on shaving, trying to ignore Halsey but glancing in the mirror over his shoulder.

'Hard to piss with a hard-on.' Halsey remained standing, his back to Gianni, for thirty seconds making grunting noises. Then he turned and brought a comb out of his pocket.

Gianni could see Halsey bending down to look in the mirror. He felt something in his back.

'You'd better concentrate on your shaving. Otherwise you're liable to cut yourself.' Halsey bent his knees and pressed the carrot up the crack of Gianni's ass.

Gianni cut himself.

'Hey, let me take a look at that,' said Halsey.

'I'm fine. I'm okay.' Gianni tried to keep the hysteria out of his voice. He stared at the bulge in Halsey's jeans as Halsey backed away towards the door. Halsey smiled and winked.

Chasen, waiting outside, edged away. Halsey came out. They went back upstairs.

Chasen grinned. 'The guy is scared shitless.'

Gianni had a pink, scrubbed look about him.

Chasen said, 'I hope you didn't have any trouble.'

'Trouble?'

'In the bathroom there with Halsey.' Chasen had a worried expression on his face. 'The thing is.' Pausing, not sure if he should say what he was about to say. 'He's not dangerous as long as you play along with him. Don't worry. I know how to handle him. It's okay.'

Gianni said, 'What's wrong with him?'

'He was in a North Vietnamese prison for two years. They turned him into a killer.'

Gianni fumbled with the clothes in his suitcase. He found a pair of pyjamas, a jade color with a chinese collar and frog ties. Chasen said he liked them. Kinda sexy. That slinky material. Gianni hadn't thought about his pyjamas as being provocative.

'Here's what we do,' said Chasen. 'I'll trade places with you.'

Gianni seemed puzzled.

'Sleep between you and Halsey. You give me some of that perfume of yours.'

'Aftershave.'

'I'm wearing the aftershave. In the dark.'

Gianni was grateful.

'If I have the pyjamas.'

Gianni reluctantly handed them over.

'It's okay, trust me.'

Gianni woke, hearing a sound in the darkness. A stirring at the other end of the room. Followed by a gentle moaning. His heart missed a beat. He turned to face the wall. An act of denial. Listening until the cries ceased. Not able to sleep for the knot in his stomach until just before dawn.

Driving to the palace, Halsey said, 'If you don't mind me saying – ' he quoted Chasen ' – "oh no, that hurts" and "give it to me, big boy" was way over the top.'

Chasen chuckled. 'The guy was playing Let's Pretend this morning. Let's pretend I was asleep and nothing happened. I put some of that detergent around the crotch. Leaves powdery white stains.'

They parked by the orange grove. Ben Sa'oud came to meet them, saluting and saying good morning.

'*Sabah al-khair* Lieutenant Ben Sa'oud,' Chasen said.

Ben Sa'oud was giving lessons in Arabic. '*Sabah an-nur.*'

'Benny,' said Chasen. 'My friend here. Our friend,' including Ben Sa'oud. 'He has a problem. Halsey is in love.' Chasen grabbed himself by the balls. 'He's got it bad.' He nodded.

Ben Sa'oud understood. He smiled.

'The problem is he can't find her. Cinderella. You know that story?'

Ben Sa'oud shook his head.

'See, the girl is a . . . she's, let's see.' Not remembering. 'A housemaid.'

'Is all this background necessary?' said Halsey.

'Let me tell the story,' said Chasen. 'Anyway, the girl goes to a ball looking like a princess. Meets the prince. They fall in love. Only at midnight she runs away leaving behind a slipper. The prince finds the slipper.'

'It's a glass slipper,' interrupted Halsey.

'A glass slipper. Okay?'

'If you're gonna tell the story, get it right. And you forgot the fat sisters. Fat, ugly sisters.'

'Who's telling this story, for Christ's sake?' Chasen stood with his hands on his hips. 'That it? Can I get on with the story?' He faced Ben Sa'oud. 'Where was I?'

'Glass slipper,' said Halsey.

Ben Sa'oud was watching this back and forth. Not really following but enjoying the humor.

'The maid goes back to being a maid. And the prince is lovesick because he has the hots for Cinderella. The only thing the prince knows about her is her shoe size. So he sends out footmen across the land to find the foot that fits the . . .' Chasen paused, waiting for Ben Sa'oud to fill in.

'The glass slipper. Fits the glass slipper. Only in Halsey's case it's a pair of panties.' Chasen smiled. 'Okay. Did you follow that story?'

Ben Sa'oud said, 'What are footmen?'

Chasen made it simple by explaining who they were talking about. The woman at the back of the class. 'German, dark hair, drives a VW Beetle.'

The smile left Ben Sa'oud's face.

Washington DC

O'Brien sat on the bench examining the cleats on his black brogues. He tossed them on the floor right way up, and slipped his feet in, bending down to tie the laces. The maroon of his Argyle socks matched the maroon of the woollen shirt. The black and white houndstooth check pants came from the pro shop at St Andrew's in Scotland. Sean Connery had a pair.

'Take five thousand from the slush fund. Elaine'll give you the money. Go down to good ol' boy country. Fayetteville. Buy hand guns: .38s, Magnums, Smiths, Colts. No Japanese imports.' O'Brien glanced up at Schultz. 'I'll call Elaine. Tell her to get the money ready. This is a low profile operation. Use cash. No names.'

Schultz said, 'What are they for?'

O'Brien was surprised by the question. Schultz knew better than to ask. He stood up, leaning forward. 'Special operations overseas.'

Schultz seemed satisfied with the explanation and O'Brien

walked off, the clatter of the cleats on the tiles echoing through the lockerroom. Schultz picked up the hide golf bag with the regulation fourteen clubs and a striped umbrella.

O'Brien held the door open. As Schultz passed him he said, 'This is straight from the White House basement.' He gripped Schultz's upper arm, leading him on. 'Why don't you put the clubs in the cart? Get yourself a drink at the clubhouse. Put it on my tab.'

A man dressed in yellow was talking to Arnie Capper, the club assistant pro, when O'Brien walked into the shop. Yellow sports shirt, cap, stretch slacks and two-tone yellow and white shoes.

Arnie Capper said, 'Gene Auric, I'd like you to meet Jack O'Brien.' The two men moved together. 'Gene's a new member.' They shook hands.

'Let me tell you,' said O'Brien. 'You have to watch out for Arnie here. He'll sell you a sand wedge for every bunker on the course. I once asked him about some new clubs. Arnie said, "How many sets do you want?" '

'Now, Jack,' said Capper. 'Why'd you have to go and ruin my chance of a sale?' He laughed, giving O'Brien a dig in the ribs with the grip of a wood he was holding.

'Say, why don't you play a round with Gene. I have to get the books straightened out before they go to the accountant.'

'Caught up with you, huh?' O'Brien turned to Auric. 'You played this course before, Gene?' He got the door.

Auric said he hadn't even been to Washington before. A country boy. Originally from Fresno. Sunny California. The golden state. Once Auric started talking there was no stopping him. He still had a place down in Palm Springs and some investment in real estate. Condo development, hotels.

They took the golf cart over to Auric's Fleetwood Cadillac. In the trunk a set of gold-plated clubs.

'I'm buying a town house off Pennsylvania Avenue. Figured I had to get close to the real money,' said Auric.

'We're gonna be neighbors. I have a place in Georgetown. A farm out in Loudon County. The town house is handy for those late nights at the office.' O'Brien grinned.

'I can see you're a man to know.' Auric lifted the clubs into the back of the cart. 'In the big city I suppose you have to drive these little cars. I think I could fit this in the trunk of my old Caddy.' He laughed at his own joke.

O'Brien smiled, stretching his face until the jaw cracked. 'What's your handicap?'

Quick as a whip Auric came back, 'Golf.' And laughed again.

They got in the cart, O'Brien driving in the direction of the first tee.

'On a good day I can hit under ninety,' said Auric. 'I'm playing off nineteen.'

O'Brien swung the cart over behind the raised tee and climbed out. 'How about a little side bet? Dollar a hole too rich for you?'

Auric showed how playful he could be, punching O'Brien in the gut. 'I'll give you the eighteen dollars now you introduce me to those chickies you do business with late nights in Georgetown.' He followed O'Brien up the steps cut in the grass bank.

The tee looked down towards a line of pine trees on the left and three bunkers on the other side of the fairway where the hole made a dog-leg to the right.

O'Brien said 'My advice, play short of the sand trap.'

'Why don't you show me how it's done.'

O'Brien hooked his tee shot into the trees.

Auric said, 'Last time I saw a hook like that there was a shark on the end of it.' He plucked a handful of grass and tossed it up in the air. He placed the yellow tee and ball together in the soft turf with a yellow gloved hand. The driver lay loose in his grip, addressing the ball, fixing the landscape in his mind. He hit a straight drive but the ball started to fade. O'Brien smiled, seeing it going towards the bunkers, landing in the sand. Then bouncing out again.

'God is smiling down on me today. Thank you God,' said Auric. 'Strict rules of golf?'

'Strict rules of golf.' O'Brien smiled inwardly.

Schultz sat on the covered terrace sipping a Tom Collins, watching the first fairway. The little red cart moving towards the stand of pine trees. A gentle breeze rippled the surface of the lake beyond.

The barman came through the open French windows and stood behind Schultz. Schultz said, 'Nice day.'

'This time of year the weather's changeable. Can I get you another one of those? Some pretzels?'

'You have any cigarettes?' said Schultz. 'Marlboro?'

The barman nodded and gazed up at the sun as though he was

expecting something to happen. He turned and disappeared through the doors.

O'Brien dropped another ball in a patch of light rough. 'Here it is. Probably bounced off those trees.' He went over to the cart, selected a four iron – one club too much – and pitched the ball near the pin, running it on past to the back of the second tee. Auric hit a six iron on to the apron of the green, leaving himself with a fifteen-foot putt.

'I flew in overnight,' Auric said. 'No one on board. Practically had the plane to myself. I'm reading some papers. This chickie sitting in back of me, blonde, nineteen years old. She says can I sit next to her because she thinks the dark, empty plane is out of *The Twilight Zone*. So I move back there. She says she's gonna go to sleep and if she should fall on my shoulder, just push her away.'

O'Brien parked the cart in front of the green. He collected his Tommy Armour gooseneck putter. Auric followed him across to where his ball lay in the semi-rough. O'Brien hit a good putt, leaving himself two feet short.

Auric continued with his story. 'I got the light on, I'm still reading.' He walked over to the flag. 'Why don't you sink this one?' She starts moaning in her sleep after five minutes. Reaches down, starts rubbing her crotch. All the time moaning. Pulls up her skirt. No panties on.'

O'Brien was lining up his two footer with the putter stretched out in a line with the hole.

'She's fingering herself, saying, "Oh yes, stick your big cock in my pussy." Makes sure she has my attention. Puts her head on my arm and slides a hand over to see what my pecker is doing.'

O'Brien bent over the ball.

'Slips her hand around the shaft.' Auric paused.

O'Brien gripped the club and tensed his muscles.

'Jerks it up and down.'

O'Brien missed his two-foot putt.

The barman carried a silver tray out to the terrace. He placed the Tom Collins and a bowl of cashews on the table, together with a pack of Marlboro and collected the empty glass.

'We're out of pretzels.'

'Thanks.'

'If you don't like the cashews we have some peanuts.' The barman glanced at the sun and squinted. 'The sky's getting dark. Clouding over. We're in for a storm.'

'My pecker is reaching for the stars. She puts the bite on.' Auric sunk a six foot putt. He bent down and retrieved the ball.

O'Brien held the flag. 'So what happened?'

'She wanted two hundred.'

O'Brien replaced the flag.

Tripoli

Halsey made a right off the Sidi al Marsri road into the university. He drove slowly along the central roadway that linked the complex of anonymous new concrete buildings down to the sports stadium that formed part of the boundary. He swung the Eagle around the stadium parking lot and headed back the way he came. At the first intersection he parked next to a long wheelbase Land Rover. The walks were lined with eucalyptus trees. Symmetry and gray anonymity were relieved by mosaics and some facing marble. As Halsey got out of the four-wheeler he gazed over to where the platform crane had been used as a gallows. He hadn't been back since then. Back to run around the track. He'd avoided the place, taking another route across the city. The only reason he was there now was because he had no leads on the woman Marielle. He'd seen her in the crowd at the hanging. The only line he had to follow was that maybe she was teaching here at the Al Fatah University. Or taking classes.

Halsey wandered past students, through open courtyards with green pools, gushing fountains. Past a black Mercedes idling at the kerb. The rear tinted window lowered with a steady whine.

'Mr Halsey.'

Halsey turned, seeing a uniformed arm. He took a few steps back towards the car. 'What's the problem?'

The door opened. 'Can I help you?'

'Help me?'

'Please get in the car.'

Halsey thought about it. Thought about a bullet in the back, and decided to get in the car. The car was an icebox. His eyes grew accustomed to the darkness. A hawk-faced man sat holding a copy of *Al-Ahram*.

'I believe you are looking for Marielle Bayer.'

'Is that right?' Halsey hadn't known her full name. 'You know who I am?'

'I have your file.'

'My file?'

'Your CIA file.'

'May I know your name, Sir?'

'I am Captain Musa.'

Halsey recognized the name. 'And Marielle Bayer?'

'I understand she has left Libya and returned to Germany,' Musa said.

Halsey looked out at the sunlight falling on a large placid pool. He didn't know whether or not to believe Musa. But he wasn't about to call the man a liar.

'What was she teaching?'

'I believe that she was a lecturer in particle physics.'

Washington DC

O'Brien craned his neck. 'Is the sky getting darker?'

Auric relaxed his grip on the putter and squinted at the sun. 'It's darker.' Auric putted long. 'Halved.'

They strolled back to the cart. 'Why don't we make this more interesting? How about we call it all square, play the back nine for a hundred a hole?'

On the tenth O'Brien's game improved. He hit a three wood straight down the fairway. Auric hit a low screamer that ended up twenty yards up on O'Brien's ball.

'What line of work are you in?' said O'Brien.

'Mostly in the clothing business.'

'Are you looking for government contracts? I have a little influence. I could introduce you to some people.'

'On what basis?'

'A percentage basis.' O'Brien put a six iron on the green. The ball rolled on by into a bunker.

Auric brought his seven iron back high. The lake surface appeared to be rising on the far side. A gray wall of water. There was a flash of lightning that skimmed along, striking Auric's club on the down swing, wrenching the shaft from his hand and casting it in the lake. Thunder sounded overhead and rumbled on. The ball bounced twice and dropped in the cup.

'Did you see that?' said the barman. He stood in the rectangle of the open French windows.

'Lightning,' said Schultz. 'It's starting to rain.'

'Yeah.' The barman had an empty glass in his hand. 'Kind of weird when a storm hits.' He sucked on his teeth. 'Guy was killed here last year. Struck by lightning. The funny thing, I saw him laid out in the trophy room. Had these burn marks on his shoulder,' pointing to his own with the glass, 'otherwise there was nothing wrong with the guy.'

'Apart from the fact he was dead.'

'You want another one?'

'Why not?'

The sound of metal slapping against concrete from across the terrace. Auric and O'Brien were running for cover, the striped umbrella held out slightly in front of them.

O'Brien reached the verandah. 'A drink. I need a drink.'

The waiter said, 'Large Gordon's.'

'And this guy needs a brandy.' He shook the umbrella and stood it against the wall.

Auric and O'Brien sat with Schultz at the table. Waves of rain driven by the wind swept across the lake. The three men sat in silence. Lightning and thunder receded. The storm was passing over in the direction of Washington. Three drinks went on the table. One, two, three, the brandy last.

The tree branches heavy with rain swayed in the rising wind. As suddenly as the storm began, it ended. The sun caught the edge of a dark cloud above the lake.

O'Brien turned to Auric. 'You wanna quit?'

Auric tasted the brandy. 'Here's health.' He upended the snifter. 'Let's play golf.'

O'Brien finished his gin and they clattered their way down to the cart.

'God loves me,' said Auric. 'I'm gonna beat the holy crap outta you.' He laughed.

Tripoli

Halsey sat in the cab of the truck, shading his eyes, searching the sand for any sign of life. A wilderness. A wilderness that men fought and died in, died for.

'Where's this ambulance?' He didn't need an answer. They had been waiting in the sun an hour and a half, Ben Sa'oud forced into a position of apologizing when the medics failed to show. It was the second time Halsey had set up the demonstration. They had to make a three-hour journey and wait two hours with temperatures in the hundreds. Halsey jumped down from the cab, kicking up sand. The sand was hot. Too hot for horsing around. Sleeping bodies lay in the shade of the three tonner. He walked over to a halftrack fifty yards away. There were bullet holes but otherwise it was intact. The camouflage paintwork and the black iron cross.

Ben Sa'oud was shouting and pointing at a sand cloud in the distance. He ran over to Halsey and gave him his binoculars. There in the oncoming shroud of sand, a red crescent.

'Okay, let's go. Wake Mr Doug.'

Chasen didn't want to wake up although the noise had woken him. He climbed out of the cab calling to Halsey. 'I was dreaming about Doris Day. She was eating a foot-long hot dog.' He fell in beside Halsey and they walked away from the truck to the Chevy Impala fender deep in the sand.

'Why are we doing this?' said Chasen.

'Generally or what?'

'Hell, I don't know.'

There was sand inside, over the seats. The Impala had been brought to this remote firing range from one of the many car graveyards outside Tripoli. The shell of the car would define the blast from the C4. At Nagasaki and Hiroshima they measured the effectiveness in bodies and buildings. Being scientific requires a scale, a unit of measurement.

The aims of the exercise had been explained. This was an indulgence. A controlled detonation to complete the story of what happens. But then the bodies in the car were missing.

Halsey observed the dark faces. The idea that anyone could turn these desert Arabs into professionals. Professional what? Render safe men.

'Okay. This is easy. Here we have a remote timer.' He had gone beyond their span of interest. A span that was getting shorter every day. Dangerously short. They were getting over-confident. Something you don't do with the boom boom. It was a matter of time. Waiting until someone got too careless and hoping you weren't around when that happened.

The explosion lifted the car off the desert floor, buckled the roof and blasted the doors open. No one looked impressed. As far as Halsey was concerned, it was good. The timer worked, the right amount of C4, the right place. He knew what they wanted. Blood and guts.

Washington DC

Auric looked down into the bunker and laughed. 'Hell you're gonna need dynamite to get that little baby outta there.'

O'Brien's head and shoulders showed above the edge from the eighteenth green. He was standing up against the slight overhang trying to figure a way out of the sand-trap. He took up a stance and tried to get his feet down in the sand, feeling the grains working their way into his brogues. There was an old maple tree spreading branches overhead that dripped intermittently on his neck. He struck down behind the ball, sending up a shower of sand, unsure of where it had gone. Auric chuckled as the ball rolled back along the slope.

O'Brien tried again, with the same result. His face flushed.

Auric was choking, holding his stomach. 'You wanna concede the hole now?'

At the third attempt the ball landed on the green together with a jet of sand. Auric walked over to his ball at the edge of the green.

Schultz was standing behind the bunker holding O'Brien's putter. O'Brien gave Schultz the sand wedge and took the putter. Then he pulled a ball from his pocket.

'Okay. Here's what you do.' When this jerk putts out, you're there holding the flag, you switch balls.' Schultz didn't reach out immediately. 'Either you shape up . . .' O'Brien spoke through his clenched teeth.

They moved out from behind the maple. Schultz over to the pin, O'Brien to mark and clean his ball. Auric played a delicate chip that ran to within five feet. He went over to the cart for his putter. O'Brien signalled to Schultz to make the switch. He wasn't ready and fumbled in his pocket, missing the chance, almost dropping the extra ball on the deck.

'This putt for a bogey.' Auric made the remark on O'Brien's back swing.

O'Brien left the ball, walked away and came back. The way he was putting it was unlikely he'd sink this. So a double bogey and Auric would get his par. The putt was short by six inches.

'Two over.' Auric bent down and replaced his ball.

Schultz stood holding the flag, the sweat running down his back. O'Brien ready to distract Auric. The putt went straight at the cup, hit the rim and jumped in. O'Brien stepped over and held out his hand, smiling a gritty smile. He put his left arm around Auric's shoulder, turning him towards the clubhouse. Schultz made the switch, pocketing the other ball. He held out the Spalding Topflite in the palm of his hand.

O'Brien watched Auric collect the ball, trying to appear confused. 'Don't you play a Wilson Ultra?'

Auric was there ahead of him. 'No, I always play a Topflite XL.'

He took the ball from Schultz and tossed it in the lake to join the seven iron.

O'Brien opened his mouth to say something but no words came out.

'Seven holes at a hundred a hole. I reckon I can afford to buy you a drink.'

Tripoli

'We're down in Egypt and Jack says let's go and take a look at the pyramids.' Katz was in a good mood, telling Francine and Halsey stories as he carefully sipped flash. 'I don't have to drink this stuff too much longer.'

'You don't have to drink it at all,' said Francine.

Katz ignored the remark. 'So we take a trip down the Nile, and we go see the pyramids, which are okay if you like pyramids. Anyway, Jack says he wants to ride a camel. Have his picture taken. We find a guy with a camel. Jack gets up there, a little nervous. I'm just about to press the tit, the camel takes off with Jack holding on for his fucking life. Cloud of dust, high ho Jack. The camel guy is really pissed. They were close.

'That's the last I see of Jack. Reported him missing. They got the army out combing the desert. Nothing. The only thing I can do is go back to the hotel and wait. Three days later Jack shows up. Looks a mess. I say what happened. Tells me the camel didn't stop till nightfall. Threw him off and kept on going. He's down in the desert and no camel. Figures the only way he's gonna get back is find the camel. The next morning starts looking. No camel. Fortunately for Jack he meets this old man. Asks the old man if he's seen a camel. The old man says, "What did the camel look like?" '

'Spoke English?' said Francine.

Katz glanced over at Francine sitting at the typewriter. 'Who's telling this story? The old man's educated at Eton and Oxford all I know.

'The old man says, "What did the camel look like?" Jack says, "How the hell should I know, they all look the same to me." The old man says, "Well, can't you even remember if it's a boy camel or a girl camel?" Jack thinks about this. Then he says, "Sure it was a boy camel. I remember. When I was riding by people would point and shout 'Look at the schmuck on that camel'." '

Francine didn't laugh. She went back to her typing.

'Hey, whattsa matter Francine? Schmuck is a Jewish prick.'

'When are you leaving?' said Francine.

'End of the week,' said Katz. 'You miss me?'

'My heart's breaking and my pussy's aching.'

'I'm gonna be back. Time to time. Jack and me still got one or two things going.'

Halsey said. 'You miss this place?'

'Let my people go.' Katz beat out a rhythm on the metal desk. 'Jack's in too deep. No, Middle East. The place to be. Lebanon, Syria, Iraq, Iran. Me and the Ayatollah go way back. Stop by see my good friend Adnan Khashoggi.'

Halsey found it hard to figure when Katz was talking bullshit. He reasoned that that made him a good salesman.

The telex clattered.

'That'll be Jack,' said Francine. 'With the latest scores.'

London

'Fifty pounds. How much is that in real money?' O'Brien peeled off a note from his dollar clip. 'Hundred should cover it.'

The young girl took the money, standing there in a shiny black PVC raincoat, and stuffed it into a leopard-skin purse.

O'Brien sat back on the pink brocade patterned couch, rearranging his blue and white striped bathrobe. The phone rang. He leaned forward and reached for it on the low table. A red double-decker bus roared past the full-length window overlooking Hyde Park.

'Yeah.' He listened for a moment, then said, 'I'll take the call.'

The girl let the raincoat fall to the floor. The rest of her outfit was black except for a wide leopard-skin belt.

'Bill. Yeah. I had the operator hold my calls. I'm in a meeting.' O'Brien smiled and covered the mouthpiece. 'Okay, take 'em off.' Into the phone he said, 'What have you got? What's the Agency computer come up with?'

The girl slipped the stretch top over her jagged dyed black hair that fell on to narrow white shoulders. O'Brien watched, impressed with the engineering in the black uplift bra. She unzipped the PVC skirt. He reached inside his robe and released his constricted balls.

'Ahuh.' O'Brien was having trouble concentrating on what Mason was saying. A list of Agency applicants. Rejected applicants. 'Okay, cut the crap and give me a name.'

Black stockings and garter belt. Gauzy see-through leopard panties, thin material stretched over a wide ass.

O'Brien wrote in the air. He covered the mouthpiece again. 'Get me a pen. Over on the attaché case.'

The girl walked over to the bed on five-inch stiletto heels and bent over slightly as she picked up the silver ball pen. O'Brien put his hand inside his shorts and tugged at loose skin. She handed him the pen.

'Gimme the name again.' O'Brien scrawled a name and number on the pad by the phone. Through the leopard material he could see the pink folds of a shaven cunt less than two feet away. He threw the pen down on the table and grabbed at the goods on display.

'Auric. Get me something on that cornfed cocksucker. Something I can use. I'm gonna cream that farmboy.'

He pulled the waist elastic down her thighs. The girl licked her finger and ran it between red labia lips. Then she unhooked the black uplift bra.

'I'm gonna hang up. Something's come up.'

O'Brien ran through Stanhope Gate in the direction of the Serpentine. Not following the paths, running across the grass at an easy pace. The lake came into sight and the sound of the brass band acted as a magnet. He veered off towards the bandstand. Sunlight slanting down through the dense canopy of branches. Bassoons, horns, timpani, the bright-sounding rhythms of an old marching song. He stopped at the back of a small audience, some sitting in striped deckchairs, others standing there for five minutes before moving on.

This was a ritual when he was in London. Running in the afternoon, stopping to listen to the band.

The man in the black trenchcoat and the brown tinted glasses said to O'Brien, 'What're they playing?'

'British Grenadiers.' Then added, 'Some talk of Alexander and some of Hercules. But nothing can compare with a British Grenadier.'

'What's a Grenadier?'

'Carries a grenade. Seventeenth-century special forces.' O'Brien marched away from the bandstand, head erect, followed by the man in the trenchcoat.

When they were far enough away from the crowd, but still within hearing of the Green Jackets, O'Brien said, 'What did they say?'

'Not as simple as we figured. No one knows what's going on down there. Somebody's gonna have to go down and take a look.'

O'Brien said, 'You go.'

'That wasn't part of the deal.'

'I'm making it part of the deal.'

'For how much?'

O'Brien rubbed his ear, pulling at the lobe. 'Five thousand.' The amount didn't matter. When he spoke to Jalloud he'd double the figure. What mattered was assessing this guy's price. It was low, but how low?

'Fly down to Chad. Act like a tourist.'

'How about I take along a lady friend. Make it look realistic.'

'Just try and come up with a plan to take out those planes.' O'Brien stretched out his arms, in the blue tracksuit, and yawned.

'And make it simple so those niggers can handle it.'

At the lake they retraced their steps.

O'Brien said, 'We have to have a name for this operation.'

'How about Serpentine?'

Serpentine, like a snake. O'Brien heard the band in the distance. 'Grenadier,' he said.

'What?'

'Grenadier.'

'Call me Grenadier?'

The band was seguing through Streisand show tunes.

'What the fuck are they playing?'

The horns standing in for Streisand.

O'Brien turned away in disgust.

' "On A Clear Day".'

'What?'

'They're playing "On A Clear Day". You know, "On a clear day, you can see forever".'

O'Brien broke into a run. 'Hey.' The man in the trenchcoat took off after him, running towards Marble Arch.

Tripoli

'Jack is looking for you,' said Francine.

Halsey slumped into the chair opposite Francine's desk. 'What does he want?'

'You're gonna have to ask him yourself. He wouldn't tell me. I think it's an operational secret. Your ears only.'

'You know they screwed up again. The ambulance arrives. This time it's a real ambulance, not a truck with a red crescent painted on the side. We open the doors at the back. There's nothing. No medics, no stretchers, no drugs.'

'Where is he?'

'He's taking a siesta. Jetlagged.'

'Am I supposed to wake him up?'

'With a kiss.'

Halsey climbed the stairs to the top floor. He decided to put his head around the door. See if Jack was asleep. Not wake him. There was a warm golden light under the bedroom door and a fetid smell in the air. He opened the door and crept in.

O'Brien was lying on a round king-size bed, white silk sheets. He was snoring, his belly moving up and down. All he wore, a pair of coral shorts, the front tented up and his hand there.

Halsey moved back. The door creaked. That woke O'Brien. Halsey swung the door closed and knocked. There was a grunt from inside. He waited.

'Yeah.'

'Sorry Jack, did I wake you?'

'No.' O'Brien sat up in the bed. 'I like to meditate in the afternoon.'

'Meditate?'

'Yeah.'

Halsey tried to imagine O'Brien meditating.

O'Brien rubbed his face. 'Power of the mind. Control of the mind. A pair of balls lying in the palm of your hand ready to squeeze. The CIA has a long-term program. A big investment in psychological research.' He reached for a cigarette and a lighter on the side table.

Halsey was surprised how quickly O'Brien came awake.

O'Brien slapped the bed, indicating Halsey should sit down. 'You want a cigarette?' Pointing to the pack.

'The guy ran the Bata shoe company used to imagine a pink feather.' He flipped the Zippo, spun the wheel, inhaling deeply with the flame.

Halsey sat on the bed.

'He would think about this feather drifting in space. He'd look up, watch it falling to the ground. When it hit, his problems were over. All his decisions made.'

'Why a pink feather?' said Halsey.

'Fuck knows.' O'Brien stared at the lighted tip of the cigarette burning. 'Tee em, transcendental meditation. Auto hypnosis. You can build up a bio-feedback. Use it to direct your energies.' He belched and glanced around the room. 'Have you ever read *Will*, Gordon Liddy?'

Halsey shook his head.

'Read it. I'll lend you my copy.'

There was a pause. O'Brien seemed distracted.

'What is it you wanted to see me about, Jack?'

O'Brien stood up and stretched. He walked over to the window and drew back the shutters. The sun outlined his body, highlighting the receding dark-blond hair. In good shape for a man in his late forties. 'Why don't we have dinner? There's one or two things I want to talk about, get your advice.' He came round with his arms outstretched, stretching. 'I'm gonna take a shower. Ya.'

Halsey, wearing a gray and black light-weave sports coat and blue chinos, said to Francine, 'Dinner?'

All she said was 'Yum yum'.

When O'Brien came down Francine had a message for him. 'A man called. Said his name was . . .' She consulted her pad. 'Said his name was Grenadier.'

O'Brien responded with a blank stare. 'That the message?'

'The message was to call him.'

'Grenadier?'

'Said you'd know.'

O'Brien shook his head. He smiled at Halsey. 'Let's go eat.'

They were leaving the office when O'Brien stepped back. 'Grenadier?'

Francine nodded.

'We'll take the BMW. You can drive.' O'Brien handed Halsey the keys.

Bumping down the track, Halsey said, 'How was London?' For want of something to say. There was a feeling that he had of uncertainty. He wanted O'Brien to do the talking.

'What I like about London, get the best fuck for a buck.' O'Brien stuck his head out the window. 'See the faggot over there carrying a purse. Makes you wanna puke.' He swivelled around. 'You get to London I'll give you a coupla phone numbers. Hang a left.'

They were on a tree-lined street. The shutters down over shop fronts. Men squatting on the stone steps outside. Halsey noticed a woman wearing a veil. It was unusual. That's what surprised him about Libya or Tripoli, Tarabalus. Unusual to see traditional clothes. He figured Gadafi would have everyone wearing them.

'When I pay for a fuck that's what I get. I'm the one doing the fucking.'

Halsey parked the car and they walked along the harbor across the Al Kabir and down Fatah Street. A very sober crowd of Russian sailors crossed over the street on their way back to their frigate, tied up alongside an Oasis tanker. They didn't look impressed with the nightlife.

The restaurant wasn't a restaurant from the outside. A brick frontage and a small unpainted door. O'Brien went ahead to be greeted by shouts of Mr Jack, Mr Jack. Halsey had been told by O'Brien the place was Lebanese, 'the most civilized kind of Arabs'. The walls were white stucco with a mural of a fishing scene painted on the long right-hand wall. An extra table appeared and a space cleared in the middle of the floor.

O'Brien said, 'Jimmy, I want you to meet a good friend of mine, Nate Halsey.'

Halsey shook hands. Jimmy had blue eyes, graying wiry hair and pale skin.

'Okay, what have you got?'

'We've got the mixed grill.' There was a slight French accent.

'You've always got the mixed grill. How about something else?'

'Kebabs. Or perhaps red mullet.'

'All right. Mixed grill.'

Halsey said, 'I'll try the mullet.'

Jimmy started to move away. O'Brien held him by the wrist. 'I'll have one of those fruitjuice cocktails.' Keeping his voice low he said, 'Two, and put something in them.'

The place was popular with the East Europeans. A woman laughed. She was hidden at a corner table, surrounded by men in heavy limp suits.

'Have you ever done any intelligence work?'

Halsey said he hadn't.

'I know you have a high security clearance.' O'Brien edged his chair closer. 'USG is trying to promote contact with moderate elements inside Gadafi's government by supplying these people with arms.

'I'm liaising with Gadafi's cousin to provide materiel for a Libyan strike force. Langley figure they can buy influence and balance out the factions around Gadafi. Selling arms to Gadafi's cousin puts Jalloud's nose out of joint.

'And the tougher Libya is, the more the Egyptians pay attention to USG.'

Halsey said, 'Grab them by the balls, and their hearts and minds will follow.'

'I've got a contract. I need someone . . .'

Jimmy came over with the drinks. Halsey tried his, wondering what was in it.

'I need someone in on this.' O'Brien took a good pull at the cocktail. 'More money and commission.' He showed Halsey the glass. 'The job's based in Europe where life is altogether more agreeable.'

So far Halsey had liked what he heard. 'What's the job?'

'What I want you to do is track down the goods on the Libyan's shopping list and negotiate a good price.' O'Brien sat back in the chair and let the idea sink in.

Halsey said he hadn't done that kind of work.

'That's okay. All you need to know is where to go and how much to pay.'

Whichever way he looked at it Halsey could see a ticket out of Libya.

The food arrived and O'Brien ordered another round of drinks.

'This is the best food in town,' said O'Brien. 'So whadda ya say?'

'Where's Jack?' said Halsey.

'He's gone. He's catching the early flight to Zurich.' Francine had her head on one side, looking at Halsey. 'Is it important?'

'No. I guess it can wait.'

Francine, arms folded across her pink sweater. There was a half smile in her eyes.

'What is it?' Halsey mirrored her gestured and stood there sullenly, waiting.

'Oh, nothing.'

'When a woman says "Oh, nothing" it means something.'

She shrugged her shoulders. 'You're in charge of the office.'

'What does that mean? In charge of what?'

'Jack says you're in charge of the office.'

'Francine.' A note of aggravation in the way Halsey said her name. 'Francine. You run the office.'

'I know. It's purely an honorary title but Jack has placed the mantle around your neck. You're Jack's golden boy.'

Halsey understood now. He and Jack had got drunk last night.

Jack had his arm around him, saying he was a good American. How he was going to take him into partnership, make him a rich man. They had been in a bar on one of the oil camps outside of Tripoli. Painted oil drums for the bar, sawdust on the floor. He vaguely remembered that Jack was under the impression that he had saved his life at the party. Taking the gun away from Crow. Whereas it was Jack who had talked the gun out of his hand.

'Mr Halsey,' Francine simpered. She smoothed down her tight white skirt. 'Are you ready for dictation now?'

'I have to go to work.'

Chasen was waiting outside, leaning against the Eagle.

'I hear you got promoted.' A hint of resentment there.

'Jack offered me another job,' said Halsey. 'Not a promotion.'

They got in the four-wheeler and took off down the track, Chasen driving, aiming for the potholes. Halsey rolled with the suspension.

'Jack wants me to go to Europe and buy arms for the Libyan Army. I didn't say I'd do it.'

'What are you gonna do, hang around here till they mail you home in a bag?'

Halsey didn't like the idea of having someone make his decisions. He had free will. The right to choose.

Musa was waiting for them at the People's Palace. Halsey had recognized the Mercedes and knew there was something wrong.

Musa was angry, incoherent in his raving. As far as Halsey followed what he was saying was that they had let him down. He was pissed off there were no bombs. He needed bombs. The reason he needed bombs was to make a punitive strike against Egypt. Musa stated what he wanted. He wanted bombs. Radios, clocks, any household item. These would be left in the streets of Cairo and when anyone touched one it would go off, killing many people.

Musa marched Halsey and Chasen off in the direction of the workshop.

Halsey mouthed to Chasen, 'I don't like this.' And to Musa he said, 'We have to check with Mr Jack.'

'There is no time. You must fly to Tubruq now.' Musa was snappy, almost snarling.

'We are in deep shit,' said Chasen out the corner of his mouth. 'The only thing to do is go along.'

They travelled on a commercial flight from the International airport. The only passengers.

'It must be seventy-five miles to the border, another four, five hundred to Cairo. How are they gonna get the bombs across the border?' Chasen said.

'We have to carry them in a suitcase,' said Halsey.

'I don't think that's funny.'

'So you don't have to laugh.'

Here was Chasen acting the part of a dickhead. Halsey said, 'Let's start worrying about how to get out of this shit.'

'I think we just go with it.'

Musa's parting remark at the airport: If they wanted to see their families, see America again, they'd better kill many Egyptians. Ha ha.

'Whadda ya have in mind? Hijacking the plane?'

There was a beat before Halsey said, 'It's a possibility.'

Chasen blanched. He turned to stare out the cabin window. Halsey wondered if they could see Egypt down there.

'Anyhow, why should you care about killing Arabs, Egyptians?'

'What the fuck do you mean?'

'I've seen that circumcised schlong of yours.'

'I don't want to kill anyone, except maybe Jack O'Brien, getting us into this.'

'Should have listened to Charlie,' said Chasen. 'He warned me about Jack. Christ, he oughta have shot the cocksucker while he had the chance.'

'Listen,' Halsey moved closer to Chasen, 'if we construct these devices so they won't function . . .'

'What happens when Musa finds out?'

'How is he gonna find out? No one's gonna hang around, see they go off. You're gonna go back to Musa and tell him what he wants to hear. "Kill many Egyptians." '

Tubruq

When they landed in Tubruq they were taken to the intelligence compound. Old concrete huts. Halsey was surprised at the efficiency of the operation. The equipment was there. Everything they needed. Ben Sa'oud had arrived ahead of Chasen and Halsey with the task of making the arrangements and kicking ass.

Halsey took him to one side to ask him what was happening. Ben Sa'oud wasn't prepared to talk, ignoring Halsey's questions, giving a poor impersonation of Musa. Halsey turned to Chasen. 'Talk to the man. I can't get any sense out of him.'

They worked in a hut with the shutters closed. Worked forty-eight hours straight, even though Halsey told Ben Sa'oud that it was the way to make mistakes. There was no choice in the matter. Musa had issued strict orders. Food was brought at intervals. Rice and meat, macaroni and meat. By noon of the third day they had enough household goods primed and ready. Halsey suggested a drink in the bar while the students loaded the truck.

'What I want to know,' Chasen said. 'How come you can get a drink here when the rest of the country is drier than a desert?'

Ben Sa'oud said that this was a training area. The bar was small and dark with metal shutters at the windows. The air still and laden with dust.

Chasen winked. 'You train your secret agents here. Right?'

Ben Sa'oud looked puzzled.

'Training them to drink and screw.' Chasen grinned. 'Hell, I could do that job, teaching Muslims how to drink.' He pulled a cigar out of the breast pocket of his sweat-stained shirt. 'Come on Benny. This is a celebration. Have a little gin in your fruit juice. Makes it taste better. Barkeep. A drink for my friend.'

Halsey put his hand on Chasen's arm. 'Why don't you get some sleep?'

'One more drink.'

Halsey had an idea that if this was a training area it wasn't for use by the Libyans. Libyans didn't drink. Could be for foreigners. Russians and the Chinese, maybe. He'd also heard about terrorist training camps.

Chasen had calmed down. Gone back to being morose. Halsey

took the cigar that Chasen was toying with and stuck it in his mouth.

Halsey said, 'Have a cigar.'

'I was saving this.'

'We're having a celebration.' Halsey picked up the matches on the bar and lit the cigar for him.

Ben Sa'oud said he thought it was time to check on the loading. That's all he said. The stillness of the bar was shattered by a blast that splintered the windows. Everyone hit the deck. Halsey lay there on the barroom floor, dust eddying, anticipating the scene outside. His stomach churned.

The end of the hut had been blown away. There was rubble over the truck. At first Halsey couldn't see any bodies. And for a moment thought the Libyans had been lucky. Then he saw a severed arm. An arm he recognized. A trail of blood.

After the ambulances carried the four survivors away, an ashen-faced Ben Sa'oud returned to the scene of the blast. He reported to Halsey and Chasen that Musa had been contacted and was on his way. He also said that one of the two dead students was a nephew of Jalloud.

Chasen looked very sober. 'One minute we're having a quiet drink and then blooey.'

They were driven under guard to the airport to meet Musa's plane.

Chasen said, 'You arm one of those devices?' He had his teeth clenched.

Halsey didn't answer straight away because he didn't think the question deserved an answer. Chasen repeated the question.

'You saw them throwing the boom boom around.'

Chasen stared out the window. 'You suppose Francine has called Jack?'

'What for?'

'Tell him we're missing.'

Halsey was doubtful. 'What's Jack gonna do, wave a magic wand?'

An hour, nearly two, waiting by the runway in the back of an open truck. The air heavy with aviation fuel. Out of the sun a Chinook came skimming in low, blackening the sky. The twin rotor blades beating the air, hovering, sending up clouds of dirt and sand. The Chinook touched down. Musa, in combat uniform, climbed down past the guns and got into the waiting Mercedes. The convoy moved off along the perimeter of the airfield and through a gate into a fenced-off parking lot of neatly-aligned new army vehicles. The convoy came to a halt. Halsey was manhandled out of the truck. Chasen dragged. Musa came over towards them, his hawk face blank. He began shouting in Arabic. A tirade of abuse. Continuing in broken phrases of English running into Arabic. Halsey understood the two essential points Musa was making. Americans are incompetent and they murder Arabs. If Musa wanted them dead they wouldn't be standing where they were. He obviously had something in mind. Musa was winding down.

'You must make big bomb. Kill many Egyptians. One explosion.' Musa's voice was strained. He pointed to a water carrier. A ten-thousand-gallon tanker.

Halsey went over to the hulk, playing for time, trying to figure how to deal with Musa. It would be possible with binary explosive to turn the carrier into a lethal weapon that could blow a small town off the map. But how would the Libyans get the fucker across the border?

'How do you intend to move it?'

'That is our problem,' said Musa.

'The Egyptians aren't stupid. You've even got military markings on the side.' Halsey hit the tanker with the side of his fist. 'Okay, you get some paint, change the color. Don't you think they're gonna be suspicious if a newly-painted water truck arrives one day outside the door.'

'No more excuses.' Musa appeared to be about to jump up and down.

The wooden horse. The Libyans leave the tanker in front of a frontier post. The border guards say, 'This is a really friendly gesture. Those Libyans, we've misjudged them. They're stand-up guys. Let's drive the truck to Cairo and show everyone what we got from our neighbors.' They go to Cairo. The President hears about the whole thing. He wants to be there to officially welcome the tanker and take the first drink. He declares a public holiday. Dancing in the streets. A festival every year on this day. The President meets the procession that's formed on the journey. He rides on top the last mile into the city. He gets down and tells the people let's have a drink on Muammar el Gadafi. Takes his cup and turns the faucet.

Halsey doubted Musa had heard the story.

Halsey kicked the tire with his boot. 'It presents some problems.' His throat was dry. 'Technical problems.'

Chasen moved within spitting distance. 'What?'

As soon as you presented the Libyans with two or more problems their abilities crumbled. Musa was beginning to falter.

'We need a pressure switch and a way of arming, solenoids, valves.'

Musa's mind began to wander with Halsey's technical double-talk. Then something caught his attention and he shouted. His eye had been attracted by a number of campers in the corner of the lot.

Halsey wondered how they got there. He hadn't figured Musa would come up with a new and brilliantly diabolical plan that fast. Instead of a tanker, motor homes.

Chasen, at Halsey's shoulder, said, 'Let's do it and get the fuck outta here.'

They followed Musa. If the guy thought he could get a tanker across the border then campers were easy.

Turning motor homes into instruments of death and destruction was simple. Also primitive, using washing-machine parts, anything available, clothespegs. And it took only a few hours. The work complete, they spent the night in a barred room. Halsey couldn't sleep. He stood naked at the window grasping the bars and watching clouds drift across the face of the moon. The shadow of the guard swayed. He thought he saw movement in the darkness. Cloud fell from the moon. Halsey saw a woman in the shadow. Something told him it was Marielle. And then she was gone, hidden in the night. He called her name.

The butt of a Kalashnikov hit the bars, narrowly missing Halsey's hand. He backed up to his iron cot. The gun muzzle following him.

Chasen woke up. 'What's going on?'

'Okay, it's all over. Go back to sleep.' Halsey lay down.

When he woke the next morning the incident had such a dream-like quality that Halsey believed it had been a dream.

Tripoli

'Where the hell have you been?' Francine glared at Chasen and Halsey. 'Shacked up with some bimbos?'

Chasen was visibly crumbling. 'We've been living through a nightmare.' He held his head. 'I feel like shit.'

'The bimbos turned out to be drillers in drag and you spent the last three days chained to a bed.' Francine shook her head slowly and deliberately. Then she laughed. 'God, you both look awful.'

'I'm gonna hit the sack.' Chasen staggered out the office mumbling to himself and yawning.

Halsey said to Francine, 'You want coffee?'

She followed him up the stairs to the kitchen. The smell of body odor sickly sweet on the grease-smeared fatigues.

'Are you going to tell me what happened?'

'What?'

'Jack thinks you ran out on him.' Francine folded her arms.

Halsey put the coffee machine on the stove. 'Kidnapped.'

'You're kidding.'

Halsey turned around so she could see his face.

'No you're not.'

'Musa came down to the Palace and had us shipped out to Tubruq.'

'Why?'

'He wanted bombs to kill Egyptians.' Halsey began recounting the bare facts in a dry, weary tone. Francine listened open-mouthed.

The phone rang. Francine went back down to the office to answer it. Halsey poured strong black coffee, brought it over to the table and sat down.

He heard Francine calling out. Jack wanted to talk to him. He heaved himself out the chair and carried the coffee downstairs.

'He's in a coffee shop,' said Francine.

Halsey took the receiver. 'Yes Jack.' His voice tired.

'What the fuck's going on?'

O'Brien watched the cars. One of the waitresses went past. His gaze became transfixed by her swinging hips in clinging nylon. Mason's Buick cruised by and out of sight. O'Brien waited for him to appear, half-listening to Halsey. Mason came through the side door wearing a Burberry trenchcoat and dark glasses. The coat worn belted.

'You're okay. That's all that matters. Just relax and take it easy.' O'Brien laughed, seeing Mason glancing round furtively. 'Listen, I'll talk to you tomorrow. I'm gonna kick ass down at Musa's office.' He hung up.

Halsey said to Francine, 'Jack was laughing.'

Washington DC

O'Brien came up behind Mason. 'Bill.' He swung into the booth.

'They've convened a grand jury.' Mason smiled. That took the stupid grin off O'Brien's face.

'What have they got?'

'The Cubans gave them conspiracy to commit murder.'

'Is that it?' O'Brien unimpressed.

'The DA's office can open up a whole can of worms with that.'

O'Brien attracted the waitress's attention. 'Two coffees, two apple danish.' He eyed her lasciviously. Her uniform stretched.

'Not for me.'

'I'll eat his.' O'Brien could see tight yellow panties through the nylon and his prick got hard.

'I don't think you realize how far this could go.'

'Are you circumcised?' O'Brien was in pain. 'Every time I get a hard-on, hurts like hell.'

'Go and see a doctor.'

'Don't worry. I'm moving out of K Street, out of Washington.' The waitress brought the order.

'What's your name honey?'

'Melanie. Says so right here.' She pointed to her name tag.

O'Brien could see Melanie wasn't wearing a bra. Her cleavage showing. His gaze came back to the table. 'Out of reach in Tripoli. They'll lose interest.' He wolfed down danish.

Mason tried his coffee. 'This is appalling.' He pushed the cup away. 'I'm thinking about leaving the Agency. Going into business.'

'What kind of business?' O'Brien dragged Mason's cup towards him.

'Shipping, export, electronics, politics. I have one or two things lined up.' Mason leaned back in the seat. He could see O'Brien was interested.

'How much you need to get started?'

Mason half laughed. 'Jack.'

'How much?'

'Say a million.'

'Let me kick this around.'

O'Brien saw Melanie bending over a table. 'You want some more coffee?'

Mason got up. The two men parted without a word. O'Brien waved to the waitress. 'How much?' She sauntered over. 'How much?' Standing, resting against the table, idly fingering the buttons of her uniform.

'Two coffees, two danish.'

'I can see something sweet that isn't on the menu.'

Melanie put her hands down on the laminate table, forcing the uniform to take the added strain. 'Fifty. Ten minutes.' She called to the other waitress. 'I'm just going on my break. Cover for me, Charlene.'

Tripoli

'Why don't you take a shower,' said Francine, 'and go lie down? Get some sleep.'

'When I get this tired I can't sleep.' Halsey stretched his back.

'Take a shower.' Francine gave an order. 'Go lie down on Jack's bed. I'll come and give you a massage. You just need to relax.'

Halsey drifted into the bathroom. There was a heady scent of jasmine in the humid atmosphere. He ran the brown water into the tub and added bath oil, shucking his clothes, kicking them into the corner.

Thirty minutes later he was still lying in the tub. A languor held him in the chill waters. Francine came in with a large pink towel. 'Out you get.'

Reluctantly he got up. His body glistening with oil and water. Francine waited for him to step out. His prick swung between brown thighs. She wrapped the towel around wide shoulders and led him to the bedroom.

Halsey plunged headlong on to the bed, the palm of Francine's hand in the small of his back. She stepped out of her flat shoes on to the undulating mattress, straddling Halsey, and sank down on her knees. Beginning with the neck she eased the muscles with downward pressure.

'Don't stop.'

Francine unbuttoned her white blouse.

Washington DC

'Oral'll cost you extra.' Melanie rolled her tongue around.

'That's fucking disgusting.'

'If I've been a naughty girl you can spank me.' Melanie sucked her finger, little-girl like. 'But it'll cost you extra.'

O'Brien ran his hand across the washbasin. 'And this is fucking disgusting.' O'Brien saw a fractured reflection of the washroom in the cracked mirror over the basin.

'You paying for the fuck, not the fucking Hilton.' Melanie was pissed off. 'You wanna do it or what? I gotta get back.'

O'Brien reached out his hand and put it on a nylon-covered tit.

'Money up front.'

'You should have a list of charges printed on the back of the menu.' He pulled out his clip and peeled off a fifty.

She tucked the fifty away in the pocket behind her name tag. 'Go in the stall and sit on the john with your pants round your ankles.'

O'Brien couldn't believe this. He thought he was paying for the fuck. 'How about you bend over the basin, I fuck you from behind.'

'You wanna fuck or what?' She looked at her watch.

O'Brien unbuckled his belt, unzipping as he went, wondering if he could still get a hard-on. 'Why can't I do business like this?'

Tripoli

Halsey went to sleep with a smile on his face. Francine sighed.

Washington DC

Schultz laid the six weapons on the large oak kitchen table. A Smith & Wesson .38 with a four-inch barrel, two Colt .45 automatics, a .357 Magnum, a Ruger Security Six and a 7.65mm Parabellum with a scarred butt.

'I thought I said American guns.' O'Brien picked up the Parabellum. 'This looks like a German gun to me. Fucking Luger.'

'American. Says so right there.' Schultz pointed.

'The Libyans aren't as smart as you are. They can't read. Take one look at this and says it's a German gun. "El no goodo." No fucking money.' O'Brien lifted the gun to his shoulder. 'I pay you money to do what I tell you to do. Instead of going around using your fucking brain. Have we got that straight?' He put the gun down on the table and moved over to one of the cherrywood cabinets on the wall. He tapped a glass panel with the tips of his fingers.

'Can you believe this?' He opened the cabinet door and closed his hand round the neck of a bottle. 'Can you fucking believe this? That bitch is using fucking Remy Martin to cook with. I'm busting my ass down in Tripoli. She's cooking with fucking Remy Martin. Gimme those glasses behind you.'

Schultz took one of the crystal tumblers from a tray by the sink and handed it to O'Brien.

'Whatsa matter, you're not drinking?'

'Not right now.'

O'Brien poured three inches into the tumbler and drank the first inch. 'I want you to take those guns and find a metal tool-box. Throw in a few wrenches, fool the X-ray machine. Have them put the box in the cargo hold with the baggage. That way they won't check it.'

'You want me to walk these through?' Schultz understood these guns were for Agency covert operations overseas. Jack had told him as much. Now it turned out they were for the Libyans. The Libyans were buying them. Why would the Agency want the Libyans to have American handguns? None of this made sense.

O'Brien put his arm around Schultz. 'Listen. When you come back I've got a new job for you. Pays more. More responsibility. I want you to take charge of the Washington office.'

Schultz brightened.

O'Brien relaxed his grip, carried the cognac over to the sink and filled a second glass. He left the bottle and brought the tumbler over to Schultz. 'Here's to the new president of International Commodities. Mr President.'

Their glasses kissed. A cold glancing kiss followed by a deep silence.

'Ah, Mr President. There are one or two papers I'd like to have you look at and sign.'

Tripoli

Halsey sat on the balcony reading a book. Wearing only a pair of white shorts, he was stretched out on a woven-plastic lounge-chair. Francine was at the kitchen table, cubing lamb on a wooden board.

'What are you reading?'

'In the dark ages the Arabs had street lighting in Córdoba. I'm talking about the Fourteenth Century.'

'Is that why they called it the dark ages? Because they had no street lighting?'

Halsey got up from the lounger and wandered into the kitchen. The sun was cooler now and he needed a shirt. Since Tubruq a calm had descended. He had nothing to do except read, improve his French with a textbook he'd bought secondhand and occasionally help Francine around the office. One day he'd gone down to the beach for a swim but he hadn't gone more than ten feet. The beach was covered in excrement and oil spillage from the tankers using Tripoli harbor.

'They had a library of forty thousand books. This is before the printing press. The centre of learning. Arabs, Christians and Jews. Then the Arabs were defeated by Ferdinand and Isabella, the Christians, it was the beginning of persecution. Arabs and Jews. The Inquisition.'

'What are you cooking?'

'Cous-cous. Stew.' Francine was now preparing a chicken. 'It's for tomorrow.'

Halsey read from the book. ' "The moorish prince Abdullah then delivered up the keys of the Alhambra to his conqueror, saying: 'They are thine, O King, since Allah decrees it. Use thy success with clemency and moderation'." ' He closed the book. 'Did you know Ronald Reagan is a Christian?'

Francine said, 'How about chopping the coriander?'

'Sure. You heard any more?'

'Jack's definitely pulling out of K Street.' She ripped the guts out of the chicken. 'Out of Washington. He has to be out of his mind. Giving up a two-thousand-acre farm in Virginia. For this.' She held her arms out, waving the chicken. 'Maybe Elaine kicked him out but then he'd move right into one of the town houses.'

'What about Jacqueline?'

Francine thought about that for a moment. 'She could be putting the screws on Jack. Okay, Jack moves to London. No, Jack moves to Tripoli.' She released the chicken.

Halsey wondered how much Francine knew about the Agency involvement. O'Brien operated on a need-to-know basis. Francine didn't need to know. She could see what was going on but wouldn't make the correct interpretation. O'Brien in Tripoli, there would be an Agency reason. He and Francine would never know about it.

'Maybe he likes the place. Maybe Jack and Connie.'

'Yeah. Maybe Jack and Jalloud,' Francine said.

Halsey washed the coriander under the faucet. 'It's hormonal.'

'Are you saying I'm hormonal? How would you like this chicken stuffed up your ass?' She brandished the chicken.

Halsey held up his hand. 'I'm a virgin.'

'Isn't it about time you lost your virginity? Take those shorts down and bend over the table.'

Jack had warned Francine that there would be someone flying in. That he'd be around the office for a couple of days. Jack had said, 'While he's around let him have what he wants and leave him alone. You don't have to ask any questions. You don't even have to ask his name. Call him John Doe.' Francine reported her conversation to Halsey and Chasen. They both accepted the information without comment. Francine was surprised at the lack of any reaction.

John Doe showed up at the villa late one night a few days later. Francine was in the office watching TV. She heard a car and a few minutes later he was there, standing in the office doorway, black trenchcoat, dark tinted glasses. When Francine told him Jack wouldn't be around until tomorrow he turned around and left.

The next morning O'Brien flew in early from Malta. He went into conference with Halsey immediately after he'd checked with Francine that there were no matters requiring urgent attention.

'We close the deal today or tomorrow. I want you over there in Belgium ready to go to work on tracking down what we want.'

O'Brien had a glass of flash and orange juice in his hand. Breakfast.

'The name of the guy in Liège is Artur Rimbaud. He's on the payroll. Ex Foreign Legion, deals in armaments. You're staying at the Holiday Inn. Go see him, give him the list. I know what I can fill. He'll run down the rest.' O'Brien poured a little more flash from a Black & White whisky bottle. 'There may be another job to take care of. I need a plane crew. Artur probably has a few names. You'll have to meet these guys, charter a plane and give them a cash advance.'

Halsey said, 'What am I supposed to tell them? You want me to recruit them?'

'No, I'll do the recruiting. Just give them a phone number.'

The door of the office opened and John Doe put his head around. 'Sorry Jack. I'll come back later.'

O'Brien went towards the door. 'That's okay. Come on in.' He gripped the door handle. 'Meet Nate Halsey.'

Halsey shook hands with the short, facially-scarred man in a beige leisure suit. The square gold-rimmed glasses with amber lenses shaded unremarkable brown eyes.

O'Brien said to Halsey, 'Could you maybe make us some coffee?'

Halsey felt a resentment at the way O'Brien dismissed him. As a parting remark O'Brien had said he'd talked to Musa and Musa apologized. Musa wasn't sorry. Bullshit. That was Jack kicking ass! Sent off to make the coffee. Leaving the office, Halsey heard voices raised in argument.

'It wasn't in the newspapers,' said O'Brien.

'Jack, I'm telling you. I saw it.'

O'Brien went over to the file cabinet and found a fat envelope at the back. He handed the envelope to Doe. 'Are you saying I'm a liar?'

Doe, anxious to get at the clippings, managed to tear several. He laid them out on the desk scrabbling to find the one he needed. Becoming more desperate when he couldn't find it.

'Maybe they didn't print the story. Or the fire looked like an accident.'

'I thought I told you to make sure it didn't look like an accident.' O'Brien with venom.

Doe was confused. Sure because he'd torched the car. Seen the fireball a block and a half away. He needed some kind of proof.

'You could call the fire department. Say you're with the insurance company.'

O'Brien made a sound in his throat, sat down at the desk.

'Did you check all the papers?' Doe chewed the cuticle on his thumb.

'And UPI and Reuters.' O'Brien poured more flash.

'The *Mail*. You read the *Mail*?'

'No, I didn't read the fucking *Mail*.'

'It's gotta be in the *Mail*.' Doe got down on his knees in front of O'Brien. 'Jack, if the story isn't in the *Mail*, if I'm lying to you about the car . . . If I'm lying to you – ' he moved from one knee to the other ' – you can have a nigger boy for a year.'

Halsey knocked twice, holding a large metal tray. He backed in through the door without getting a response. The sun behind O'Brien shafting through the half-closed shutters fell in a rectangular grid. And Doe there kneeling, abasing himself before O'Brien.

Paris

Louis XIV had his architect turn a hunting lodge into a château at Versailles. Paris was getting too crowded. He moved sixteen miles away, three hours in a coach. The sheer size of the place was unbelievable. Every time Brecht walked across the cobblestones of the forecourt she had the same feeling. And if Louis was bored and wanted to get away from the 'incessant demands of grandeur', as one guidebook she'd read put it, he could escape to one of the small villas nearby in the grounds. Then everyone, well, those people who had money, started building their own villas on the road to Paris. The exodus to the suburbs had begun.

Brecht recognized Krupps's heavy, dark, military-style topcoat. He was walking away from the Galleries des Glace that faced the gardens and linked the halls of war and peace. They hadn't met since the parking garage at La Défense over a month ago. A month was an agreed laying-off period before planning a new action.

Their paths met at the head of the stone staircase that led down to the fountain and the Grand Canal. Brecht linked her arm with his. As they descended the steps a woman in a smart beige raincoat with a Chanel scarf around her shoulders called out in broken French, asking if they would take a photograph. Krupps replied in German, saying he didn't understand. Brecht smiled. The woman held out a compact camera. Brecht saw the man, obviously her husband, dressed in the same raincoat, standing ten yards back. She posed the couple, taking two shots in front of Versailles and handed back the camera.

The woman offered to take their photograph. Brecht smiled and shook her head. She was superstitious. She thought she'd lose her soul in the camera. The man stepped forward and introduced himself as Harold Stein from Baltimore. And his wife, Rachel. Rachel said, '*Je suis enchantée.*' Harold smiled. They were in town for a couple of weeks staying at the Holiday Inn, Place de la République. A second honeymoon. Harold said a third honeymoon. Rachel corrected him, saying that Moscow was business. Harold Stein worked for Pepsi-Cola.

Rachel Stein said why didn't they get together and have a drink at the Ritz. The couples parted with Rachel Stein saying to Brecht to call them at the Holiday Inn.

At the end of the Grand Canal Apollo rises out of the water on his chariot. As Brecht and Krupps reached the statue, the sun, shadowed by cloud, hung over the avenue of trees. They discussed changing the death list. Krupps was in favor of moving the Americans to the top. The publicity was better. Brecht wanted to stick to the original order. She didn't believe in change for the sake of change.

Here in the grounds of the Sun King's palace, she was aware of herself and of being outside herself. She watched the people strolling in the autumn sunlight. She was aware of playing a part. The feeling of parallel worlds was uppermost in her mind. It was an idea that persisted.

The name at the top of the death list was Moishe Gal, a cultural attaché at the Israeli Embassy and known Mossad agent. Rarely seen around the embassy, he spent most of his time travelling. Although he had an apartment just outside the *periphérique* in Clichy, when he was in Paris he usually stayed with one of four women he saw on an irregular basis. He kept his car, a dark blue Alfa Romeo, in the embassy compound, preferring taxis or occasionally the Métro.

Three weeks of surveillance revealed no pattern in Moishe Gal's life. A note stapled to the weekly report from the Lille Group said simply, 'Query continue – confirm.' The cost of the surveillance – vehicles, hotels, etc. – was running at around ten thousand dollars a week. The financial equation: death against expenditure, had to be considered. There was also the additional risk that increased with each day, of the subject becoming aware of being under surveillance. The decision had to be made whether to go for a softer target or wait another week.

Krupps cabled Lille a one-word cable: Terminate. Then something happened. By chance four days later Chantal Monceau nearly bumped into Moishe Gal in the street. She had been doing research for her doctoral thesis at the Musée de la Publicité near the Gare de l'Est and was on her way to the Métro Château d'Eau when she saw him parking a red Renault in the Rue Martel. She followed to an address in the Rue des Petites Ecuries. Moishe Gal was visiting the dentist. Monceau made enquiries over the phone. She said she had recently arrived in Paris from Bordeaux and was having trouble with a loose crown. A friend, Moishe Gal, had recommended the dentist. The receptionist volunteered the information that Gal was having a course of treatment for root canal work. Very painful.

The car Moishe Gal was driving that morning was checked out through Lille. A hire car rented for seven days.

From the start Krupps had wanted to use a car bomb. As the reports arrived each week, that no longer seemed viable. But as soon as Krupps heard about the hire car he resurrected the idea. The gun had jammed at La Défense. Using a remote device eliminated that factor in the equation.

Krupps delivered a coded list to the dead-letter drop in the Père Lachaise cemetery near the mass grave of the Communards shot against the Federalists' wall in 1871. There were five items: the keys to the Renault hire car, a copy of the dentist's appointments' diary, two Uzi sub-machine-guns, an unmarked panel truck, a car bomb and transmitter. With six days' delivery.

Three days later Krupps collected a package from a post office box in Drancy. In the package were the keys, a photocopy of the diary, delivery instructions for the other three items and an invoice for two hundred and forty thousand dollars.

The Lille Group provided every back-up service at a price and with a guarantee.

Moishe Gal's appointment was for eight thirty on Wednesday morning. Five days after the first appointment. The dentist's chair provided the right framework for the assassination. A time and place and the added advantage of an anesthetic that would slow the Israeli down.

At seven fifty-five on Wednesday morning, Krupps left the Gare de l'Est Métro and walked through the main train station, crossed over to the Avenue du Verdun, making his way to the canal. In the Rue Varlin he found the green panel truck with Monceau behind the wheel. He climbed in the back. Strapped to the floor between the axles were two black cases. He unhooked the straps and opened the left-hand case. Inside, packed in foam, were the two Uzi machine-guns. He ran a check on each gun in turn, then snapped in the right angle clips, two joined together for rapid changeover. He handed one to Monceau, the other he slid under the passenger seat.

In the second smaller case was a package wrapped in brown paper. Packed in foam alongside the package, a transmitter. Krupps closed the case and carefully handed it over to Monceau. He squeezed through to the front between the seats, made sure the Uzi wasn't about to start moving around and then took the case from Monceau.

Since five a.m., Brecht had taken four Valium. It was now eight twenty. The half-empty bottle of tablets lay flat on the dashboard of the Citroen CX parked at the intersection of Rue Martel and Rue des Petites Ecuries. If Moishe Gal was driving the car he wouldn't have a problem finding a space to park. She could see the green panel truck in her rear-view mirror.

At nine twenty-five the red Renault with Moishe Gal at the wheel came down Rue Martel and made a left into the one-way system on Rue des Petites Ecuries. He parked illegally outside the charcuterie in front of the Citroen. As he walked back down the street he glanced over at Brecht and smiled.

Monceau and Krupps watched the Israeli coming towards them. He should have crossed to the street to the dentist. He didn't. They sat framed in the windshield of the truck, transfixed. There was a moment when Krupps knew he could reach under the seat, lean out the window with the Uzi and blow the Israeli's head off from no more than two feet away. But he had the case there and shooting was the secondary action. In the mirror Monceau saw him turn the corner. She looked at Krupps. He sat impassively, his gaze fixed on the side mirror.

A full five minutes passed before Moishe Gal reappeared carrying a pharmacy bag. He was walking along the street on the same side as the truck. Right before he came level with the truck he started making moves to cross over. Monceau watched her driver's side mirror, waiting for him to come out from behind the truck.

What happened then Krupps wasn't sure. The next thing he registered was the driver's door being wrenched open and the Israeli standing there pointing a Beretta at Monceau. Monceau was turning, and the two bullets she took in the chest sent her rocking back. With the impact, the Uzi in her hands fired off the full clip of thirty-two bullets in a line diagonally bisecting the upper torso of the Israeli.

Brecht watched the lunchtime news on the TV set in Marie Claude's office at the bank. The gun battle in the Rue des Petites Ecuries was the lead story. She watched with the sound down. There were shots of the covered body on the road. There were shots of the green panel truck with a shattered windshield. There were shots of the ambulance and gendarmes standing around, the street cordoned off. There were no shots of Monceau's body. She had to imagine the lifeless form stretched out across the floor of the truck.

Beyond the white tapes the hungry crowds looked on.

Tripoli

In the morning the air was dry and the sun pale behind golden clouds. Now, as Halsey gazed up at the sky, it had turned from vivid blue to gray. The sea, usually calm, had become angry with foam-flecked waves. He looked over at Francine. Francine engrossed in the accounts.

'Rain or what?'

'The weather,' she sighed.

A hot wind rising in the Sahara carrying sand across the Hammada al-Hamra, gathering pace. The red-hot breath of the desert. Francine pressed 'total' on the calculator and a ribbon of paper shot out.

Airborne sand whipped across the road, occasionally settling, patterning the black surface with a desert landscape, moving on to become a part of the beach.

'You have your ticket?'

Halsey patted the front of his coat.

'You want me to drive you to the airport?'

Halsey cleared his throat. Then shook his head.

'Uh huh.'

'Listen. I'm gonna be back.'

'You might not.'

The Eagle horn sounded saving him from having to say any more.

He kissed her gently on the lips.

'*Fi'aman allah.*'

'Yeah. Write when you get work.' There was a tear hanging on her eyelash.

Halsey threw his bags on the back seat and climbed in beside Chasen.

'You are one lucky son of a bitch getting outta here.

'Amen.'

They drove in silence towards the airport, the Sahara, their backs to the sea and into the oncoming sand. Halsey wondered if he would ever be back in this place, this city of minarets. The muezzins calling: 'I witness that there is no god but Allah. Come to prayer, come to betterment. *Allah akbar.* There is no God but

133

Allah. Come to betterment.'

Halsey was heading in the other direction.

Liège

After delays Halsey caught the flight to Zurich. From Zurich on to Brussels, Zaventem. A train from Brussels Nord for Liège.

The carillon of the cathedral chimed five o'clock along the Rue Destenay. Halsey stared out the cab window. He had the impression that Liège was a gray town. The gray stone buildings ingrained, blackened with debris from heavy industry along the steep-sided valley of the Meuse. The cab was following a funeral procession across the Pont J. F. Kennedy. At the head of the cortège a silver Buick hearse decked with wreaths and lit with four carriage lamps at the corners of the black vinyl roof.

Halsey checked into the Holiday Inn and was given a room on the ninth floor facing west across the river. The town stretching north along the west bank. The number of churches surprised him.

'God is good for business,' Rimbaud said to Halsey, the two men sitting at a small leather-topped table sipping Duvel beer in the Quinquet bar of the hotel. Rimbaud also had a glass of Peket, the local brandy, in front of him, which Halsey had declined, sticking to beer.

A group of dark-suited businessmen entering the bar attracted Rimbaud's attention. 'I have to talk to these guys.' He called to the barman, '*Encore une fois, Henri,*' stood up, draining the Peket and weaved his way over towards the lobby.

They were too far away for Halsey to overhear their conversation. Salesmen. Rimbaud couldn't be mistaken for a salesman or a businessman, even though he wore a conservative suit. He had the unmistakable way of holding himself of a career soldier. Halsey and Rimbaud had that in common. O'Brien had said the man was an ex-colonel in the Foreign Legion. Halsey had recognized him as soon as he walked into the bar. Dark skinned with a grizzled gray and black beard. A scar disfiguring his mouth. His accent was strong and Halsey had trouble understanding him in French. They spoke together in a mix of French and English.

Rimbaud came back to the table. '*Ce mec*. At the left.' He inclined his head, indicating the man he'd been talking to. 'I have to lick his ass.' He lit a Disque Bleu with a match and ran the flame between finger and thumb. '*Vous connaissez le business?*'

'I'm a soldier,' said Halsey. 'Ex-soldier.'

'*Bon. Screw les hommes d'affaires.*'

They drank to that. Then to the *Régiment Etrangère*, followed by Halsey's outfit.

Halsey couldn't remember how he got to bed. The phone woke him. 'Artur. What time is it?'

Rimbaud said it was time to get up. He'd pick him up in an hour. Halsey stumbled out of bed and straight into the shower, turning the jet to cold. After three minutes he adjusted the temperature to warm for two minutes, soaping himself, and then shut the control off. He stood in the white-tiled stall towelling vigorously. The white tiles reminded him of the milky-white arak. Why had he switched to arak?

Breakfast was a cup of coffee and some lightly scrambled eggs from room service. At nine o'clock Halsey was waiting outside the hotel. Rimbaud swung the pale gray Mercedes 280 SE convertible in front. The sky was overcast, a blanket of cloud, and Rimbaud had the hood down. Across the river, south along the Quai de Rome, neither man speaking until they hit the ramp for Ougrée.

'When do we talk business?' said Halsey.

Rimbaud had on a pair of heavy-rimmed dark glasses, a black and white silk suit, hair mostly gray. The only color in his appearance the deep-brown skin. He left the question unanswered, lighting a Disque Bleu with the burning element in the car lighter. Nicotine stains on his fingers barely discernible.

The three-storey warehouse in the back of the gas plant had all the openings bricked up in the same red brick as the main structure. Electronic steel shutters rolled back and the Mercedes inched into the narrow loading bay. Rimbaud told Halsey to take a look around while he made a few phone calls.

Green-shaded bulbs at intervals along cage-lined corridors failed to illuminate the racks and crates of weapons. Shadowy shapes appeared and receded with proximity to the yellow circles of light. The cages held military armaments. No sporting guns. In numbers not enough to supply armies. Automatic and semi-automatic rifles – Armalite, Kalashnikov, FN Mitrailleuse à Gaz from the Fabrique Nationale twelve kilometers down the Meuse. All secondhand, collected from battlefields throughout the civilized world. Halsey could only speculate about where they might be used next and how long before they would be back inside the cages ready to be sold on again. He saw Rimbaud sitting in a glass-partitioned office, talking to a man and a woman. Pale light spilled out, eaten by the shadow. Halsey headed down a narrow passage between boxes of grenades stacked next to empty cages.

Rimbaud introduced his secretary Solange Duprey and Jean Hullos, the warehouse manager. Hullos pointed to an open crate on the floor and said, 'Do you want to check them out?'

In the crate were factory new Parabellums, Mauser replicas of the German army pistole 08 in 9mm caliber.

'Jack ordered these?'

Rimbaud said, 'We have a small firing range.'

Halsey didn't know anything about handguns. He'd fired one occasionally. What was there to know apart from how to pull the trigger? He selected two guns from the crate.

In the cold dark basement Halsey loaded the two clips with 9mm ammunition. He was paying close attention when Hullos explained how the Parabellum worked. Slide the clip in, pull the toggle mechanism and that chambers the shell. All you do then is point the thing and pull the trigger.

Blam. Flame came out of the barrel and the shell casing shot by Halsey's shoulder, ricocheting off the ceiling. The noise was unbelievable. Even though he had earplugs in, he was momentarily deafened. The cardboard soldier in a camouflage uniform with a rifle had a hole in his neck. Too high and to the left.

Halsey emptied the clip into the target, tearing a wound four inches across over the heart. With the second gun he lacerated the soldier's face after putting the first through his helmet.

Satisfied as he could be that the guns worked, Halsey bought them back up to the office and returned them to Hullos. 'Noisy bastards.' Halsey took the plugs out of his ears, his head ringing with the percussion.

Hullos smiled, packing the guns back in their crate. He showed Halsey a box of silencers that went with the Parabellums. 'I think you need these.' Everyone's a joker, Halsey thought.

Rimbaud stepped forward. 'Now we must have the money.'
Halsey said, 'What are they for?'
'They're to be delivered to Tripoli.'
'If Jack hasn't paid for them, talk to Jack.'
Hullos picked up the phone.
Rimbaud said to Halsey, 'Let's get some coffee.' He moved over
to a two-drawer file cabinet with a filter machine and cups laid out
on a black and red lacquer tray. With a shrug and to no one in
particular, Rimbaud said, *'Ce mec est un juif.'*
The office area was divided into four boxes by glass and black
metal partitions, each equipped with a metal desk and chairs in
gun-metal gray. Three boxes of varying dimensions arranged
around the largest box, the reception area. Rimbaud poured coffee
from the glass jug into white octagonal cups and handed one to
Halsey, then led the way through the door marked 'A Rimbaud'.
'Okay, we talk business.'
Halsey placed his cup on the edge of the desk and sat down,
ready to listen.
Rimbaud rested his weight against the door, the gold lettering of
his name. He began explaining the nature of the arms trade, how it
worked, how business was transacted. 'This money,' he said, 'this
money for the Mausers.'
'Talk to Jack.'
'Jack said you have the money.'
'I don't have it. Jack didn't mention the guns.'
'This is bad business.' Rimbaud aimed a finger at Halsey.
'I'll talk to Jack. Get this straightened out.'
'I make a force of argument. When you make a deal. When you
shake hands, be sure of the money.' Rimbaud betrayed no anger.
He was making a point.
Halsey knew he had to tread carefully. Not antagonize
Rimbaud. He needed him.
'There's a couple of things we have to talk about.' Halsey
looked at Rimbaud to proceed. 'You've seen the list.'
Rimbaud went around his desk and took a file out of the top
drawer. He flipped it open. 'There are three things that are not
possible to find. The others I supply or I know where they are. For
those that I find I get ten per cent.'
'Jack won't buy from you if he can get the goods cheaper
elsewhere. And he'll only go to five per cent as a finder's fee.'

Rimbaud either smiled or sneered. Halsey couldn't tell, with scar tissue dragging the mouth down on one side.

Rimbaud lit a cigarette, exhaling blue smoke in Halsey's direction. 'Ten per cent, in cash, on delivery.' Exhaling again. '*Ce mec*. He should have his ass handed to him.' These words were delivered in a slow and deliberate manner.

Halsey had no reply. He changed the subject. 'Jack wants me to locate a pilot.'

Rimbaud nodded. 'I know what he wants. Someone who flies anywhere at the right price.'

Paris

'An Israeli diplomat, Moishe Gal, and his unnamed female assassin died yesterday in a fierce gun battle on a quiet Paris street.' Brecht gazed over her day-old copy of the *Herald Tribune* at the water cascading down beneath the feet of a naked Acis and Galetea. 'Moishe Gal, forty-six, a cultural attaché at the Israeli Embassy, was gunned down in a hail of bullets in the Rue des Petites Ecuries.'

Golden carp swam in the dark pool shaded by overhanging plane trees.

Brecht asked Krupps, beside her on the bench, if he had read the newspaper report. He glanced up from the article he was reading in *Life* magazine and shook his head. Brecht reported the comments from a spokesman blaming Gadafi.

Alongside the two-column story a three-column photograph of the funeral. And below, in Washington Ronald Reagan had given himself the right to withhold information for National Security reasons. Brecht stared at the photograph, the dark figures staring back. She gripped the paper and flung it in the water. Brecht surprised herself with the violence of her action. Fish darted forward, biting at the newsprint. The sodden paper sank beneath the surface.

Rumors had begun spreading about police reaction. At the Sorbonne a number of students had disappeared in the early hours of the morning after the shooting.

Although Monceau hadn't been named in the media, it was obvious the police knew who she was and had 'rounded up the usual suspects'. Perhaps some good would come of her death if her death provoked a riot at the Sorbonne. What was it like in sixty-eight? Brecht felt sure everything would have been simpler then. The lines were drawn when the barricades went up. In America people were being killed on the campuses for taking a stand. Opposing the war in Vietnam. Justice and humanity were words that had a meaning. Not Reagan rhetoric. Brecht envied the Arabs their belief in a holy war, Jihad – was she losing her faith?'

As she continued to stare at the point where the newspaper had sunk she realized that her hand had found its way into the patent leather purse on her lap. She was fingering a glossy postcard as though it were a holy relic. The card had arrived that morning from Germany. The image, creased and torn, showed the Electoral Palace in Bonn – the University. On the back the four word message read, 'Having a lovely time.' Signed with the initial 'M'. It was a coded signal arranging a meeting in Bonn.

At that moment Brecht believed the postcard was her only link with sanity.

Liège

The red awning arched in space above the sidewalk, shadowing the wall. A yellow light rippled the semi-obscure glass. The bar on the Quai Orban appeared to have no name apart from Stella beer.

Rimbaud exhaled blue smoke and said, '*J'attends ici.*'

Halsey hesitated, half expecting Rimbaud to say something more. He swung the heavy gray door on the Mercedes. Rimbaud was watching the canal. The water fragmented.

The yellow light came from imitation candles in pairs along the panelled walls. A soccer game with the sound down was showing on a TV hung from the ceiling in the corner. Halsey couldn't see the faces of the two men bellied up to the rail. They had their back to the door watching the game.

He ordered a beer. The tall one looked around. Halsey nodded. '*Voulez-vous prendre un verre?*' He had no doubt from the description that this was Guy Tallien. And the other one had to be Hablinski. Hablinksi stayed watching the TV and ordered a large vodka. Tallien had a Ricard in the same glass.

Tallien led the way over to a table at the back. The Polack

followed reluctantly, moving backwards. He stood by the table and lit the butt of a cheap cigar with a match, his head on one side trying to get a look at the game. Hablinksi took time out to ask what the deal was.

Halsey laid it out in limited terms. A charter. Hiring a DC3 legitimately. Filing a flight plan and then disappearing for a couple of days. Pick up a cargo. Fly it somewhere. Take the same cargo back. He paused and Hablinski indicated with the cigar to go on.

Halsey said all he could say beyond that the fee was ten thousand dollars each. Hablinski wanted to know where. Halsey said Africa. Tallien rolled the ice around in his glass. Hablinski looked away from the TV and at Halsey. He had a one word question: Chad? Halsey pulled an envelope out of his jacket and held it up in front of Hablinksi and Tallien. He told them that inside the envelope they'd find a two thousand dollar advance and a phone number. Hablinski jabbed the air with his cigar. Did Halsey know there were *Légion Etrangère* down in Chad? Did he understand that they wouldn't fight against them? Halsey said that as far as he knew there was no fighting involved. No action against any Frenchmen.

Hablinksi snatched the envelope and returned his attention to the game.

'They didn't seem surprised,' said Halsey as he got into the Mercedes.

Rimbaud threw the burning cigarette out of the window and turned the key in the ignition. The engine caught first time. He put the car in gear and started north along the canal. 'What do you want to eat? Vietnamese?'

The Brasserie Flo on the Quai sur Meuse served Boudin Blanc, the local sausages. Rimbaud ordered crayfish, and sausages for Halsey. Halsey wasn't missing Tripoli.

'Tallien, Hablinksi?'

'Those guys,' said Rimbaud. 'OAS.'

Halsey only vaguely recalled OAS, a French army faction that had tried to bring down De Gaulle's government. 'De Gaulle betrayed them over Algeria. Giving it back to the Algerians.'

Rimbaud crushed the empty pack of Disque Blue and signalled to the waiter. '*Algerie Française*.' An edge in his voice. 'They are *pieds noirs*. French born in Algeria. We fought together in

Indo-China, Vietnam. Then in Algeria. I had my feet mutilated. Arrows of bamboo. Tortured by the ALN and left behind part of my stomach. They lost everything. Tallien's brother was killed by a bomb, drinking beer in a café. Hablinski's wife was shot by a stray bullet. A French bullet.' The waiter brought the cigarettes on a tray. Rimbaud tore the cellophane, ripped the silver paper and snapped the pack with his index finger. 'Alors, ça y'est?'

Halsey wasn't sure what Rimbaud meant. 'Did they buy the deal?' Halsey shrugged his shoulders, puffing air through a closed mouth. He was learning how to say nothing in French.

'If I ask, Tallien would tell me.' Rimbaud rolled the cigarette in his finger tips. 'Are you a good friend with Jack?'

'Jack doesn't have any good friends.'

'You work for him.'

'I work for the man.'

'Dis moi. What's his angle?'

'Angle?'

'What is this with Gadafi?'

Halsey shrugged again.

Rimbaud leaned forward on the table. 'Gadafi and the CIA. Yes?'

Halsey smiled and shook his head. 'Let's talk M-16s. Five thousand shouldn't be too hard to find.'

Tripoli

The man, code name Grenadier, known as John Doe around the villa, also had another name. The name he was born with forty-three years ago in El Paso, Texas – Gordon Wilder.

Wilder sat slumped in a canvas chair resting a polystyrene cup on his crotch, picking dog hairs off his lime leisure-suit and listening to Jack O'Brien.

'I want you to get something heavy. Give him a couple of whacks with it around the legs.' O'Brien brought his glass down on the desk, making his point. The glass cracked into three pieces. Flash and orange juice flowed over the paperwork.

Wilder reached forward and picked up a sheaf of papers, sluicing the juice into a bin.

O'Brien waved his hand around, blood running down the wrist. 'Gimme the handkerchief.' Pointing to Wilder's suit.

'It's part of the suit.'

'Don't shit around. I'm bleeding to death here.'

'I ain't kidding.' Wilder tugged at the material in his breast pocket.

'Christ!' Not really believing. O'Brien found a shirt over the back of a chair and wrapped it around his hand to halt the flow.

'What if I can't find what's his name?'

'That's a pretty dumb fucking question. Just do it and no fuck-ups. I'm not going to have that cocksucker around saying he screwed me out of money.' O'Brien started looking around for another glass and the bottle. 'And the fucker's name is Auric. Gene Auric.'

Francine heard the shouting coming down the stairs. The office door opened and Wilder, his face red with drink, came out. He saw Francine on the stairs above. 'Where's a glass?'

'A glass what?'

Wilder puzzled over this then said, 'Jack wants a glass.'

'Try the kitchen. I have a lot of luck in that area.'

Wilder barged past Francine.

'Hey. It's unlucky to cross on the stairs.' Francine descended the last three steps and kicked open the office door. 'Not only does he look like a pig, he has the manners of a pig.' She carried on down the staircase.

O'Brien shouted, 'Don't forget the orange juice. None of that guava shit.'

Wilder had found a nearly empty peanut butter jar and was trying to get the rest of the contents out with the end of a fork, spooning it on to a plate of congealed pasta.

O'Brien came in the kitchen. 'Where's the glass?'

'I'm just washing it.'

O'Brien had a quart bottle of flash in his hand. He flipped the screw top with his thumb, took a swallow and said, 'Any of that coconut juice around?' He put the bottle on the table and opened a cupboard. 'Schultz'll give you a gun. Don't kill the fucker. I want the money.' He couldn't find the coconut.

'What if he don't have the money?' Wilder rinsed the jar.

'He's got the money.' O'Brien took the jar still smeared with butter and poured. 'Put the gun to his head. Don't fuck around. Put the gun to his head, don't fuck around showing everyone what a great shot you are. Spread his brains over the wall. Maybe his wife'll have them framed.' He drank. 'Use a Magnum or a Blackhawk. Blow him the fuck away.'

'I thought you wanted the money.'

O'Brien smiled at Wilder, moved along the table, leaning closer. 'After you get the money.' Hard to believe that Wilder was a Green Beret, the élite fighting man.

'Jack's been acting strange lately,' said Francine. 'You know what I'm talking about.'

Chasen made the turn off the ring road to Bab al Azizia, giving a wide berth to a cattle truck, and had to swerve to avoid a dead dog in the road. 'He's been spending more time in Tripoli. That would account for it.'

'But why is he spending more time here?'

'He's running away from those ballbusters.'

'I think it's more serious than women.'

Chasen parked the Eagle in behind a Datsun Cherry. Francine made to get out. Chasen put his hand on her arm. 'What's on your mind?'

'Two or three things. A lawyer for the Green Berets going stateside. Newspaper articles. Talk about a Grand Jury.'

'Shit. It's that stinking Irishman, Lynch, mouthing off.'

'We're talking about conspiracy to murder.'

A kid climbed on to the hood and began cleaning the windshield with a rag.

'Come on, Jack gets a little wound up, has a drink, starts in about how someone should be dead. Christ, he doesn't mean anything by it.'

Francine watched a goat wandering along a third-floor balcony of one of the new apartment blocks. 'Tell me this. And think very carefully before you answer. Would you elect Nixon for a third term?'

Bonn

Brecht held a copy of the Bonn *Rundschau* over her head. Rain dripped on her neck from the tall chestnut trees.

She looked at her watch, then up at the Palace across the lawns.

Marielle Bayer was coming towards her along a gravel path, holding a black umbrella.

Rivulets of water from Brecht's hair ran down her forehead across her eyes, meeting Marielle Bayer's lips as the two women kissed. Linking arms, they moved off down the path to the Rhine.

'We can stay at Lotte's place,' said Bayer. Brecht glanced over her shoulder.

'No one's following me,' said Bayer. 'I checked, I've been through the Kunst museum on the U-Bahn to Bad Godesburg and back.' She could feel the tension in Brecht's body and sensed something behind it. Maybe disapproval. 'I crossed the border into Tunisia in the desert. Flew into London on my French passport. Stayed a couple of weeks with Greta and flew into Frankfurt on my own passport.' She would have added: you see I can take this seriously, but held back.

'It's not a game.'

'No, it's not a game.'

'Monceau is dead.'

'How?'

'Shot by the Mossad agent.'

'The one on the list?'

'Yes.'

'What happened?'

'He must have noticed something. He came up behind the truck that she was driving.' Brecht turned to Bayer, salt tears ran together with the rain. 'It isn't a game.'

They walked on under the black umbrella held between them.

Around behind the university in the Munster Plaza Brecht bought aspirin in the pharmacy while Bayer sat in the café bar opposite ordering drinks. The *fin de siècle* façade of the Munster Apotheke a brown stone color next to the gray stone of the Pizza Hut restaurant. Bonn was a city of muted tones. They had spent three years here, Bayer studying physics, Brecht studying French. Three years. Comparing Bonn and Tripoli. Hard to compare. No point of similarity, except they were capital cities. Lutheran Christians and desert Arabs, Bedouin tribesmen. Gadafi's seat of government a tent inside a fort.

'What are you laughing at?' Brecht sat down at the table.

'I was just thinking about Gadafi.'

Brecht unscrewed the cap of the aspirin bottle, took three, washing them down with straight Geneva gin. 'Did you see Gadafi?'

Bayer shook her head, sipping white wine.

'What did they teach you?'

'How to fire a Kalashnikov. How to strip it down blindfold. How to use a grenade launcher and a mortar.' Bayer paused. 'There was an East German banker teaching business. Accounting, currency dealing. He wore a heavy suit and wouldn't take the jacket off with the temperature in the nineties. The armpits of the jacket were stained. She glanced at the light refracted through the glass. 'And American soldiers were there teaching survival techniques and unarmed combat.'

'Did you talk to Musa?'

'He has silver teeth.'

'What did he say about the Americans?'

'He made a joke. He said, "Now the CIA are working for us." '

'That was the joke?'

'Well, he thought it was funny.'

'Will he give us any money?'

'What a son of a bitch he is. No. He'll give us small arms and C4. As much C4 as we can carry.'

'And detonators?'

'And detonators.'

'We'll have to rob a bank.'

'Musa did make an offer.' Bayer let the words hang.

'He'd give you the money if you went to bed with him?'

'If we kill two men he will give us a million dollars.'

'These men.'

'Arabs. Libyans.'

'You said no.'

'I also said no when he asked me to suck him off.'

Brecht laughed.

A blond man at a nearby table looked around. Bayer said, 'He probably thinks we're a couple of dykes.'

Petaluma

Wilder called the house on Grant Avenue, Petaluma, from the Mexican restaurant. A big barn of a place at the north end of the main street. He was the only customer. The Libyan's wife answered, saying her husband wasn't home until six. Wilder said he was calling about translation work, explaining that his secretary had made an appointment.

Wilder paid for the meal and drove the rented Oldsmobile south, making a right at the 7–11. Should he give the wife a little something with the sap, tie her up. And maybe check on the color of her panties.

The Olds cruised along the street of nineteen-thirties clapboard houses. Wilder turned the car around and parked opposite a yellow single-storey house with a square tower. Out the back was an open field with horses grazing. He pulled the attaché case on the passenger seat towards him and twisted the release buttons before snapping the case open. There were a selection of guns in a bed. They were arranged in caliber from .22 up to .44. One automatic and three revolvers. The automatic was a beauty, a Welrod he'd bought on R and R in Bangkok.

Wilder wasn't about to use an automatic. There was the possibility the guy would be armed. He couldn't take the risk of it jamming on him. The Police Positive was going to be too noisy. And he liked the .22 Magnum. Checking the load, he slid the Magnum in his shoulder holster.

The fifth of rye in the glove compartment was nearly empty. Wilder unscrewed the top and drank a good amount. He checked the level and trickled the last down his throat.

Across the street Khadija Jadalla was lighting the lamps either end of the sofa in the front room. It wasn't dark but the house faced east and only had the sun in the morning. She glanced out the window and saw a man in a pale car, parked, drinking from a bottle.

Bonn

Brecht saw herself standing in the lobby of the Holiday Inn on the Place de la République. She could pass for American. All she had to do was slip the case she was carrying in with the other baggage. She could see the driver taking the baggage and loading it in the bus. Then the bus on the way out to Charles de Gaulle or Orly, blasted all over the highway.

Above, the arch framed the clouds obscuring the moon. The rain had made the roof slates a deeper gray.

Bayer handed a joint to Brecht. Ash fell on the bed.

'What is this?' Brecht inhaled deeply.

'Thai sticks,' Bayer said. 'In Libya they had Triex and Quadrex, binary explosives. You mix the two liquid components together and they become volatile.' Bayer outlined her idea of using planters in the lobby as a bomb.

'The bus will contain the explosion.'

'But think of the publicity value of the Holiday Inn.' Smoke wreathed Bayer's head.

Together they watched the first star appear in the sky.

Bayer said, 'I went to a party in Tripoli. At someone's villa. I went to get a drink. The next day I had to leave for the desert. One drink for my thirst.' She grinned. 'A Green Beret told me about the party. He wanted to take me along. I said I was leaving. He gave me the address in case I changed my mind.

'I had one drink there.' Bayer stared at the ceiling. 'I met a man. He was the one who taught explosives. Very attractive. I was very drunk, under the stars.'

Brecht said, 'It sounds like a cheap romance novel.'

Petaluma

At ten minutes of six, a full five minutes after he'd parked, Gordon Wilder checked the pocket of his maroon knit suit for the sap and got out of the car. The tape holding a flat knife to his leg tore at the hairs. He winced, and started limping across the street.

Khadija Jadalla was slicing lamb when the door chime played the first bars of 'Clementine'. From the kitchen she could just make out the dark outline of a short man in dark glasses through the reeded glass. Approaching the front door she noticed the maroon suit, and the blurred face a lighter red.

'Who's that?'

'Mrs Jadalla. My name's Gordon MacArthur. I called.'

The sound of a chain guard being slid back and the heavy clunk of a dead bolt. Wilder was confronted with a black woman, Black African, maybe, wearing a yellow velour tracksuit. In her hand by her side a big knife.

'I came about the translating.' He stared at the knife.

'I was just cutting up some meat.' She waved the knife. 'Come in.'
The whiskey on his breath hung in the air.

'You better go in there and sit down.' She indicated with the knife. 'I'll get you a drink.'

'Yeah.' A beer chaser was about what he needed. 'A beer would be good.'

'We don't have any alcohol. We're Muslims.'

'Right. I was over in Libya.' He held his hands clasped across his crotch. 'A Coke'd be fine.'

Khadija Jadalla went off to the kitchen, leaving Wilder undecided about his move. The idea was to hit her with the sap and wait for the Arab behind the door. Clip him as he came in. Get out fast. The knife had thrown him. And the manner. Aggressive. No, not aggressive, but something of an edge there. He thought about following her into the kitchen.

A car horn sounded along the street and an old Volkswagen Rabbit swung on to the cement slab drive. Wilder had to rethink the whole thing.

The room fronting the street was an extension of the hall. To the left there was a dining nook. Across the far side was a brick fireplace with crossed axes above a beam shelf hung with flagons. The shelf was eaten away, showing brown fiber. The room was full of furniture. There were four chairs and two sofas in plastic hide, red and green. In the center a low ceramic-tiled table. If this had to be the killing ground there wasn't much space. And the picture window gave anyone going by a grandstand view of the action. Like a big Japanese TV screen.

Wouldn't it be fucking amazing to have a tape of the whole thing? Play it over.

'Why have you closed the drapes?' Khadija Jadalla stood over by the dining table with a glass in her hand. Behind her Haamed Jadalla came through the front door.

'My eyes. I have trouble with my eyes.' Wilder moved away from the window, watching the skinny Arab come in the room and stand beside his wife. He decided that the Arab couldn't weigh much more than a hundred and forty pounds fully clothed. Wilder smiled and held out his hand. 'Mr Jadalla.' He took the limp offered hand. 'The name's MacArthur. My secretary talked with you about translating.'

Jadalla nodded. 'Please sit down.' Half turning to his wife he took the coke. Khadija Jadalla went off back to the kitchen.

'You have a cigarette?' Wilder patted his side-pockets.

Haamed Jadalla handed the drink to Wilder and went hunting for a pack of cigarettes. 'I only have menthol.'

Wilder said, 'Let me tell you a little about this translating.' He reached in his jacket as he put the Coke down.

Jadalla found a pack of Salems down the back of the green sofa by the window. The blows to his head startled him. He didn't go down, staying bent. A trickle of blood ran across his forehead. Wilder lifted the gun barrel to the Arab's head and fired. There was a loud crack followed by a scream from the kitchen. Blood oozed from Jadalla's scalp where the bullet had cut a groove in the skull. Wilder fired again and a small hole appeared in Jedulla's cheek. Blood from the exit wound by the jaw spattered the sofa.

Wilder stepped back. Two shots. One on target.

Jadalla kneeling forward ran his fingers through his hair. It was sticky. He wasn't sure if part of his head was missing.

Wilder was bringing the barrel up again when Jadalla grabbed the gun, catching him off balance. They went over on to the rug, wrestling for the gun, rolling around the floor. Wilder was too close to have any advantage. He tried to bring his knee up into the Arab's balls but caught it on the leg of the table. That weakened his grip on the gun but he got an arm around the Arab's neck and choked him enough to get a good hold, dragging him into a near sitting position. The gun went off against Jadalla's right ear. Wilder released his hold and the Arab slumped to the ground, falling on the hard edge of the brick hearth.

'Jesus fucking Christ.' There were dark patches over the knit suit. 'I got blood on my suit. Look what the fuck you did to my suit.' He kicked the inert body. Then he remembered the woman.

There was broken glass over the kitchen floor. Wilder took cartridges from his pocket and stood at the open window as he reloaded. Khadija Jadalla was struggling to get over the barbed-wire fence at the end of the back yard, shielded by a gum tree. Wilder holstered the gun, drew up his trouser leg and slid the flat knife from its sheath.

The time it took him to climb out the window, the woman was over the fence and making her way up the steeply-inclined ground towards a barn at the summit. It was rough terrain but she moved easily in track shoes. Wilder crossed the yard and tried to jump the wire fence using the tree as a pivot. He made it but ripped the leg of his pants, drawing blood, and landing heavily.

After twenty-five yards he had to stop and regain his breath. He looked up. Above, the yellow tracksuit, the barn doors were opening and someone was leading a horse out into the field.

'Shit.' Wilder twisted round and started back down the hill. 'Christ. Ain't my fucking day.'

He put the knife away and took care with the fence, made his way around the house almost bumping into a woman coming the other way. Wilder took out his gun and showed it to her. She reacted by putting her hands up, defensively, covering her face and backing away.

'Get down and eat dirt.'

The woman cowered against the wall and slid down among the red poppies. He put the Magnum away before he reached the street. Checked his pockets for the car keys, a cigarette, found both. A kid on an Italian ten-speed racer cruised by. Wilder watched him go, sprinting to the intersection.

In the car he punched the cigarette lighter and started the engine. He didn't check his mirror and didn't see the kid until the kid and the bike went over the hood.

Tripoli

'Jack is drinking a quart a day,' said Francine.

'I don't believe you can drink a quart and live.' Halsey's voice on the phone sounded distant.

Francine picked up the cradle and walked round the desk. 'Take my word for it.'

'What's he like?'

'One minute he's on top of things, the next he's screaming and shouting. Listen. He wants to talk to you.'

'What about?'

'Does he ever tell me anything? Is the Pope a Catholic?' There was a break in the conversation. Francine said, 'How's your French?'

Halsey didn't want to talk. 'Where's Jack?'

'You'd rather talk to Jack?'

'He's the one wants to talk to me.'

'Jack's in the kitchen making a Velveeta and jelly sandwich. There, I told you he's acting strange.'

'Is he on anything?'

'Yeah. About a quart of flash a day.' Francine ran her fingers through her hair. 'By ten o'clock in the morning he's on his ear. From then on its downhill.' She heard O'Brien on the stairs and said cheerfully into the phone. 'Here's Jack now.' She called out through the door. 'Jack. It's your lover-boy.'

O'Brien came round the door. He was looking haggard, drawn. His hair greasy. He scowled at Francine. 'I don't like that obscene talk.'

Francine spoke into the phone. 'He's in a mean mood.' And handed the receiver to O'Brien.

'How's it going?' O'Brien talked and a smile appeared around his eyes.

'There's something I want you to do back here.' O'Brien waved Francine away out the door. 'Don't worry about the appliance shipments. That can wait. And this won't take you more than a coupla days.

'It's those Frenchmen you hired.'

Halsey hadn't. He let it go.

'They're having a problem down there in Chad. I can't go. I want you to go and straighten it out. You speak the language.'

Halsey wondered what had happened. What kind of trouble the Frenchmen were in. This sounded dangerous. Going into a war zone.

'It's very simple. A labor dispute. You go down there as an arbitrator.'

Halsey didn't know what to say. He didn't say no.

Paris

When he checked into the Holiday Inn on the Place de la République, Krupps used the name Carlos Fuentes. He'd dyed his blond hair black and restyled it with grease. Applied fake tan and wore heavy-rimmed tortoiseshell glasses with blue tinted lenses.

He shared the elevator with an elderly American Jewish couple and overheard their conversation. 'Sidney. It's a fairytale castle.

We're stopping at a fairytale castle.' The reply, 'Yeah. At a strictly fairytale price.' Later that day he met Brecht at the Medici fountain in the Luxembourg and repeated the conversation. She responded by saying, 'So many fairytales have violent endings.'

The end was violent when it came.

The ten pounds of C4 plastic came from the Libyan People's Bureau in Bonn. The Lille Group made the collection and delivery in Paris. The material had been transformed into an explosive device contained in the attaché case that Brecht gave Krupps in the Luxembourg. She had also given him a label to fix to the handle of the case.

The bus for Orly airport was late. The noise level in the lobby of the Holiday Inn was getting louder. Jews from the El Dorado tour party were raising their voices in complaint. Krupps was standing at the desk, checking out. He heard the old man from the elevator saying, 'These people need a kick up the ass.' His wife was trying to keep him quiet.

Trouble in never-never land.

Brecht and Bayer were parked around the corner in the Avenue de la République. They were waiting to collect Krupps when he came out of the hotel.

Ten twenty on Saturday morning. Krupps was late unless the clock on the dashboard of the Mazda was fast.

Krupps glanced at his watch.

The blast shattered windows in direct line.

Traffic on the Place de la République had slowed to a crawl, with people trying to get a look at the hotel. The lobby had contained the explosion. All the devastation was on the inside. Mutilated bodies arranged in a tableau like a Delacroix painting.

It wasn't until two days later that Brecht and Bayer knew for a fact that Krupps was dead. They saw the TV news. The police had identified all the bodies except one. Fingerprints from the unidentified corpse matched those found on the case that had held the bomb.

After that Brecht started popping Valium like candy.

She had been desolated when Monceau was killed by the Israeli, and since her death she had been having nightmares. Brecht would wake up from the nightmare and experience a waking dream. The waking dream was always the same. Standing in the lobby of the Holiday Inn with the Jews from Florida. The Jews on the El Dorado tour. All wearing loud clothes, talking loudly. An old lady would say to her, 'You got a nice kid. He's a nice looking boy. He'll break his mother's heart.' Brecht would look down at her son. There were men and women coming out of the elevator, smiling bleeding, gummy smiles. They tossed gold teeth into a stainless steel bowl. The old lady would say, 'Don't worry. It's under gas.' Brecht always came awake shouting, 'But my son, he isn't Jewish.'

Bayer called the Lille Group and asked them to make arrangement for the termination of the operation. Collect the weapons and close the apartments. She called Marie Claude at the Banque National and explained Brecht's absence, telling her that Brecht had received news of her mother's death. She couldn't say when or if Brecht would return to Paris.

Chad

Flying never appealed to Halsey. It was nothing fundamental. As a kid he'd even thought about becoming a pilot. There were associations in his mind that he didn't care to recall. Mornings looking out over green forest and blue sky lit up with napalm, catching a lung-full of black smoke. The chopper going in fast and low, picking up ground fire.

The sky was blue over the desert. Bluer than the sky over Da Nãng. Tripoli to Sabhah, baking in the belly of the C-130 transport. On the desert oasis airstrip he'd met the Libyan captain, the other passenger in the back seat of the Cessna. The single-engined four-seater bounced around on the thermals rising from the desert floor. Halsey's stomach heaved. Out the window an eagle soared on an air current. Volcanic forms of the Tibesti mountains shimmered in the heat. The captain struggled to get out of a sweat-stained dress jacket, swinging his armpit in Halsey's face. Halsey reached for the brown bag. He gagged but didn't throw up.

The plane landed on the dirt strip, hacked out of a rock-strewn plateau, taxied to the far end of the runway. A collection of huts made out of sheet metal and stones were grouped together at the base of the mountain. Brushwood concealed the primitive camp.

'*Vous êtes l'Americain?*'

Halsey followed the pilot and the Libyan out under the wing. He was confronted by an African in heavy-rimmed glasses wearing a brown combat uniform with matching forage cap.

'*Oui.*' Halsey could see that behind the huts the cross-shaped lean-to he'd seen from the air housed a DC3.

The Libyan captain introduced the Chadian as General Mbaya. Halsey expected an exchange of some kind. But the general was all business. He gripped Halsey's arm and propelled him towards the mountainside. The three men scrambled up above the huts for about fifty yards.

Two guerillas leaning on assault rifles straightened up. They were standing in front of a cave, the entrance barricaded with stones and a woven wooden panel forming a makeshift stockade. Halsey saw the Frenchmen through the slatted wall.

'*Alors. Bienvenu.*' Tallien laughed a hollow laugh.

One of the guards dragged the panel back and Halsey felt a gun barrel in his side, sending him into the dark, foul-smelling prison.

Halsey glanced over his shoulder. The Libyan and the general were sliding down the slope in a cloud of dust. 'Let's talk English.'

'Sure.' Tallien was nervous.

Halsey hunkered down. 'What the fuck's going on?' He hadn't expected to find the legionnaires being held prisoner. And he wasn't too sure what his own position was. What Mbaya had in mind. 'Tell me about it.'

'Have you a cigarette?' Tallien sat on the rock floor holding his knees.

Hablinski had his back bent along the roof of the cave, resting his weight against the wall, '*Pourquoi êtes-vous ici?*'

Halsey smiled. 'That is the question.' He looked up into an impassive face. 'I came down here to talk you guys into taking that DC3 out there over to Atti.'

'*Merde.*' Tallien shrugged. 'Three days ago we fly to Atti. Most of the soldiers have not flown before. We have bad weather and they are sick and cannot even stand up. Rolling around the floor in their own vomit. The stench was very bad. We must land at this airbase. But the power is dead. There are no lights on the runway. Without lights it is too dangerous to land.'

'What were you planning to do down there?'

'We are to signal for an emergency landing. When we get on the ground these pathetic soldiers must place explosive charges on the fighter planes. And engage the forces for five minutes. Then we take off.' Tallien let his arms fall by his side. 'They cannot stand. They will all be killed.'

'This accounts for why the general's so pissed off.'

'He wants us to fly again. I say it is too dangerous. There are no weather reports. They do not know if the lights work. Also the fuel is not enough.'

Halsey's assessment of the situation was simple. 'Listen. If we're getting out of this alive, you're gonna have to fulfil your contractual obligations and tool down to Atti.'

'That is easy for you to say. It is not your ass on the line,' Hablinski said.

Tallien added, 'These soldiers will all be killed on that airfield. There are legionnaires on the ground. We are also killed.'

'Okay. Let's figure this out fast. The longer we take, the more edgy Mbaya is going to get. He wants his pound of flesh. Either you go through with the deal or he takes his slice right here.'

'What difference does it make?' Tallien wanted to know. He seemed lethargic, fatalistic. The Polack was resigned in a different way. A man who believed every day brought death.

'The difference is,' said Halsey, 'that if you go you stand a chance. And if you stay we're all gonna get shot.'

Tallien narrowed his eyes. 'I don't think I will shed any tears when they put the gun to your head.'

'Jesus fucking Christ.' Halsey couldn't believe it.

The light was fading on the mountainside. Halsey gazed up at the sky between the gate and the rock. Stars were already appearing.

Movement down below and the sound of distant voices signalled the presence of the returning army, absent when he'd landed. Thirty men. Not one of them had a complete uniform, some no more than fourteen, fifteen, all carrying different assault rifles. Halsey was trapped between two embittered mercenaries and a rag-bag guerilla army that wouldn't think twice about spilling someone's guts. Fighting over land that wasn't worth fighting for.

'How long has this war been going on?'

'Fifteen, twenty years. I don't know.' Tallien was in a petulant mood.

'Why are they fighting?'

'Who knows. The land is called *inutile*. No good. But I think there is oil and minerals to the north along the border.'

'How does Mbaya fit into this?'

'He is the local warlord. He fights for Gadafi today; tomorrow for someone else.'

'That doesn't give me any leverage.' Halsey heard the sound of a propeller turning over. The Cessna taxied down the runway and took off over the huts, leaving Halsey with an empty feeling in the pit of his stomach. He watched as the plane circled south and, gaining height, flew off north.

Halsey beckoned to Tallien and Hablinski. They reluctantly shuffled closer.

'Here's what we do. Fly the mission. Somehow put the plane down. Unload and get the fuck out of there. I'll come along as a guarantee.'

'These men will die certainly.' Tallien's concern surprised Halsey.

'You said they'll die anyhow.'

There was a brief conversation in heavily accented French that Halsey couldn't follow. Then the two men nodded.

Halsey called to the guard. '*Attendez! Je veux parler avec le général.*'

Tallien repeated the request. The guards ignored them.

Shadowy figures appeared on the slope. Halsey could make out the general with his forage cap sat on a brush of wire curls.

'*Prenez les trois prisonniers . . .*' A voice in the darkness.

The woven gate was pulled back.

'*Allez.*'

'*Allez vite.*'

Across the mountainside, flares that marked out the landing strip guttered in the rising wind. The prisoners stumbled down towards a fire among the huts. The guerilla army gathered around a sheep roasting on a spit.

Halsey said, 'What's this? The Last Supper?'

'*Peut-être.*' Tallien gave Hablinski a questioning look.

'Seems our fate's been decided.' Halsey tried to catch the general's attention. '*Qu'est ce qui se passe?*' The general ignored the question.

Hablinski, Tallien and Halsey were ordered to sit on the ground. They sat in silence and waited. Within the circle of soldiers the fire crackled and sent sparks shooting into the void.

After maybe ten minutes the camp-fire talk started getting louder. A jagged shape lurched out of the darkness holding a large curved knife and attacked the sheep. Halsey sensed a ritual element in the butchering of the carcass. The first meat went to the general.

'I ordered the Big Mac and fries to go.' Halsey accepted the offered tin plate. Fat lamb and cous-cous. He gave his food to Tallien and Hablinski. 'Here, I don't have the appetite.' Watching as they divided the meat.

The meal was over in a matter of a few minutes. One of the guerillas appeared in front of Halsey. '*Levez-vous. Allez.*' A gun barrel jarring his ribs.

Stumbling, trying to find his footing in the dark. Away from the firelight, the night cold and black, illuminated by the flames. Halfway down the runway the gun barrel reached out and forced him into a kneeling position. The steel on his neck so that he had to bow down and touch the earth. Halsey knelt there, the stones embedding themselves in his flesh and leg muscles aching. Waiting there. Waiting in the darkness on this mountain you couldn't find on a map. Eating dirt. Waiting for what? For some guerilla to put a bullet through his head? He tried to get a look at the guy. Only seeing the white eyes before feeling the blow that sent him rolling. Having to fight the pain, struggling to get back on his knees.

Jack O'Brien.

An hour went by. Or maybe two. There was a numbness in Halsey's limbs, causing him to fall over at intervals, resulting in a kick to the ribs. One time he tried to anticipate, bringing his arms down, but his reactions were too slow. Two hours and the DC3 hadn't taken off. He had no idea what had happened to the Frenchmen. Unless they had a problem with the plane. The possibilities were limited. If the DC3 took off leaving him behind as a hostage and the plane didn't come back . . . that was the favorite. The general was probably waiting until after midnight when everyone was asleep down in Atti. But why light the flares so early? Could the Cessna be coming back? God knows.

Bonn

'In the early hours of this morning an American soldier was found dead in a forest outside West Berlin. The soldier had been shot through the head at close range.'

The Sony portable was raised up on a cardboard box between two Breuer cantilever chairs. The screen showed shots of a dark pine wood, shafts of light falling between the treetrunks. Bayer placed a tray of food in front of the TV. Bratwurst and beans with a glass of sparkling mineral water. Brecht said nothing, made no sign, sitting on the Misrātah rug, staring.

'An update later. And now the war in Lebanon. The news yesterday that a British churchman held hostage by Hezbollah was working for the CIA, has been met with strong denials from the White House and the British Foreign Office.

'Next we have an interview with a French doctor just back from one of the Palestinian refugee camps, who says that he had to watch as children starved. The relief agencies were not able to get supplies through.

'That and more after this.'

A station break.

They had been back in Bonn for two weeks. In that time Brecht had not left the house. She had sat in front of the TV. Returning to Germany had made no significant change to Brecht's behavior. Bayer was certain that Brecht needed professional help. But that was impossible. The only solution was to sedate her and hope that she came out of it. Bayer became the keeper, Brecht the prisoner.

Tripoli

O'Brien said, 'I see how you feel but there wasn't a damn thing I could do about it.' He checked for a reaction, found no response and went on. 'Jesus, I had to go down on my knees there.' His face was pale. He hadn't had a drink. 'Down on my knees to Musa. I had to beg him.' Letting the words trail away. 'You need a drink. I have some scotch here. The real thing.' He winked. 'Came in the Saudi diplomatic pouch.' He went over to the gray file cabinet and opened the second drawer. There was a case of Black & White scotch. O'Brien took a half-full bottle from the carton. Also two tumblers from a pack of twenty-four. His hands were shaking.

'A drink for medicinal purposes.' He poured two glasses and put the other on the desk. 'I know you were over in Vietnam. You're a soldier. I fought that war.' The scotch was going down well. 'Vietnam, I was in the Marines. One night we were ordered to take a hill.' O'Brien reached for the bottle. 'Those gooks knew we were coming. We didn't have a chance. I was in a shell hole. I could hear my men calling out to me. Crying and moaning. I don't mind telling you I couldn't go through that again.' There were tears welling up in his eyes. 'I still have nightmares about those men. Good men every one of them.

'Christ, those Frenchmen. Shit. Garrotted on a mountain in the middle of fucking nowhere.' O'Brien chugalugged the scotch and a little dribbled down his unshaven chin. He wiped his mouth with the back of his hand.

Halsey said, 'I'm gonna go back stateside.'

O'Brien thought about that. 'I'm sending money to their families. Out of my own pocket.'

'You let me have my money.'

O'Brien put his hand on Halsey's shoulder. 'You need some R and R. I want you in good shape. You're important to me. I want you on that arms deal. Come back, we'll talk about your bonus.'

Halsey had a weariness in his voice when he said, 'I'll go back to Belgium, find the M-16s, fulfil the contract.' He left it there. Walked to the door.

Francine knocked.

'I don't want you to talk about this.' O'Brien said.

Halsey opened the door.

'Francine,' O'Brien said, 'I want you to wire some money.' She went over to the desk and picked up a spiral notepad.

Halsey started up the stairs.

'Have you got a pen?' Francine sat down behind the desk and pulled open the top drawer.

'What for?'

Francine found a red ballpoint and checked to see it worked. 'Okay.'

'Okay what?'

'You wanted me to send some money.'

O'Brien shook his head. He moved around behind Francine, leaving the glass on the front of the desk and slid his hands around her tits.

Flames swam around the base of the espresso machine. Halsey watched the gas shooting out of the burner. Blue, a lighter blue, yellow where it hit the aluminium. He couldn't stop thinking about the Frenchmen. He could feel the wire round the neck and the boot in the back. Death was there waiting for them on the mountain. It could have happened flying for Somoza. In combat over Angola. Anywhere in Africa or South America. It happened in Chad. About the poorest stretch of land on Earth. Halsey couldn't understand why he felt the way he felt. Maybe it was the realization of his own mortality.

'I got the coffee you like.' Francine leant against the wall. 'Did you find the cups I bought? I got them in the souk. They're Italian. I bought the pot as well but it's cracked.' Francine wandered over to the sink. 'I knew it was cracked. I had to have it though.'

She found the cups and laid them out on the table.

Water rose as steam under pressure through the ground coffee and percolated up into the top half of the machine. Halsey poured coffee into the black and white pattern china.

'The coffee tastes better out of these,' Francine said.

Halsey nodded. 'I'm going back to Belgium, straighten out a few things. Collect the money coming to me and go back to the States.'

'What are you gonna do when you get back?'

Halsey didn't have an answer. There weren't too many options.

Liège

The water was warm, about eighty degrees. The tiles a moving mozaic on the ceiling. Halsey ploughed along doing lengths in a lazy backstroke. The only one in the pool. Sound reflected off the glass walls. He drifted, kicking his feet to stay buoyant and watching the waves bouncing off the side. Various thoughts reached his conscious mind and fell back. Here he was at the Holiday Inn in Liège, swimming, relaxing, planning changes in his life. One marriage behind him, a five-year-old kid. Resigning from a hundred thousand a year job. All the facts. And none of the answers. The only plans he'd made were a couple of drinks in the bar and a slow walk along the Meuse to the brasserie off the Place du Vingt Août. Having the *potée*, which was good there.

A heavy outline came into his field of vision. The face side on and in shadow.

'Hey.'

Halsey started swimming again.

'Gordon Wilder.'

Wilder got down on his haunches. 'We met down in Tripoli.' The words echoed.

Halsey was away now at the end of the pool. He recalled the squat shape.

'How about a drink? I'll see you in the bar and buy you a drink. I guarantee it'll taste better than this.' Wilder ran his hand through the chlorinated water.

The blonde in the gold spandex dress, showing a lot of leg, was paying a good deal of attention to what Wilder was saying. Throwing her head back and showing expensive teeth when it was time to laugh.

'Mad'moiselle Monique.' Wilder didn't remember her other name. 'I'm interviewing her for a job. Translation work.' He was struggling to get a cigarette out of a pack of Marlboro with a bandaged hand. 'What'll you have?'

'Stella.'

'Is that a beer or a woman?' Wilder laughed and so did Monique. 'Here.' He had the barman's attention. 'Give this guy a Stella and two more the same.'

'*Qu'est-ce que c'est Monsieur?*'

'That's a bourbon and . . . what are you drinking? Pina Colada. Yeah, Pina Colada.' Wilder slid off his stool on Halsey's side. 'Monique speaks French. She Frenches.' He grinned. 'The only trouble her American ain't so good.'

The woman smiled at Halsey and sipped from the long glass.

'Listen. Do I need French to get around in Algeria?'

Halsey said yes, if you wanted to get out of the big towns.

The barman brought the drinks. Halsey took a long swallow.

'I guess you heard what happened?'

Halsey hadn't. He made no reply.

'I know your background,' Wilder said. 'I've seen your file.'

Halsey paid attention. The blonde concentrated on her second Pina Colada.

'Tell me, what do you think of mercury loads? When you use a .22 caliber bullet you need an edge. Right? I'm using a reduced load, lower muzzle velocity. Shit I don't need to tell you. Right? I have to get hold of a silencer for a Beretta.'

Halsey drained his beer. 'Why don't you try an ad in *Soldier of Fortune*?'

'Hey. You're shittin' me. Aren't you?'

Monique was bored. Wilder took a room key from the jacket of his black cowboy suit. The narrow cut did nothing to hide the gun and shoulder rig. 'Hon, why don't you go and freshen up. The men have a little business to talk here.'

She held the tag between her fingers, smiled and pouted at Halsey.

'I'm meeting someone,' Halsey said, and made to get up.

Wilder put pressure on his shoulder. 'One more drink.' He pointed to the glasses. '*Encore.*' Waved Monique bye bye. 'I'm picking it up, the language, from Monique. I thought about enrolling in one a those Berlitz courses, but I don't think they could compete on the oral.' His eyes became thin slits when he laughed.

'Jack says I have to take care of you. And that's an order. So whether you like it or not.' Wilder punched Halsey in the shoulder with his good hand. 'Listen good buddy, would you do me a kindness?'

'Do what?' Halsey said.

'Would you reach in my pants pocket here and get my lighter. See I can't get it with my hand.' Wilder thrust his hip forward. 'In the pants.'

The pants were tight. Halsey reached in delicately with two fingers and a thumb and pulled out a solid gold Dunhill. Wilder got a cigarette. Halsey flipped the top and pressed the side of the lighter. The gas jet nearly burned Wilder's eyebrows.

'By rights the son of a bitch oughta be dead.' Wilder seemed pained. 'Christ, I put two bullets in his head. The son of a bitch oughta be dead.'

Halsey adjusted the flame. 'What did you use?'

'A .22 Magnum.'

'If you use a .22 you got no guarantee. A .357 on the other hand . . .'

'Too big. Too noisy. I coulda used a knife. But that can be messy. Right?' Wilder sipped some Jim Beam. 'Never used a garrotte. I used to carry one but I never had occasion to use it. You gotta have the height. Two bullets in the head and that son of a bitch Arab is up running around. The wife is screaming her head off in the kitchen.'

Halsey toyed with the Dunhill, running his thumb across the lettering engraved on the side. 'What happened to the woman?'

'Took off out the window.' He picked up the pack of Marlboro. 'Hey, you want one of these?'

Halsey shook his head.

'About that silent appliance?'

Halsey said he'd ask around but wouldn't promise anything.

Wilder clapped him on the shoulder. 'That's all I'm asking, good buddy. How about one more drink? Then I have to get on with my *parlez vous*.' He looked for the barman. 'Hey. Do all these Frenchwomen move their asses around like that when you're balling them?'

'Depends whether they're Flemish or Walloons.'

Wilder nodded, understanding.

'I won't have that drink.' Halsey checked his watch.

'I'll be around a coupla days.'

Halsey held out the Dunhill and read the inscription. 'Try gas. Six million Jews can't be wrong.'

The river was blue gray, the same color as the rooftops. Apart from the darker reflections of the buildings and the yachts moored in the marina under the Pont Roi Albert. Halsey crossed the terraces by the bronze King Albert on his bronze horse. A broad sweep of steps led down to the Parc d'Arroy. Liège was all parks. Parks and churches. The stone staircase reminded him of a Hollywood musical. Gene Kelly would come walking down humming a tune, see he was on the staircase and start to dance. Music by Gershwin.

'Music's good.'

'*Si tu aimes le jazz.*'

The Pierre Levée club was a cellar bar in a yard off the Rue Serbie.

Rimbaud was wearing dark glasses, although the bar was dark, and a blue-black double-breasted suit, a black silk tie with a white shirt. The band got a good hand at the end of the piece.

Halsey lifted his glass of Peket.

'You are supposed to drink in one.' Rimbaud took his and threw it back.

Halsey did the same. And didn't like it. 'Let's order some beer.'

Rimbaud said, 'I know about Chad.'

Halsey nodded. He couldn't see Rimbaud's eyes. He sounded offhand. Halsey wondered if Rimbaud held him responsible for what happened to Tallien and Hablinski.

'I spoke to Tripoli today.' Rimbaud lit a cigarette and exhaled blue smoke. He peeled tobacco off his tongue. 'I hear you want to get out.'

Halsey said yes.

'Because of Tallien and Hablinski?'

'Perhaps.'

'*Ils sont morts.*' Rimbaud drew a lateral line with his cigarette. '*C'est fini.*' He relaxed back in the chair. Halsey listened to the saxophone imitating John Coltrane.

After a space Rimbaud said, 'Why don't you go to work for me?'

Halsey said, 'I'll think about it.'

'*Oui. D'accord.*'

They ordered beer. The beer arrived and went down. They ordered another.

'I want you to do something for me,' Rimbaud said.

'A favor?'

'I want you to look at something for me.'

'Look at what?'

'Some papers.'

'What's in these papers?'

'They are plans.'

Halsey didn't commit himself.

'I will pay you five hundred dollars.'

'To look at some plans?'

'*Oui.*'

'When did you want me to look at these plans?'

*   *   *

The air was cool and damp. A shower had left pools along the roads. The trees dripped rain from their leaves. The car tires sucked at the surface water and droplets streaked the paintwork. The Mercedes went south through narrow streets.

Halsey had agreed to look at the papers, provided he could get something to eat. Out of the car stereo came 'In the beginning'.

These plans were obviously important. Rimbaud wasn't saying why. Over the Pont de Fragnée following a barge up river towards Angleur.

It was around one a.m. when the car turned into a street of solid brick houses. Rimbaud killed the engine, coasting down a gravel drive overhung with trees, coming to a stop in front of a double garage. There were no lights showing and the only sound came from the wind in the branches above.

Rimbaud let them in with a key and showed Halsey across the shadowy hall into a room illuminated by the moon. When Rimbaud switched on a reading lamp Halsey saw a harpsichord under the window and the walls lined with books.

'*Qu'est-ce que tu veux? Du bière, du vin. Un autre Peket?*'

'Some coffee,' Halsey said.

Rimbaud closed the door after him, leaving Halsey standing, staring at the dying embers of a wood fire burning in the grate. Looking around. Three photographs in silver frames arranged along a shelf caught his attention. A woman in her twenties with a boy and a girl. Flanked by separate photos of the boy and girl, older, about the same age as his son. He picked up the photo of the family. And carefully put it back.

The books were mostly on insects, entomology. Halsey examined a leather-bound volume of nineteenth-century gravure color reproductions of scorpions. He also noticed shelves devoted to music scores and poetry.

Rimbaud came back with a glass of beer and handed it to Halsey. 'I have put some coffee on and something to eat.' He went over to the poetry bookcase and opened a false panel, revealing a wall safe. He worked the combination and took out a heavy folder.

'I would like you to look at this and tell me what you think.' Handing it over.

Halsey put the beer down on the wood-block floor and took the file. Inside the cover was a single word on the first page:

Manhattan. He glanced at Rimbaud and said nothing. On the next page there was a general statement about the balance of power. Simple geopolitics. It didn't take him long to figure what the preamble was leading to and why Rimbaud would be anxious to keep the file a secret.

'You want to sell the Libyans a bomb?'

Rimbaud shrugged.

'You and Jack?'

'*Oui.*'

'What do you want me to do?'

'*C'est possible?*'

'From these plans?'

'*D'accord.*'

Halsey was also curious to know if it were possible. He sat down on a Louis Quatorze chair and started working through the dense text.

Rimbaud went out to check on the food. He came back five minutes later pushing a cart, laid out with a meal of frankfurters and beans. A full two-pint cafetière stood alongside a blue flower-pattern cup and saucer matching the plate.

'*Bon appetit.*'

Halsey carried on reading for a few more minutes. Then slammed the file closed and stood up. He handed it to Rimbaud.

'*Qu'est-ce que tu penses?*'

Leaning over the cart Halsey pressed the plunger down on the coffee, sending the grounds to the base of the glass pot. 'It's meaningless crap.'

Rimbaud paused for a moment before returning the file to the safe. 'Do you think the Libyans will believe this document?'

'It took me less than ten minutes to figure out it's bullshit.'

Rimaud seemed to doubt what Halsey was saying.

'The Libyans aren't stupid. And where are you getting the plutonium from?' Another question occurred to Halsey. 'Why would the Libyans believe you want to sell them a bomb?'

'For money. And I will say to them I am a servant of Allah.'

'If they can't see through those plans then you truly are the son of Allah.'

Brussels

Fog was given as the cause for the three-hour delay of the flight from New York, Kennedy, into Brussels. Halsey had been waiting there since seven. That had meant getting up at four thirty, allowing an hour and a half for the drive from Liège. The three-hour delay didn't bother him that much but a couple of other things did.

Standing to the side of the small crowd at the arrivals gate Halsey watched and waited. A chauffeur in a uniform held up a panel with movable lettering, spelling out a name, Herr Kissing. A nurse stood by an empty wheelchair.

'Hey there, good buddy.' Halsey turned, recognizing the voice. Ten yards away, struggling across the concourse with a suitcase and a toolchest. Sweat pouring off his face collecting where the aviator glasses touched his cheeks.

Gordon Wilder in a black trenchcoat. One of the things that bothered Halsey.

'Good buddy. I surely appreciate your coming out here.' Wilder dropped the suitcase and the box. The box hit the ground with a loud crack. 'I have to take a break.'

Halsey said. 'I came because Jack told me you'd have some money for me.' Trying hard to keep the edge out of his voice.

'The money's in Bonn.'

'In Bonn?'

'Jack figured you wouldn't mind driving me to Bonn, collect the money.'

'Driving you to Bonn?'

Wilder held out two bandaged hands. 'See. I can't drive.' Jack O'Brien.

Halsey said, 'Why didn't you fly into Bonn?'

'Jack said to go to Brussels, give you the money and have you drive me into Bonn.'

'But you don't have the money.'

'The money's in Bonn.'

'Yeah.' Halsey shook his head. 'The money's in Bonn and you're here.' Jack O'Brien.

'What happens when I get to Bonn and the money isn't there?' Halsey said.

'I have to make a delivery and collect cash.'

Halsey stared at the toolbox without seeing it. Trying to figure out what his best move was.

'Jack is gonna be in Bonn day after tomorrow.' Wilder said.

'The money better be there or it's your ass on the line.'

Wilder didn't take Halsey seriously. He smiled and picked up the case and the toolchest. There was a small brass padlock securing the top folding panels.

Halsey said, 'What do you have in there, guns?'

They left Brussels on the Autoroute 40 for Louvain, driving Rimbaud's gray Mercedes convertible. Rain falling on the top with a dull thudding sound. The wipers had trouble clearing the windshield. Spray kicking up from the road made visibility hazy.

Halsey had use of the car while Rimbaud was down in Tripoli making his presentation. He had an image of Rimbaud and O'Brien on camels, dressed as Bedouins, riding up to Gadafi's tent in the desert. Gadafi embracing them as brothers.

'I got a pint of Jim Beam in that case in the trunk there. You want a drink?' Wilder said.

Halsey shook his head.

'Hell, I could sure use one.'

Halsey checked the fuel gauge.

'I'll look for a gas station.'

An Elf sign appeared out of a wall of rain. Halsey swung off the road and pulled up in front of a line of pumps.

'You fill the tank. I need to take a piss.' Halsey got out of the car.

Wilder watched the blue figure disappearing. He had the trunk open and the case. The bottle of Jim Beam was resting on top of his black suit. He unhooked the padlock from the toolbox and folded the panels back. Inside, underneath the wrenches and the lengths of pipe, were five handguns. Three Smith & Wesson .38s, a Colt Police Positive and an Interarmco Luger. He wrapped the guns in an old army shirt from the case, carried the bundle round to the passenger side and slid the guns under the seat.

Halsey arrived back to find Wilder struggling with the pump.

'It ain't easy killing for a living.' Wilder had the Jim Beam to himself, the bourbon slipping down his throat easily. 'Sure you won't have one?' He showed Halsey the bottle. 'Job has to be done.' He stared off into the mist. 'A sacred duty.' Down to the white edge of the label. 'You remember that conversation we had. You gave me a piece of advice. You said get a garrotte. I got one.' He took a swallow, throwing the bourbon at his neck. 'Ayrab had his hand inside the wire.' He held out a bandaged hand. 'I shouldna carried those cases. My hands hurt like hell.'

Halsey could see the Frenchmen down on their knees. Wire biting into the soft flesh of the neck. He put his foot to the floor. This guy thought killing was a sacred duty.

'I'm gonna get me one of these Mercedes. Little coupé. I know women who'd blow you just to sit in one of those.'

They crossed the border where the Meuse river forms the divide north of Aachen. The German border guards waved the car through.

Halsey had no desire to see Wilder eat but hunger got the better of him and he found the first service area on the autobahn.

A Volvo truck swung out in front of the Mercedes. Halsey hit the brakes. The guns under the seat slammed forward.

'What's that?'

'Machine parts.' Wilder bent down to push them back. A gun barrel poked out of the bundle.

Halsey reached over and pulled out the Luger. The butt was scarred. 'Machine parts.'

Wilder shrugged. 'Christ, we're across the border.'

Halsey grabbed Wilder by the collar. 'Get rid of the guns.'

Wilder laughed. 'What do you want me to do – throw 'em in a trash can?'

'Just get rid of them.'

'Hey. Let's eat. You'll feel better when you get something to eat.' Wilder reached for the door.

Halsey tightened his grip. He glanced around the parking lot. Maybe he should kick this asshole out of the car. Leave him there with the guns.

Wilder said, 'Hey. Let me explain something here. Ayrab's taking delivery of these pieces is handing over an envelope with twenty-five thousand dollars in it. That's your money. The money you got coming to you.'

There were two choices. With about forty thousand saved he could quit and tell Jack to stick the money and the guns. Or drive

Wilder down to Bonn and collect what was coming to him. The twenty-five for the sale of the guns. Guns that sold for five a piece. It didn't leave much room for doubt what they were for. He'd see the rest on the six o'clock news.

Bonn

The rain was making waves on the surface of the water. Crossing the Rhine for the second time, from the east now across the Adenauer Brücke. Entering Bonn through the Freizeitpark. Lakes and trees in the river bend. Halsey was forced to make a right off the bridge and had to run alongside the U-Bahn, dividing the road, into the town before he found a place to make a turn south to Bad Godesburg. He almost made the mistake coming back of getting funnelled on to the bridge.

The ruins of a tower stood above the tree-lined slopes on a point jutting out into the valley. Godesburger Allee became Moltke Strasse.

'Around here some place.' Wilder held a map up to his face. 'Can't see the print without my glasses.'

'Left or right?'

'Left.'

Halsey made a left under the U-Bahn. 'Plittersdorf.'

'No good. Hang a right.' Two wrong turns and the car was into the one-way system going north. 'Okay. Right, and right again.'

Halsey made two rights and then pulled over to take a look at the map.

'Beethoven?'

'Beethoven off Moltke.'

'Beethoven Allee?' Halsey had found Moltke. 'It's a left right here.' He stabbed with his finger.

There was a tap-tapping at the window. He looked up and into the barrel of an automatic weapon.

'*Ihre Papiere bitte.*'

Wilder said, 'What's he saying?'

'Hand over your passport.'

'*Was machen Sie hier?*'

'What's he say?' Wilder said.

'He says, What the fuck are we doing here?' Halsey said.

'Hey. I thought this was a free country.' Getting aggressive. 'War's over, buddy. You lost.'

'Let's not fuck with these guys. There's a gun to my head. They don't get much call to use them and that makes both of us nervous. Him because he has a gun and me because he has a gun.'

Another uniformed torso was checking the car.

Halsey held out his passport and the car papers.

'*Wir suchen die Beethoven Allee.*' Halsey said.

'*Dies ist Beet. Allee.*'

Halsey glanced in the mirror out the rear window. Were they going to search the car?

'*Welche Hausnummer suchen Sie?*'

'He says what number? He says this is Beethoven. What number?'

'Twelve.'

'*Zwölf,*' Halsey said.

'*Nummer zwölf ist das Lybische Konsulat. Vielleicht haben Sie sich geirrt.*'

'He says we've made some mistake. I don't think we've made a mistake.' Halsey said. 'I think I made a mistake.'

'*Wir suchen die Amerikanische Botschaft. Unser ganzes Geld und alle Travelers Cheques wurden gestolen.*'

'*Die Botschaft liegt zwei Kilometer die Koblenz Strasse und Mainzer Strasse hinunter. Biegen Sie links ein.*'

Halsey said, '*Danke . . .*'

'*Ihre Papiere.*'

'*Dankeschön.*' Halsey said.

'*Es tut mir leid, dass Ihr Geld gestolen wurde.*'

'What's he saying?' Wilder said.

'He's sorry we lost our money.'

'What money?'

Halsey had the car in gear, checking the mirror. '*Guten Abend.*' Pulling away, checking the mirror again.

'Hey. Where are we going? I thought that was Beethoven.'

'You were making a delivery to the front door?'

'Why not?'

'What do you suppose would have happened if those two guys had searched the car? They would have found the guns and arrested us.' Halsey drove slowly round the corner and south down the Koblenzer Strasse following the directions he had for the US Embassy. 'And you tell them, "Hey. I'm just delivering these machine parts." All the time they're thinking we've hit the big time here. Caught us a couple of tourists.'

Halsey circled around until he was sure they weren't being tailed. Then drove back up to Bad Godesburg. He parked in the Winter Strasse outside a small hotel. He leaned over and opened the passenger door.

'Okay. Get out.'

An expression of pure surprise appeared on Wilder's face.

'I said get the fuck out the car.' Halsey controlled his anger.

'Check into the hotel. Make the delivery – the People's Bureau is right across the street. I'll call you. Come by and collect the money.'

Halsey found another hotel a block away in the Waldburg Strasse. He had a little trouble at the desk without any baggage but smiled at the woman in his boy-blue outfit and paid in advance for a double room with a shower. He called the Burgblick hotel to ask for Herr Wilder who had just checked in. No Herr Wilder had registered. Halsey was insistent. Perhaps Herr Wilder would check in later and if he wanted to leave a message . . . Halsey hung up and made a call to Tripoli.

'I'm calling from a hotel in Bonn.'

And Francine said, 'I just had that creepy guy on the phone calling from Bonn.'

'Where is he?'

'Maybe you're staying at the same hotel. I have it written down right here somewhere.'

Halsey could hear papers rustling.

Francine searched. 'Are you planning a social visit? Okay, here we are. Burgblick on Winter Strasse.'

Halsey felt stupid. Checked in using another passport.

'Can I talk to Jack?'

'Jack's at a meeting. You'll have to talk to me,' Francine said. 'Did you book a double room?'

'Single beds.'

'We could push them together.'

'I hear Jack is over in a couple of days.'

'And you'd rather get in bed with Jack.'

'Jack is already shafting me,' Halsey said. There was a silence at the other end of the phone. 'Francine?'

'Yeah.'

'Everything okay?'

'Sure. Why not?'

'You sound pissed off.'

'I am.'

Halsey hung up, then picked up the phone again to call room service but changed his mind. He showered and dried himself with a white bath towel, wrapping it around and over his shoulder. He lay down on the bed near the window. The battlements of the Godesburg showed over the houses. How should he play this? The sun was setting behind the tower. A song was going through his head. He recalled the tune 'Murder She Said'.

A black car on a black night driving along the autobahn in a steep valley lined with trees. The sun setting in the distance beyond a v-shaped horizon. Deep in the forest a dark tower rises above the trees. Leaving the car and stepping through tall wrought-iron gates that lead to the tower. Up the ivy-covered path to heavy oaken doors. No response to echoing blows on the wood. The doors are open. Inside, a large hall hung with tapestries of hunting scenes. A fox being torn to pieces by a pack of dogs. Wild boars butchered on the ends of lances. A wooden gallery around the hall, lit with torches, and a stone staircase leading to the gallery. Through a gothic arch the valley below falls away. At the base of the wall, round striped tents form an encampment.

Then, standing at the entrance to a tent, a Hassidim pulls the striped flap to one side. Inside, a group of black figures, Hassidim, gathered around a bed. They separate, a divided sea, staring. A woman dressed in white lies on the bed. Pale and weak. She pushes up, spewing blood.

'*Das reicht.*'

Halsey came awake choking on blood and pieces of filling. A wall of black bullet-proof vests leaning over the bed.

'*Steh auf, schnell!*'

Handcuffs biting into his wrists brought Halsey fully awake. Then he was in the back of a truck trying to get his breath, staring down at combat boots and listening.

Engine noise and traffic penetrated the steel plate walls. Nobody spoke. No one answered Halsey's questions. The truck roared on.

Tripoli

The shutters were nailed closed with rough planking. On the inside, plastic garbage sacks stapled around the window frames blocked out any light. Bare bulbs illuminated the rooms day and night. In the last week an army unit had mined the beach in front of the villa. There were no markers indicating the minefield. A fisherman beaching his boat had lost a leg and a wandering camel had been blown apart. The dismembered corpse of the camel lay rotting on the sand. A stench of decaying flesh penetrated the barricades.

'Fucking Jew media. Trying to fucking nail me. Jesus. Cocksuckers.' O'Brien picked up the newspaper on the desk and brought it down hard, making the sound of a gunshot. 'Christ. Who you gonna believe? Some fucking Jew? This paper stinks higher than that camel out there.' Holding the phone on his shoulder, dragging a finger around the dial. 'And that laywer of mine's playing kissy-ass with a greaseball from the DA's office. He should be suing the ass off those scumbags.' He ran his hand over the filmy black sheeting covering the window, examining the edges for gaps.

'That fat little fuck Schultz's disappeared. I found him, he was pumping gas for a living. Running out on me. I'll fix that son of a bitch. Cause him pain.' The phone was ringing in his ear. 'Answer the goddamn phone.' O'Brien found a chink of light in the plastic blind. He reached for the staple gun resting on an upturned slatted crate and jammed it up against the frame, firing staples into the pulpy wood. Ten staples in a three-inch area. 'The phone for fuck's sake.' Glancing around. 'Where's that fucking drink?' He located a tumbler behind files and made an exchange for the gun. On the desk a war comic cover showed a German SS officer in a black uniform with a sabre scar across his cheek standing in front of barbed wire fencing and a guard tower in the background. A speech bubble had him saying, 'Achtung, achtung. Release the dogs.' In his hand held out, pointing down, was a Luger.

Bonn

'*Sie sind Amerikaner. Ihr Name ist Halsey. Und Sie sind Soldat.*' A white-haired man in a black suit, a white shirt buttoned to the neck and no tie, read out the information from Halsey's passport. The voice was tired. He went over the discrepancy in the Libyan stamps, then he asked the question – what were you doing in Libya?

Halsey focused on a point in space about waist level, sitting on the steel chair bolted to the concrete floor.

Halsey thought about the answer. 'What's this all about? Why are you holding me here?'

'*Warum waren Sie in Lybien?*'

Halsey said, 'I want to talk to someone from the US Embassy.'

'*Wir möchten, dass Sie uns ein paar Fragen beantworten.*'

Halsey couldn't remember how long he'd been there in the gray concrete cell, fifteen by fifteen, with a video camera high up in the corner angled down. Two hours sitting alone or being softened up. Occasionally staring into the lens trying to figure if his performance was monitored.

Tripoli

O'Brien glugged the flash, the phone in his hand, waiting for someone to answer. 'I'd like to ream that scumbag.'

Checking the blind again he tore the plastic. Shouting and throwing the glass in one action, lengthening the word to fit the movement. 'Fuck.' The shattered fragments bounced off the far wall and hit the floor shattering a second time into shards. The heavy base remaining intact.

Out the window, through the narrow opening, a yellow dog, a scabby hound, urinated over the wheel of the Eagle. 'Get the fuck away from there. Go piss on the beach.' The dog looked up to where the voice was coming from and carried on pissing. O'Brien took up the staple gun and emptied the clip into the window frame.

Bonn

The Kaiser passage turned out to be a small shopping mall with café tables under a glass vaulted roof. Wilder sat in one of the cane chairs with the blue toolbox by his feet. He had a beer in front of him. Everything was black and white. Mostly black. Black shop fronts, a black and white tile floor, black metal struts supporting the glass roof. Wilder sat behind a black-edged white pillar with his back to the wall, waiting. He blended right in with his black trenchcoat.

The Libyan made a final selection of postcards from the rack. He wandered over to a table at the perimeter of the café, by the blackboard listing the menu. He sat down in a chair and unbuttoned his camel hair top-coat.

Wilder had been waiting fifteen minutes and was fifteen minutes late when he'd finally found the place. The Ayrab wasn't going to show. He was hungry and needed something to eat. He saw the chalked-up menu and went over to take a look, try to figure out what it meant.

The Libyan was writing postcards to the many members of his family. Photographs showing the brown slab Parliament buildings, the University and Fantasy Land. He wrote the address and in the space for the message on all the cards: 'Bonn very good.' The waitress brought him an orange juice with a double vodka in it. He reached for the drink as the waitress turned to the man in the black trenchcoat by the menu.

'What's this . . . ?' Wilder wanted a hamburger. 'Hamburger. That's German.'

They had no hamburgers and he settled for the wiener schnitzel.

The Libyan recognized the American from his photo and asked him for a light. The arranged signal.

Wilder pulled out his Dunhill. 'Where you been, buddy?' He held out the flame, leaning on the table.

'I don't smoke.'

The Libyan got up and collected his postcards. 'We go.'

'What about my food?'

The Libyan started off towards the staircase leading to the street. Wilder made his way back to the pillar where he'd left the blue box, sending over a couple of chairs. By the time he got back to the menu the camel coat was lost in a group of nuns descending the steps. He caught up with the Libyan as he was getting into a green BMW and was about to hand over the box when the Libyan told him to follow his car.

'How'm I gonna do that?'

'Get taxi.'

Wilder hailed a cab and the two cars rode in convoy south out of Bonn and up into the Siebengebirge hills overlooking the Rhine valley.

'Why are you holding me?'

The interrogator had his jacket off. '*Wer ist Herr Vargas?*'

'I never heard of this Vargas. Vargas means nothing.'

'*Warum sind Sie hier in Bonn?*'

'I came here on vacation. And to collect some money.'

'*Was für Geld?*'

'A severance cheque. I'm flying home to the States.'

'*Sie wurden gefeuert?*'

'I resigned.'

Halsey was tired. Tiredness audible in his voice. The questions didn't change. Repeated over two hours. He was answering more questions, those questions that were easy to answer like the questions about Vargas. The harder ones about Libya and what work he was doing he refused to answer, demanding representation and maintaining an ignorance of any reason why he should be in a German prison cell. The ignorance was genuine but a nagging doubt was eating away at his mind, sapping his energy.

'*Herr Vargas? Wer ist Herr Vargas?*'

'*Sie wurden mit Herrn Vargas in einem Auto vorm Lybischen Konsulat von einem Polizisten vernommen.*'

Vargas was Wilder. Wilder had another passport. Wilder must have a half a dozen passports. They wanted Wilder. That made sense. But if they had Wilder he would be involved. Wilder hadn't checked into the hotel as Vargas or he'd be in the next cell. Maybe he was in the next cell. Okay, keep it simple, try and stick to the truth.

'This Vargas. I gave him a ride,' Halsey said. 'Called himself Wilder.'

'*Von Liège?*'

It was possible Wilder had used the same passport crossing the border. That put them together in Belgium. But there was no reason to mention collecting him from Brussels.

'*Erzählen Sie mir mehr von dem Mann.*'

'I met him once in Libya.'

'*Und weiter?*'

'That's all I can tell you.'

'*Was macht er?*'

'I don't know what he works at.'

'*Warum fuhrt er einen falschen Ausweis?*'

Why was Wilder carrying a false passport? An easy question to answer and one Halsey wasn't about to, without getting himself involved. He caught the stare from ice-blue eyes.

'*Sie sind mit einer Deutschen verheiratet?*'

'We were married. Now we're separated.' Halsey felt safe again. Off the subject of Wilder. 'I haven't seen my wife in two years. And I'm not planning to visit her while I'm here in Germany.' Straightforward, simple.

One thing that occurred to him, sitting there for two hours. What if Jack had arranged this? He could see himself on Jack's shit list walking out on him. Jack not wanting to hand over the twenty-five thousand. It was a possibility.

Tripoli

'The bomb is el no goodo.' The words drawn out as though O'Brien were speaking to a child. 'I'm surrounded by fuck-ups. I have to do every goddamn thing myself.' He paced the office, glancing from time to time at the four-inch thick file on the desk.

Rimbaud sat facing the plastic-covered window from across the desk, his eyes closed. Not making any attempt to straighten Jack out on the essential points, such as Jack knew all along that the plans were no good. Letting him rage.

'I could've had my own intelligence agency. I could've gone into politics. No reason why I couldn't've ended up in the White House.' O'Brien took a slug of flash straight from the bottle. 'Where the fuck am I? Where the fuck am I now?' He pointed the bottle at Rimbaud. 'Tell me.' Poking Rimaud in the chest. 'I'm living in a garbage dump. In a country that has to be the armpit of

Africa. The Jew media is crucifying me. And you're hammering in the nails.'

Rimbaud was sweating. His skin yellow. He hardly listened to O'Brien.

'I'm being persecuted,' O'Brien said. 'By my own country. By America, the land I love. From sea to shining sea. I own three thousand acres of prime farmland. A prize herd. Three houses in Washington. I'm an exile. An outcast. I can't go back. I can't even step out of here at night in case the Marines come up the beach and grab me. You can't know how that hurts me.' He had a drink and sank to his knees. The bottle between folded hands, he said, 'Dear God, why hast thou forsaken me? Send me a sign O Lord.' O'Brien bowed his head for a moment of silent prayer.

'We thank thee O Lord for thy boundless mercy.' Opening his eyes on a level with the desk he saw the file. The answer that he'd prayed for was right there. He got up and reached for the phone. Rimbaud was slumped in the chair, his breathing shallow.

'Senator. Jack O'Brien.' O'Brien smiled. 'This is important. I want you to do your patriotic duty. I have something here that you should take a look at. Tripoli. I want you to help me stop a third world war. Hell, no. It isn't dangerous. How? By exposing a plan by Gadafi to get hold of the bomb. *The* bomb. You could ride this all the way to the White House. The White House.'

Bonn

'I don't think you understand.' The white-haired interrogator spoke in English for the first time. 'I said that your wife has been shot and severely wounded by a policeman at the airport. She opened fire with an automatic weapon on a group of Hassidic Jews at the Pan Am check in. Three were killed and a member of the ground crew was wounded. There was no choice but to shoot her.'

Halsey shivered.

'Your wife is a terrorist.'

Tripoli

Wilder got through, finally. O'Brien answered the phone on the second ring.

'This is Grenadier.'

'Huh?'

'Grenadier. I delivered the machine parts.'

'Machine parts?'

'I had to go way out to a forest in these mountains. The Ayrab handed over this envelope and went off into the woods. I get the envelope open, its deutschmarks.'

'And the money?' O'Brien found another gap in the blind and started searching for the staple gun. The yellow dog was back in the yard. A Green Beret was bent over the animal.

'I did what you said with the money.'

O'Brien wasn't paying attention.

'I had to get a ride with this tour bus.'

'What about the money?'

'I said. I did what you said with the money. I couldn't take care of the other problem. But the way I see it you don't have a problem any longer. Halsey's in jail.'

'That's disgusting.'

'What's that?'

'It's disgusting. This pervert is jerking off a dog.'

Bonn

Halsey stood naked in the cell. Stood naked in front of the TV camera, staring at the lens. The white-haired interrogator sipped chocolate from a plastic cup. He glanced at the TV monitor.

And carried on looking.

'Ist er Jude?'

'Is he Jewish?'

The hospital was the reverse of the cell, of darkness. White painted walls, nurses dressed in white, illuminated by banks of fluorescent tubes filling every shadow. Halsey was wearing black. Black fatigues they'd given him. He stood inside a phalanx of Grenzschutzgruppe Commando. Not all of them would fit in the big steel elevator. The six men left out had to run up the five flights.

The fifth floor had been sealed off by the Commando. They stood at intervals along the blank corridors. Halsey was aware that he was the only one without a bullet-proof vest. Or without an automatic rifle for that matter. Forced to stand facing the wall, his weight forward, he watched with one eye. Saw a communications center being set up in a glass office. Out the corner of his eye he could see a man in a white coat and steel-rimmed glasses having a whispered conversation with someone who had his back turned.

Words and unintelligible phrases drifted over.

Ten minutes and they led him away behind the elevator shaft. The white-haired interrogator was there beside an open doorway. He indicated that Halsey should go in.

He wasn't prepared for the shock of seeing Eva lying there in the bed. She lay lifeless against the white pillow surrounded by machinery that pulsed and flickered. Halsey sat down and took her hand. Eyes that were half closed opened and Eva smiled weakly. He returned the smile, not knowing what to say. Eva moved her lips trying to say something. He found a water bottle with a glass straw and brought it to her lips. She took a little.

'I'm sorry.'

Halsey couldn't hear her. He brought his handcuffed wrists up and rested them on the bed.

'I'm sorry.'

Her breath stank of decay. Halsey kissed her on the cheek and she smiled again.

They sat in silence. Halsey holding her hand. They had nothing to say to each other. He wanted to ask her why but knew she couldn't give an adequate explanation. She wanted forgiveness.

After only five minutes Halsey felt a hand on his shoulder. He swung around. The white-haired German gripped his arm, lightly. Halsey got up out of the chair, glancing back at Eva asleep. Tears came to his eyes.

Led down the corridor past the elevator, Halsey heard someone talking about a second operation, a severe loss of blood. Figures in the communications room. Eva's face on TV monitors. A shadow bending over her. Her face a mask of terror.

* * *

The cell door opened and in walked a tall fair-haired man in a herring-bone topcoat. He put out his hand. 'Bill Mason. I'm from the Embassy.'

Halsey was sitting on a bench that served as a bed. He half rose and shook Mason's hand, falling back as he released the firm grip.

'The police are planning to let you go. They would like you to leave Germany but I understand there will be no formal pressure. At least not until after the funeral.'

'What?' Halsey wasn't sure he had heard.

'I'm sorry,' Mason said. 'I assumed you'd been told. I'm afraid your wife died under the anesthetic. She didn't regain consciousness. Listen. Why don't we get out of here and I'll buy you a drink. You could use one.'

Outside, the streets were dark. Mason guided Halsey to a Mercedes coupé, treating him like an invalid, helping him into the passenger seat. Halsey felt numb. Eva was dead. Murderer or martyr, she was dead. Vague shapes drifted in front of his line of vision. There was a sensation of heightened perception. He was overcome with weariness. Events, half-images on the windshield. Living a nightmare. He tried to piece together the elements of this dreamworld into something coherent. Had he really seen Eva in his dream or was that a rationalization? Where was the beginning, where was the thread that linked this all together? At the back of his mind there was still Jack O'Brien. Jack O'Brien, a nagging area of doubt. Everything seemed to be just beyond his reach. The shapes of a simple puzzle. All you had to do was rearrange the order, then slot them into place. And Mason. How and why did Mason get him out of jail?'

'What color is this car?' Halsey said.

'Silver gray. 500 SL. You can't tell in the dark. All cats are black at night.'

The bar had a big illuminated sign outside. *Lederhosen der Angst.* A jolly Tyrolean place decorated with alpenhorns, alpenstocks, paintings of mountains covered in snow. Above the bar a collection of steins and at the back a glass case with a pair of lederhosen in white kid-skin. The three-piece band in traditional outfits played dance tunes. A blonde girl with pigtails pinned around her head, wearing a white apron, took their order and left a menu on the table.

Mason glanced at it then at Halsey. 'There are some questions I have to ask you.'

Halsey picked up the menu.

'*Was sind Knödel?*'

'Dumplings,' Mason said. 'I don't believe they're on there.'

'Your German is good. How long were you stationed here?'

'Two years.'

'CIA? Army intelligence? Where?'

'*Wiesbaden*,' Mason said. 'I'm supposed to be asking you the questions.'

'Routine debriefing?'

Two heavy steins went down between them. Halsey asked for two schnapps.

'*Zwei.*'

'I'll drink yours.'

Mason brought out a small cigar case, sliding the two burgundy leather halves apart. 'So why don't you tell me what the Germans wanted to know?' Without offering a cigar he pulled one out and rolled it around his finger tips.

'About my wife?'

'It would be had to believe that you happened to be in the same city having not seen your estranged wife for, what, two years?' Mason removed the ring from the cigar and placed it in a triangular ashtray.

'Life's funny that way.' Halsey collected the ring with his little finger. 'Havana.'

'Anything else?'

'Not that I recall.'

Mason clipped the end with a guillotine. 'Jack O'Brien. Did they ask you about Jack O'Brien and Libya?'

Tripoli

'He told me the CIA were planning to hit Gadafi. That he knows all about it. Read the story in *Time* magazine. Said I had a poisoned dart and a blow gun. That I'm gonna sneak into Gadafi's tent one night. This dart is made to look like a fly.' O'Brien snorted. Chasen sniggered, trying not to laugh openly. O'Brien's face was pale. He appeared to be severely shaken by the meeting he'd just had with Musa. 'Christ. I had to think on my feet. I said I had a lot of enemies who would print that kind of shit. Jews.

'Then I told him there might be a grain of truth in the fly story. The CIA had a training programme. Flies carrying poison dropped from high altitude in special containers designed to release on impact. They could be targeted on the barracks at Bab al Azizia.'

'Musa believe you?'

When O'Brien didn't respond Chasen went back to pecking away at the typewriter. It was hard to read Jack's writing in the candlelight. Tripoli was blacked out, a power failure. O'Brien was searching through the desk drawers. He found what he was looking for, a hand mirror, and began examining the reflection. Running his hand over the bones of his face, pulling at the loose skin. There was a lot of gray hair. It wouldn't take much to change his identity and he'd take ten years off his age.

Chasen returned the carriage and the candle guttered. 'Castle Dracula.'

Dye his hair black, get the photographs changed in his passports. Find another country to do business in. Syria. Damascus had to be better than this. Katz was in Damascus. It wouldn't be too hard to move in on Katz and squeeze him out. He could even maintain the office in Tripoli but at arm's length, using Chasen. Maybe with a new face he'd go and visit that bitch Elaine down on the farm. Figure out a scheme to get it away from her.

'I worked my balls off to build up that farm.'

Chasen kept his head down over the typewriter, trying to concentrate. He was getting used to these outbursts. They were becoming more frequent. Jack was losing his grip. Mood swings that might begin with a telex or for no clear reason. Francine was the only one capable of dealing with him when Jack was like this.

O'Brien sat by the door making a list on a legal pad with a pencil. On the first page he listed his assets, the farms, the houses, with valuations alongside each property. Most of the money was tied up in real estate in America, South America, England, Spain, France, Malta. Cash and securities in Switzerland. On the second page he wrote a shopping list: rice, tomatoes, beans, pasta, peanut butter, jelly. Canned goods, beef, fish. He ran a line through fish and put down scuba diving equipment. Then printed the word *dhow* in capitals and underlined it.

'You ever do any sailing?'

Chasen twisted round. 'Sailing.' He thought for a moment. 'Messed around on one of those little sailboats when I was a kid.'

'When you go into town see if you can pick up an atlas. Any maps of the Indian ocean and the South Seas.'

'Planning a trip?'

Overland across Egypt down to the Red Sea. Find a boat and hire a crew. O'Brien drew a sketch map on the pad. Filled in the open spaces with pyramids and a palm tree. Crossing the border could prove to be hazardous. What would happen if he got caught by the Libyan border patrols? Musa would have his balls. He sat back and reconsidered the options. Better all round to fly to Zurich. It looked natural. He could take care of business. Check into a clinic and leave with a new face. He screwed up the pieces of paper and threw them in the metal waste bin near the desk.

Bonn

The Tyrolean band had been joined by the blonde waitress in the white apron. She started to yodel. The barman, built like a mountain, moved in time to the music.

Mason edged closer. 'Had you made any plans?'

'I'm going back to the States.' Halsey finished his sixth schnapps. He watched the accordion player in his green hat with the feathers in the hatband and the white embroidered shirt.

'Would it surprise you to know that you've been subpoenaed to appear before a Grand Jury?' Mason leaned back.

'Let's have another round.' Halsey waved the stein.

'You don't seem unduly worried.'

The barman was lumbering in their direction. 'The mountain comes to Mohamed.' Halsey laughed. '*Zwei Bier und zwei Schnäpse bitte. Könnten Sie die Band fragen, ob sie* Edelweiss *kennen?*'

'They want you to testify against Jack O'Brien.'

'Against Jack? On what?'

'Arms law violations. And conspiracy to murder.'

'I thought Jack was working for the CIA.'

Mason shook his head. 'Jack used to work for the agency. Five years ago. He resigned. Certain financial irregularities.'

'I checked this out when I was in Washington. I told Langley what I was getting involved in.'

'Jack may have wanted you to believe you were involved in a CIA operation.'

'Jack never mentioned the CIA.'

'You may have wanted to believe it was an agency operation.'

'Hell. This isn't a question of my beliefs. I talked to a guy from Langley.'

'What was his name?'

'Smith.'

'Smith? That sounds highly plausible. What did this Mr Smith have to say?'

'That this was an agency operation. He checked it out on the computer and the computer blocked.'

'If you talked to Mr Smith and Mr Smith said the computer blocked, that doesn't make it an agency operation. Ask yourself this question. Why would the Central Intelligence Agency, an arm of government, monitored by a Senate committee, why would the US government get involved in the export of explosives and arms to a flaky Arab dictator who believes in terrorism as a political tool? That would make America responsible for the bomb outrages in Europe, responsible for the hundreds of dead and mutilated victims, some of them American servicemen serving overseas. Soldiers brutally murdered in the line of duty by the bullet from an M-16 rifle.'

Halsey felt he was losing his sanity. 'I have to take a piss.' He got to his feet unsteadily, dragging the table along and half staggered to the restroom.

Facing the white tiles, urinating. Water from the automatic flush cascaded down the porcelain. Halsey said, 'I'm going crazy.' The words bounced off the walls.

Two punks in black leather, yellow spiky hair, grabbed Halsey from behind. He fell, pissing his pants. They kicked at his head and kidneys.

'*Juden, Juden.*'

One of them slid on a pool of urine. Halsey caught him off balance, grabbing his hair, throwing him across the cement floor. The other ran out. Halsey managed to get to his feet, staggered over to the door and fell through at the feet of the man mountain.

Tripoli

O'Brien wrestled with the cork on the clear glass bottle that had once held Smirnoff vodka. 'I'll fix us a coupla drinks.'

A pattern of rings where the paint was down to the metal decorated the desk top. 'You'll feel better.'

Rimbaud sat the other side of the desk, shivering in the heat. He was running a temperature. His skin and eyes were yellow.

'You need a few drinks. Get some sun.' O'Brien's lips drawn across his teeth in a leering grin. He had on a crumpled white linen suit and a black and white polka dot tie with a dark stain. A lattice of red blood vessels fractured his face.

'Visit Bangkok. I hear the women only cost a buck a fuck.' He held up his glass. '*Votre santé.*'

O'Brien sipped his flash and orange juice. 'We'll talk when I get back from this meeting. I may have a big order.' He was in a good mood. The phone rang. He made a grab for it and fumbled, recovering finally. 'Yeah.'

O'Brien listened, making animal noises into the mouthpiece. Rimbaud saw his expression change, heard him shout into the phone, telling the caller not to fuck him around. He held the receiver away from his ear and emptied the glass.

'What's happening? Are they going to extradite?' O'Brien listened again. 'I don't give a shit what you think. I'm gonna nail the fucking bastard.' He slammed the phone down.

'Chickenshit asshole. Who the fuck does he think he is. Telling me what to do.' O'Brien poured more flash into his glass. 'Come on. Drink up.' Freshening Rimbaud's untouched cocktail. 'Christ. Who's running this operation?' His anger spilling flash over the desk. He looked at his watch and scooped the straw hat off the top of the typewriter. 'Tell Francine I'll take care of that shit when I get back.' Indicating a pile of papers with a wave of the hat.

Rimbaud watched O'Brien go through the door, wondering what he looked like. And couldn't decide.

O'Brien killed the engine of the BMW. The engine ran on. He was parked in a side street near the souk in the old city. It was hot inside the car. He tipped the straw hat back on his head and wiped sweat from his forehead with the sleeve of his jacket. Someone knocked on the rear window. A small Arab boy carrying a cake box. He got out and followed the boy in white flowing robes and skull cap down a narrow alley between two crumbling buildings. The air was cool. Harsh sunlight reflected off the white wall in the next street, blinding him out of the darkness of the alley. Then a blackness descended. A bag went over his head and he was bundled on to the floor of a waiting car. The car pulled away. He wasn't held but could feel something digging into his ribs.

The hour and a half drive was painful riding on the floor. O'Brien had trouble standing. Had to be helped the few feet from the car to the base of a staircase leading up into a building. He stumbled over the worn wooden treads. At the head of the staircase an arm guided him through a narrow opening and led him to a chair.

When the blindfold came off he saw himself reflected in a broken fragment of mirror resting on a bamboo table against the wall. In front of the mirror was the white cake box. He looked around. There was no one there. The primitive door stood half open. Light filtered in through the closed shutters. O'Brien stood up. He could make out palm trees, the tower and egg box roof of a mosque.

'Your hat, Mr O'Brien. I'm afraid it is damaged.'

O'Brien turned. He took the crushed straw hat from the short bearded man in the kefiya with a face he recognized from newspaper photographs, but couldn't put a name to.

'I think you know Mr Gianni.'

Fredo stepped from behind the Palestinian. 'Jack and I go way back.'

O'Brien said, 'Listen. I'm sorry. I'm not gonna have any business dealings with that faggot.' He pointed at Fredo.

'Mr Gianni is here on another matter. That has nothing to do with our discussions.'

Fredo said, 'I'm just leaving. Thought I'd say hello.'

O'Brien punched the straw hat, straightening the crown.

'You need a new hat there Jack.' Fredo smiled. '*Ciao*, Jack. *Va fa ncula mamma'de.*' Fredo shook hands with the Palestinian and left.

The two men standing in the white room watched him go.

'Mr Gianni has been very helpful to us. Even though Colonel Gadafi is our friend, it is often useful to have many friends.

Particularly since we are in a strange land. You must tell me how you find living in Libya. This must seem a very alien culture. Perhaps you need our friendship.'

'I need to get out of this shithole,' said O'Brien.

'Libya is primitive. You shouldn't judge the Arab people by what you see here.'

O'Brien grunted. 'I want a villa or apartment a little closer to civilization. I don't care where.'

'And in exchange we would receive the benefit of your knowledge. Your business skills.'

'You know the kind of set up I have here. I can supply your requirements, if you have the money.'

'Money is not a problem. Our only problem is whether or not we want to do business with you.'

'Can you trust me?' O'Brien grinned.

Bonn

Halsey had woken up in his hotel bed. There was a moment as he came awake when he thought the last forty-eight hours had been a dream. Then he'd felt the pain in his ribs and stinging skin abrasions. He couldn't remember how he'd got back to the hotel. He did remember drinking schnapps and had a hangover to remind him anyway.

Halsey came fully awake as he dived into the ice-cold water and swam the short distance to the other end of the plunge pool. As hangover cures went, this was more severe than he needed. He heaved himself out, collected his towel from the base of a fluted stone column. The steam from the steam room drifted over the pool like a fog. Halsey put the towel between his legs, defrosting his balls. The circle of Greek pillars supporting the glass roof appeared and receded in the mist. He walked around the pool, up the steps and past the steam room to the lockers.

Out of the shadows came a figure Halsey knew, draped in a towel. In that instant Halsey realized why Wilder was there, even before he saw the automatic come out of a fold in the towel. He saw the gun level with his chest and heard the click.

Wilder said, 'Would you believe it?'

They stared at each other for an instant. Wilder ejected the jammed shell and extended his arm. Halsey was gone, disappearing in the mist.

Wilder said, 'You lucky son of a Jewish bitch.' He could hear shadows whispering.

'*Was ist los?*'

There was no other exit. Halsey had to be in the baths somewhere. He was cornered. Wilder moved towards the open spaces around the pool where he was sure Halsey was hiding. He glanced in the steam room and carried on by. The mist eddying, falling down the stone steps leading to the water. Droplets of steam gathered on the pillars and ran down, forming rivulets. Sweat collected in Wilder's eyebrows and fell as salt tears on his cheeks.

A loud splash ended a shallow silence. Wilder went down the steps, the gun hidden. A sound like thunder boomed from the direction of the locker room.

'You're dead, Halsey.'

The words came back in low German tones.

'*Tot.*'

'*Sie sind tot.*'

'*Tot.*'

Salt from his sweat stung Wilder's eyes. White figures loomed out of the mist, disappearing in the space of a few feet.

Halsey sat on the steps by the pool, leaning against a pillar, his head shrouded in the towel. It would soon be time to make a move. He had to depend on seeing Wilder before Wilder saw him.

Movement sent steam sweeping across the pillar. Halsey prayed.

Wilder wiped his head with the towel, showing the gun resting on his chest. He was aware of the bent form near the pillar but he had to get in front by the pool. It would be unprofessional to shoot the wrong guy. What should he say? Good morning was about right. He could say good morning in German. With his back to the pool Wilder said, '*Guten Tag.*'

Halsey sprang off his toes without even looking up, hoping to catch Wilder under his ribs.

The gun fired, setting light to the towel and grazing Wilder's shoulder. He fell, arms thrust out, falling backwards into innocence. The step under the water met his head and blood billowed out carried by the waves. The gun dipped through the surface and spiralled to the bottom, coming to rest on the star and crescent tiles. Blood clouded the water.

Halsey threw on his blue shirt and jeans. He had no idea what the fuck was happening but he surely didn't want to be around when they hauled the body out the pool. He fumbled with his shirt buttons, hearing the sound of distant sirens.

There were no windows in the mahogany panelled locker room, only air vents. So one entrance, one exit, the main lobby.

The halls were deserted. No one around to try and stop him leaving. The ambulance and a police car were arriving as he hit the main staircase. By the time he got to the ground floor the ambulance crew were bringing in a gurney. The uniformed desk man was talking with the police car driver.

It was all down to timing. All he had to do was walk out very slowly, keeping the whole thing relaxed. If anyone said anything he might say he heard there was an accident, leave it like that. Or pre-empt the questions by asking one of his own – where's the accident?

Halsey stood to one side of the lobby as the gurney went by, followed by the second policeman.

He waited until the ambulance men were across the lobby and halfway up the marble staircase before making his move.

The desk man and the police driver were deep in conversation. He got as far as the kerb.

'*Ein Moment, bitte, mein Herr.*'

Halsey was level with an Alfa Romeo Guillietta. The Alfa engine came to life, catching his immediate attention. A woman behind the wheel, wearing dark glasses leant over and opened the passenger door.

'Get in.'

Halsey recognized her. He turned to face the two men on the steps of the entrance and smiled. He held up his arm and waved, backing into the car.

'Let's get out of here.'

The Alfa took off into the traffic.

After the first corner, Halsey said, 'Listen. I may be in some serious trouble with the police. Why don't you just pull over and let me out?'

'What did you do? Piss in the pool?'

'Just pull over and let me out. Thanks for the ride. I don't want to see you get involved.'

'I have my own reasons for not wanting to talk to the police. We will leave the car by the market and walk away. I will buy you a drink.'

Halsey sat back. 'Why'd you walk out on me that night in Tripoli?'

Marielle Bayer laughed. 'I flew out for Sahbah the next day. There didn't seem much point in saying goodbye.'

The marketplace was hemmed in by eighteenth-century buildings. They zig-zagged across the square between the stalls under striped awnings, around the back of the university and into Munster Plaza. Bayer found a table at the café across from the Pizza Hut. They sat down and ordered beer.

'Up until now my most serious run-in with the law was a box full of unpaid parking violations. Now I'm on the run.' Halsey thought for a moment. 'And what were you doing hanging around outside the baths? Waiting for a pick up? What the fuck am I doing sitting here having a drink?'

Bayer took off her dark glasses.

'I was a friend of Eva's.'

A couple of pieces fell right into place. 'You used to work with Eva?'

Bayer nodded.

'And that explains what you were doing down in Libya.' Halsey slowly shook his head. 'Was Eva down in Tripoli?'

'She spent some time there a year ago.'

Halsey was silent, watching people go by.

Bayer said, 'I'm sorry.'

Halsey said, 'You were good friends?'

'We went to the university together.'

'I hadn't seen Eva for two and a half years. That's the same period as our marriage. Did Eva ever talk about me?'

'Eva and I were apart when she married. I went off to work in Lebanon. She wrote me letters about you and Willhelm. I came back, you had split up. She was depressed and didn't want to talk. She cut herself off from the past.'

'I don't think we had much of a marriage. She married me because I'm a Jew. Not much of a Jew. Her mother told her not to marry a Jew. That was reason enough for Eva. I was exotic. A rare fruit. She was fascinated. I was attracted to Eva for the same reasons – the daughter of a Nazi war criminal. She found me attractive and I was attracted to her. A mutual bond, but it wasn't enough to keep a marriage together.'

'Please don't be sad. Eva wrote many good things in her letters about you and Willhelm. You were the family she never had as a child. Eva was depressive, I think. She was haunted by the past. I will show you the letters.'

Halsey said, 'I don't think I want to read them. I feel like I'm sinking in a lake of quicksand. How the fuck am I going to drag myself out?'

'Let me help.' Bayer covered Halsey's hand on the table with her own. 'Why don't we go for a walk?'

'In the deep dark forest.'

'In the Hofgarten.'

They strolled across the grass under the chestnut trees in front of the Friedrich Wilhelms University. The sun was shining out of a pale blue sky. A couple the same, apparently, as any other. Tall trees shadowed them. Shapes that tremored at the edges.

'So how did you track me down?' Halsey said.

'One of our group has access to the GSG9 computer.'

'What does the computer say?'

'Nothing of interest. But there is a code after your name that could not be identified. Possibly alert CIA.'

'Does Jack O'Brien appear?'

'I can't recall the name.'

'And you don't know who Jack is?'

There was no sign of recognition on Bayer's face.

'That was his villa in Tripoli.'

'I heard about the party from an American soldier. I wanted a drink.' Bayer allowed a beat, then said, 'You don't trust me, do you?'

'Right now I don't trust anyone.'

'Why are you running?'

'Because I have trouble explaining my life.'

'Are you going to tell me what happened in the Turkish bath?'

'I killed a man,' Halsey said. 'Now that may be something you do for a living.'

'And you just supply the means.'

'If I hadn't killed him, he'd have killed me.'

'Why did this man want to kill you?'

'It's Jack O'Brien wants me dead. This guy Wilder was a hired gun,' Halsey said. 'And I don't know why Jack wants to see me dead.'

'Will he send someone else?'

The question hadn't occurred to him. He thought about it for a moment and had to conclude that O'Brien might. 'It's a possibility.'

'What are you going to do?'

'My future may be written in the stars but right now I'd feel better with a gun in my hand and a plane ticket in my pocket.'

On the bus to Plittersdorf they sat close together on a bench seat. Halsey could smell Bayer's perfume. Their thighs were touching. The perfume haunted him.

From Plittersdorf they walked down to the river and along the quay to catch the car ferry. On the far side they turned and came back. Halsey said it was good to get out once in a while. Visit that far shore. Bayer was in a serious mood. Halsey felt that was his problem. He didn't take life seriously.

They rode another bus along the Kennedy Allee getting off near the cemetery, walked over to the line of taxicabs and got in the back of a white Mercedes diesel. There were one or two things on Halsey's mind. Uppermost was Bayer saying, 'Trust me.' Right, that's how they say 'Fuck you' in New York.

A red light. At the center of the intersection a tall roadside cross. The light changed. Seeing the funny side of things. Remembering O'Brien saying, 'I have trouble with your humor.' Where was O'Brien now? In church? On his knees, asking for forgiveness, delivery from evil. They rode in silence.

Bayer paid off the cab at the train station. She said, 'I'll see you back here in a half hour.'

Halsey had a question.

She smiled and said, 'Trust me.'

Inside the door of the Jesus Kirch there was an iron cage keeping the merely curious away from God. Beyond the iron bars the aisle led up along a line of gray pillars to an ornate altar. Carved cherubs smiled down from a sunburst on to a painting of the baby Jesus with Mary and Joseph, framed by pink marblized columns. Bayer did not see the light-skinned Arab in the camel topcoat come up behind her. He had a McDonald's take-out bag in his hand. A Luger and a Walther with a box of 9mm shells to go.

Halsey had his feet apart, hands down by his sides, standing on the Misrātah rug in front of the TV. In one hand he had the Interarmco Luger, in the other a full clip.

The bathroom door was open and he could hear the shower running. Music came from the TV. An orchestra playing on the small fourteen-inch screen.

Bayer came out of the bathroom, wearing a white robe.

'What are they playing?' Halsey said.

'Wagner. Siegfried. Siegfried is about to kill the dwarf, with his sword. Notung.'

'The sword has a name?'

'He has forged the sword because he knows no fear.'

Bayer ran a towel through her hair. 'What shall you do?'

'Find Jack O'Brien. Talk to him.'

Halsey ran a finger over the scarred grip of the Luger, before putting the gun and the clip on top of the TV. He was sure it was the same gun Wilder had and was due to deliver to the Libyans.

'You should kill this man before he kills you.'

Halsey thought about it. Kill O'Brien in cold blood. Did he have a choice? Kill O'Brien or run. Run where? His ribs ached and there was a tenderness around his kidney area. He'd killed Wilder. But that was in self defense. So wait until O'Brien tries again? Then kill him. That makes a lot of sense. Jack's there with a gun in his hand. Then kill him. If he was lucky again and the gun jammed.

'You seem in pain.'

'Yeah. My ribs.'

'Have you seen a doctor?'

'No.'

'I'll examine you. Take off your shirt.'

'Are you serious?'

Her face was close to his and he could smell perfume. See her breasts under the robe, the belt loose.

'Any blood in the urine? Concussion? Difficulty seeing? Ringing in the ears?'

Halsey unbuttoned his shirt.

Bayer looked at the severe bruising. 'You should have this X-rayed. I don't think there is any permanent damage.'

'Where did you study medicine?'

'In Lebanon.'

Halsey reached forward and untied the robe. She had on a gray camisole. Her skin was cool to the touch.

Bayer said. 'I can't find anything wrong with you.'

He kissed her on the lips.

She said, 'Lie down on the floor.'

He obeyed. She straddled his chest, kneeling. Throwing off the robe. The thin band of silk pressed against his face. She pulled the material to one side. He tasted her. She leaned forward, riding his face. The rough stubbled against her thighs. He ran his hands up her buttocks and slid his right up the leg, tracing the line of her ass and fingered her anus. He was drowning in her cunt.

Bayer began unbuckling the belt and unbuttoning his Levis, releasing his prick. Her hand grasped the root and she bent over, taking him in her mouth. Halsey watched her lips slide over his hard length reflected in the TV. He closed his eyes.

He opened his eyes and she stood there above him slipping the camisole slowly over her head revealing her breasts. She knelt on the rug, showing Halsey her ass. He got up on his haunches and his hand against her cunt. The soft flesh parted to the touch. He held his prick and mounted her, sliding his length up to the hilt.

He drew their flanks together in even strokes, glancing at the reflection in the TV and seeing the orchestra playing. Thinking what a great ass this woman has. He lay along her back and grazed her breasts with his right hand gliding the other across her belly to find her slit.

He could feel her coming and fucked her hard, slapping against her ass. Fucking her harder. Then, grabbing her and holding their bodies together, letting go, feeling her cunt spasm, his prick jerking sperm into her.

They lay together on the rug. After a while Bayer said she was cold, so they moved to the carved four-poster under the eaves. The bed was draped with heavy patterned linen. The design showed medieval hunting scenes. The bed was a room within a room. In the semi-darkness, exhausted, they fell asleep.

Halsey woke up vomiting blood. A voice said, 'It's gonna be okay.' He was moving past panels of light. A face wearing a green mask loomed up. He saw the eyes upside down above the mask and recognized the face.

'Has he had a pre-med? Get him in the theater.'

Circles of green uniforms merged into one articulated sculpture that was breathing. He became part of the mass, drawn into its center, raised up, engulfed. A black muzzle was held up to his face. Another voice said, 'I'm having trouble with this valve.' Halsey saw the face, the same face, sure now that beyond his reach was the name.

A woman's voice this time said, 'What music do you want on Doctor O'Brien?'

'Let's have the Wagner.'

Halsey woke sweating, hearing the faint music from the TV. Without disturbing Bayer he climbed out of the bed and padded across the bare boards in the dark over to the rectangle of light. He hit the power button and the tube stopped pumping. Blue shadows spread out from the window. Below, the silent street, trees rimmed with sodium yellow. The scene was familiar and alien. He wondered what it would be like if the sun didn't rise in the morning. Twenty-four-hour night.

She touched his arm. 'What's wrong?'

'I'm afraid of the dark.'

They awoke just after seven. Bayer was awake minutes earlier. It took five minutes with her mouth to wake him. She had a wide mouth, taking him down deep. Releasing him and running her tongue over the domed head. Halsey rose up on his knees and slid an arm between her legs to finger her cunt. He grabbed her ass, pulling her under him. They were sinking in the feather mattress. He held her buttocks, using his weight, thrusting. Her orgasm made him empty his balls.

She had to slip out from under his body. There were droplets of sweat clinging to her skin. She collected the bathrobe from the rug and went in the bathroom. Sitting on the bidet, she urinated and watched the sperm trickle out of her.

Halsey found her in the shower. He stepped in and they wrestled for the jet. She soaped his back, his front, his legs, finishing up with his prick. Soaping and masturbating him until he ejaculated against the triangle of hair between her legs, rubbing it in between her lips.

Bayer left him showering to fix breakfast. He switched the flow valve to cold. The icy water sharpened his skin. Also shrank his balls, now drained.

He gave Jack O'Brien his full attention. The first thing, find out where Jack was. Call Francine. Go talk to him. Put the Luger to his head. Get some straight answers.

There was an absence of color in the kitchen. Everything black and white with silver appliances.

Bayer was loading a Krupps espresso machine. 'Do you eat bacon, ham?'

Halsey said, 'I'm hungry, not religious.'

They ate Westphalian ham and scrambled eggs, drinking bitter black coffee.

Bayer said, 'What are your plans?'

'We sound like a regular married couple. You asking me what I have planned for today,' Halsey said. 'Listen, that night in Tripoli, you knew who I was.'

'Yes.'

He wondered about her motives. Why he was there with her in what had to be a terrorist safe house?

'Eva and I were very close,' Bayer said.

'Were you ever in a place called Zlitan down the coast out of Tripoli?'

'Yes. I have been there.'

'To see the palm trees and the mosque.'

'There is a PLO house.'

'You're very trusting.'

'So are you.'

'Green. I'm a prize prick.'

Bayer smiled. 'I have no complaints.'

'Were you and Eva . . .' Halsey searched for a word. 'Lovers?'

'At university.'

'You see I was wondering if Eva left me for you.'

'That has symmetry. But it is not true.'

Halsey got up from the table with a cup in his hand, shaking his head. 'What the fuck am I doing here?'

'Kismet.'

He put the cup down on the saucer. 'Is it safe to use the phone? I want to make a call to Tripoli.'

'The house is checked for listening devices and the phone has a warning signal that cuts in.'

'Very professional.'

'We have to be professional if we want to stay alive.'

'I heard about those Mossad hit squads.'

'It had occurred to me that you might be working for the Israelis.'

'Why?'

'You're Jewish and have skills that Mossad need. Also you don't look Jewish.'

'Sounds like I have a career in this business?' Halsey smiled.

Bayer pointed out to him that he was already in the same line of work. Supplying arms to Gadafi. Halsey didn't want to get into an argument. Try and explain that he thought he was working for the CIA, justify himself by saying that he was obeying orders. And taking the money. Gadafi's money.

'Why don't I make that phone call and get out of here.'

'What will you do?'

'Find Jack, get the money he owes me. And blow his head off.'

Halsey had to dial the number three times before he got through. Once Chasen picked up the phone and he hung up. Finally Francine said, 'Concentration Camp Erhardt.'

'Francine?'

'Yeah.'

'Is that funny?'

'Depends where you stand.'

'Where's Jack.'

'In jail.'

'Jail?'

'He spent a few days in a Maltese jail. Doug had to go over with a pile of money and buy him out. We're planning a big party. Come on over.'

'Francine. Jack and I aren't exactly good buddies.'

'You and Jack. He loves you as a son. You know what Jack's like. Forgive and forget. Have a drink.'

When Halsey put the phone down he asked Bayer how she felt about a party in Tripoli.

She surprised him by saying she'd get dressed and what should she wear.

Tripoli

'I'm gonna kill that dago bastard.' Doug Chasen wondered which dago bastard Jack was talking about. It didn't pay to interrupt, asking questions.

'The cocksucker's jealous. He knows I pay more in tips than he earns in a year.' O'Brien was working his way down a bottle of Chivas Regal. And a revised hit list. He had reached an assistant US attorney. Now recapping on important listings. 'PLO mother-fuckers. Giving out PLO diplomatic passports that aren't worth shit.'

Chasen made the mistake of saying he thought the Palestinians didn't have a country. And if they didn't have a country, how could they issue passports? O'Brien explained carefully that the scumbag Israelis had made the Palestinians exiles. Israel belonged to the Palestinians. At this point Chasen made a joke, saying they should have given him an Israeli passport. O'Brien didn't find that funny. He became more morose.

'Jews and the Arabs, who gives a fuck? As long as I make a buck. The Arabs can finish what Hitler started. Then the Arabs'll kill each other. Dumb fuckers.' O'Brien poured another glass. 'You know. CIA need me as an analyst.'

'Man of your experience Jack,' Chasen said.

'Right. Those jerks out at Langley are small minded. Ivy growing up their asses. Jesus, if the President gave me DCI, and I agreed to go back there to Langley, I'd kick ass. Have Bill Mason as head of station in Tripoli. Make the punishment fit the crime.'

Chasen said, 'The punishment fit the crime?'

Jack repeated, 'The punishment fit the crime. A source of innocent merriment.'

'What?' Chasen said.

Francine came in, passing through the office.

'Francine.' Jack slapped her ass. 'The punishment fit the crime.'

Francine said, 'What?'

'The punishment fit the crime. It's a song. Working with fucking pygmies.' He shook his head.

O'Brien's mind moved on.

'That wop pansy. That son of a bitch deviant.'

'Are you talking about Fredo?' said Francine. 'If you're talking about Fredo, say Fredo.'

'Fredo.'

'What about him?'

'I saw the little faggot. He's working for the fucking PLO.'

Francine said, 'What is the world coming to?'

'What time are those freeloaders arriving?'

'Jack. These people are coming to welcome you home.'

'Drink my liquor.'

'Even Musa is calling by.'

'Shit.'

'You'd better sober up and hide the booze.'

'What the fuck does Musa want?'

'Like all your good friends he just wants to say how glad he is to see you back.'

O'Brien finished the whisky in one swallow.

Francine said to Chasen, 'That's the easiest way to sober Jack up, bring Musa into the conversation.'

'Any business to take care of?' said O'Brien, sober already.

'Nothing that can't wait.'

'Any phone calls? You hear from Wilder?'

'Grenadier. Nope.'

'Where's that . . .' As O'Brien looked for an expletive they heard a car coming down the track.

'Musa.' O'Brien grabbed the bottle and glass, beginning the mouthwash run.

'Breath fresh and minty,' said Francine. 'This is going to be a great party.'

The two men reached the bathroom. Francine called out after them, 'I forgot to put mouthwash on the shopping list.'

O'Brien searched the cabinet. All he could find was bleach and aftershave.

Chasen hit the stairs first. O'Brien struggling, catching his breath at the top.

Chasen had the kitchen cupboards open. 'Vinegar, oil. Oh yeah. Here's some lemon juice at the back.'

Jack had some of each and some catsup. Every bottle he said, 'Jesus I have to get out of this shithole.'

Airborne

'Jack's not going to throw his arms around me and say you're back in the fold.'

Halsey and Bayer were over the Mediterranean in a Swissair DC9.

'Probably pick up a metal bar and break my head.'

'That's why you have a gun.'

Bayer was wearing dark glasses and a Chanel suit in raw silk. She peered over her copy of Vogue, watching the aisle. 'What's the movie?'

'The Jewish Hamlet. "Maybe to be or Maybe not to be".'

'What?'

'Let's have a drink. Get in the party mood.' Halsey called the stewardess over. 'How about some champagne, since we're travelling first class.'

They drank two half-bottles of Moet Chandon. Bayer said that it was a very poor champagne. Halsey said that it went right down and wasn't flash. The delights of Tripoli.

'I haven't tried this flash,' Bayer said.

Halsey raised his voice. 'Flash is not something you try. You drink it.'

Bayer gazed out the window at the first stars. 'Have you ever killed a man?'

'No. Sixteen years. I never had to kill anyone. I never had to think about killing anyone. I saw bodies. Plenty of dead bodies. I could tell you what napalm will do to a body. What a tracer bullet will do. In sixteen years I never pulled the trigger.'

'And Jack O'Brien?'

'Jack tried to have me killed. Killing him is self defense.' He wanted to get a clear picture in his head of O'Brien standing there holding a smoking gun. And a glass of flash. He thought about the two French legionnaires kneeling in the dirt on that mountainside. Jack with a gun in his hand.

Bayer crashed her champagne flute against Halsey's. 'Drink.'

He raised his glass. 'A toast. To stars in the sky.'

'Okay. To stars in the sky.' She drank and ran her free hand along his thigh under the fold-down table. She said, 'Have you ever fucked a mile in the air?'

'Why not?'

In the shadows Bayer hitched up her skirt, revealing white flesh above her black stockings. She untied a bow at the side. Halsey watched, unbuttoning his jeans. She dipped a finger in the champagne then into her cunt.

Tripoli

'Musa made a joke. It wasn't a very funny joke but he cracked his face in what could have been a smile. A lot of teeth. Showing a lot of teeth.'

Everyone who came to the party heard Jack O'Brien tell the same story. Katz had flown in on his way from Angola to Syria. He and O'Brien greeted each other like brothers, kidding around, back slapping. They even talked about a business deal. Katz had brought Jack a gift. The mounted head of a gazelle. He made a presentation and said there was a story went with it.

'You'll have to get Halsey to check that out. The one identical to that was given to an African diplomat. The guy's plane mysteriously exploded over the desert. They can't locate the pieces of the fuselage, let alone the bodies.'

O'Brien wasn't smiling.

'Hey, Jack. I think I hear it ticking.'

Everyone was laughing except O'Brien.

'Jack. There's a call.' Francine was shouting from the other side of the room.

O'Brien left Katz with the audience of Green Berets and a couple of C-130 pilots.

'Yeah, who is it?'

'Wouldn't say.'

O'Brien was glad of the chance to get away from Katz. The fat kike. Don't do business with a kike. His father had said that to him. Even a dumb dirt farmer knew better than to do business with a kike. He followed Francine down the stairs. She had on a tight black cocktail dress, cut low at the front and back. When they got to level ground O'Brien ran his hand across her ass.

'Nice material.'

Francine said. 'Don't get your dick caught in the door.'

O'Brien went over to the desk and picked up the receiver. 'Yeah.'

The voice on the other said, 'It's Bill. I'm in town. I just checked in to the Al Kabir Hotel. Why don't you come over and we'll take care of business, then I can get on to the first plane out of here.'

'We're having a party over here. Why don't you come on over?'

'I can't do that, Jack. I have no desire to be seen at a party in your villa.'

'Right. You can take my money, but you won't have a drink. Well, fuck you.'

'Jack, you stand to make a lot out of this deal.'

'If I'm in this for the biggest piece, how come I'm not an officer of the corporation?'

'We've discussed this Jack. Your name could prove to be potentially embarrassing.'

Laughter came from the room above. O'Brien looked up at the ceiling.

'Big formal state dinner to honor the Minister of Transport, only he doesn't show.' Katz paused to take a little scotch. 'They go ahead and have the meal anyhow. After the soup the President gets up and says he knows that someone sitting at the table is working for the CIA because the Minister of Transport has told him. He goes around the table asking everyone, says how it's nothing, he has a big heart, he can forgive and forget. They keep their mouths shut. The waiters bring on the food on these big fucking covered trays. Three trays. The waiters step forward, take the covers off and it turns out the Minister of Transport could make it after all. But I think he should have stayed away because he doesn't look so good. His fucking head on one tray, his feet on another and the mess on the third was probably at one time his fucking dick. So the minister working for the CIA tries to make a run for it. Gets about as far as from here over to the door. The bullet takes the side off his head and spreads it across the wall. We finish the meal with the Minister of Transport on the table and the Minister of Trade on the floor and running down the fucking walls. You shoulda seen the look on his face when the cover came off that fucking tray and he saw the head staring back at him.'

'We still have half an hour to kill.' Halsey buttoned the fly of his Levis.

'Why do you kill time?' Bayer climbed into the black leather skirt.

'We could have a drink in the bar if they had a bar.' He slid the blue blazer on over the shoulder rig. It showed. But then he hadn't been wearing the gun when he bought the jacket in Bonn along with the jeans and a matching polo shirt. Two shirts, one for Marielle.

The Luger together with a 9mm Walther were waiting for them in Tripoli, hidden in the back of the sand-colored Toyota Land Cruiser parked across from the hotel. The guns had arrived in the East German diplomatic pouch. Halsey and Bayer were travelling on East German passports.

Bayer said, 'Why don't we go now?' She pulled the polo shirt over her head.

'Okay.' He looked at her breasts. 'I wouldn't know what to do with half an hour if we couldn't have a drink.'

Halsey went over to the door and stepped out into the corridor. The elevator doors were opening and Jack O'Brien and another man carrying a grip were getting into the car. He took a pace back into the room. The elevator doors closed and the car began to descend. 'Jack O'Brien just got in the elevator.' Halsey waited to a count of five and went back out the room, heading for the stairs.

When they got down to the lobby O'Brien and the other man were standing outside on the sidewalk beside a taxicab idling at the curb.

The yellow interior light showed Bill Mason fall back into the rear seat and O'Brien slide in alongside him, slamming the door. The cab pulled away past the gray outlines of tankers, a frigate, crammed in behind the arc of cranes that enclosed the flat oily slab of sea. Metal jibs stretching out over the water.

O'Brien said, 'I had Wilder take care of that problem.'

'I said take care of, not eliminate.'

O'Brien was trying to dislodge a shred of meat from his teeth. 'Either way we no longer have a problem.'

'You, not me.'

It pissed O'Brien off listening to Mason's holier than thou shit. Ivy growing up his ass. Headlights raked the rear window.

O'Brien said, 'Musa's men. Musa has an idea that I'm about to get the fuck out of this shithole.'

'The tight-assed little shit came to my welcome home party. Cracked a joke.'

They rode along in silence. The distant waves breaking on the shore audible above the rattle of the engine.

Half a mile on along the coast road, O'Brien said, 'That money doesn't belong to me. I'm investing it on behalf of some "friends" of mine.' Leaning on the word friends.

Mason read the warning.

Halsey behind the wheel of the Toyota said, 'They have to be headed for the villa.'

Bayer checked the clip on the Walther.

'This makes it easier.' He eased the Toyota around the bend. 'They're slowing down.'

A hundred yards from the track that led to the villa the cab stopped abruptly. Halsey swerved the Toyota on to sandy scrub littered with debris and killed the headlights.

'Why aren't they going down the track?' Halsey said.

'Something's happening.'

Ahead on the road the figure of Jack O'Brien.

They heard the door slam and saw the cab turn around. Halsey waited for the cab to go by. He crept the Toyota forward across the sand, making up the distance on O'Brien walking along. At twenty yards O'Brien stopped and looked over his shoulder. Halsey hit the lights and gunned the engine. O'Brien ran. In the space of five seconds the Toyota was level. Halsey braked, skidding the Toyota in front of O'Brien. O'Brien hit the side panel, doubled over the hood and sagged down into the ditch.

O'Brien returned to consciousness. 'You killed me.'

'You're not dying, Jack.' Halsey squatted down.

O'Brien recognized Halsey's voice. 'I thought you were dead.'

'Why would you think that?'

'Christ, the pain. I think I'm paralyzed.'

'I just shoved a gun up your ass, Jack. Now, why would you think that I was dead?'

'I heard.'

'Could it be because you told Wilder to kill me?'

'Why would I tell anyone to kill you?'

'Yeah. Why?' Halsey stood up and kicked O'Brien in the leg. 'Okay, let's go.'

'I can't move.'

Halsey kicked him again. He staggered to his feet, staring open-mouthed at Bayer.

Halsey pushed him towards the track.

The villa was flooded with light from the lamp suspended alongside the TV camera on the pole opposite the entrance.

'I want you to walk slowly ahead of me, Jack. We don't want to attract anyone's attention. When we get inside you're gonna send a telex to Zurich authorizing the transfer of twenty-five thousand dollars to my account. No argument.' Halsey jabbed O'Brien hard in the ribs with the gun barrel and he went down on his knees. 'Anyway. On your knees. I don't care, Jack.' He put the gun to his head. 'Take off your shoes. Don't fuck around, do it.'

O'Brien kicked off his shoes. The stones dug into his feet.

'Now take your belt off and unzip the pants.'

'Fucking deviant.'

'I want you to hold on to your pants, Jack.'

They were getting near the pool of light. Halsey took hold of O'Brien's collar, gripping tightly, pushing with the gun at the same time. The villa was in darkness. Sounds of shouting and a Supremes number belting out.

'Sounds like a good party.'

'We'll have a drink,' said O'Brien. 'Talk this over.'

'There's nothing to talk about, Jack.'

The lobby was empty. The telex machine under the staircase.

Bayer closed the front door. 'I'll get us a drink.' Starting up the staircase, singing, 'Oh tell me the way to the next whisky bar.' Looking back. 'No don't ask why. No don't ask why.'

'Sit down, Jack,' Halsey indicated the chair by the machine. 'Go to work.'

O'Brien sat down with Halsey at his shoulder watching. 'Out on the road there I thought, that's it. A hit team. Any second I'm gonna get a bullet in the head.'

'Why would anyone want to kill you, Jack?'

'I have enemies. That's why I can't go back to the States. My farm, my home, that old tractor of mine. I'm just a farmboy at heart. You know I had to sell my prize herd. That almost broke my heart. 'Hey, where's that drink?'

'You can have a drink when you finish the telex.'

Bayer came down the stairs holding three clear plastic cups full of whisky.

'How's the party?' Halsey said.

'There was a soldier with a dog on the table, masturbating.'

'The dog or the soldier?' Halsey said.

'The soldier masturbating the dog. Everyone was standing around watching. Some creepy guy kept putting his hand up my skirt.'

'What happened?'

'I kicked him in the balls.'

'Was he upset?'

'He cried.'

Halsey tried the drink. 'Johnny Walker. Is this Fredo's? Are you two back together?'

'What do you mean together?' O'Brien raised his voice. 'That son of a bitch faggot is working for the PLO.'

Bayer said, 'The PLO also sell whisky. No, don't ask why.' She held up her cup. 'Prosit.'

'Send the telex.' Halsey waved the gun over the machine.

O'Brien inserted the punch tape.

They heard heavy footsteps on the stairs. Halsey moved around behind O'Brien, the gun hidden. Bayer stayed where she was, staring up, waiting.

'Hi there, honey. I brought you a drink.' Gordon Wilder saw Jack first. 'Jack.' Thinking he might have caught him with his pants down. Since they were round his knees. Halsey came out of the shadows, the gun extended. The first thing he noticed was the Frankenstein stitching across the side of Wilder's face. That side was blue. The other his natural red.

'And I thought he was dead,' Halsey said. 'And Jack thought I was dead. Maybe we're all dead and this is heaven.'

Bayer said, '*Götterdammerung*.'

'What's that?' Wilder was looking for somewhere to put the drinks.

Halsey said, 'You better check him for guns. And he has a knife strapped to his leg.'

Bayer put her cups on the floor. She ran her hands up inside Wilder's jacket and found a small Beretta clipped to his belt.

'Hell, I could get to like this. Doesn't cost a cent neither.' Wilder thrust his crotch forward. 'Don't forget to check inside my shorts. I have a dangerous weapon located there.'

Halsey said, 'I'm glad we're all having fun.'

'What's this?' Bayer prodded the front of Wilder's pants with the gun.

'Hey, watch out, that's loaded.'

'What is it?'

'A surprise.'

Bayer slipped the safety catch of the Beretta and pushed the barrel against the tight white outline.

'Christ, it's only a sap.'

'Take it out,' Bayer said. 'No. With the other hand.'

Wilder produced a nine-inch blackjack from the pocket.

'Drop that and hold out your legs one at a time.'

Wilder dropped the sap and held out his right leg. The knife was strapped on with broad white linen tape. He screamed as Bayer ripped the flat blade away.

'You should shave your legs.'

'Hell, that hurt.' Wilder sank down on the stairs, nursing the leg.

She said, 'You must now take your pants down.' Wilder looked over at Halsey and O'Brien.

Halsey said, 'Do what she says.'

Wilder unzipped, unbuttoned and let them fall. Bayer burst out laughing at the fat legs and the shorts with the printed guns.

O'Brien swung round from the telex. 'How about that drink?'

'Hold on there, Jack. I think you slipped up. You forgot to type in the authorization code.'

O'Brien thought about altering the code but decided he didn't need to. All he had to do was call the bank.

'One more thing, Jack. We need a letter of authorization.' Halsey found a letterhead in the carton under the telex machine. 'Anyone got a pen? Or maybe you'd like to open a vein, write it in blood.' He handed O'Brien the sheet of paper.

O'Brien took a Mont Blanc fountain pen from his pocket, scrawled three lines and signed J. M. O'Brien. Halsey read the text and told O'Brien to fold the page.

'Okay.' Halsey took the letter. 'Time to hit the road. Let's go.' He waved the gun at O'Brien and Wilder.

'What?'

'Jack. We're all going for a ride.' Halsey smiled and pocketed the letter. 'Just trust me, Jack.'

Back outside in the half light behind the villa, Halsey opened the trunk of the BMW. They stood together out of the line of the camera in the shadows of the flood lamp.

Halsey said, 'Now, Jack. I'd like you to climb in there.'

O'Brien backed away from the car and into the knife Bayer held up around his ribs.

'Listen. All I have to do is shout and the whole United States Army'll be out that door.'

Bayer said, 'Don't breathe too deeply.' Making the point with the pressure of the blade.

O'Brien climbed in, holding on to his pants.

Bayer said, 'And now you, big boy.'

'Jesus Christ. I'm not having that fat fuck in here with me.'

Bayer ran the knife up the rear seam of Wilder's shorts. He was left hanging on to the two halves.

They fitted together, O'Brien and Wilder, head to foot. Two bloated sardines.

'Keep your hands off me.'

'Sorry, Jack. I can't move.'

Halsey said, 'Now you boys behave and be quiet.' He shut the trunk and said to Bayer, 'Okay. Get in, I'll give you a ride to the Toyota.'

Halsey drove slowly with the lights out up the rutted track. Low moans came from the back.

At the road Halsey put the brake on. 'Why don't you follow me?'

Bayer got out the BMW and went over to the Toyota. Halsey waited until she had the lights on and the engine running before he made a left down the coast highway, the car heading straight, the sea on the right, headlight beams glaring in the rear view mirror. The moon standing above the desert. A song was running around in his head. He hummed the tune, searching for the words. The tires making a noise like a stadium crowd cheering.

He listened hard but couldn't hear anything from the back. Then he hit a pothole and had to straighten the car out. The sound of moaning and groaning reached him. He smiled. The name of tune came to him, written in ten-foot-high letters carved out of rock, Murder She Said.

Ten miles from the border at around three a.m. Halsey made a signal for a turn, swung over the white line and slowed to a crawl. He glanced over at the map spread out on the passenger seat.

Half a mile, Halsey saw the lights and heard the noise about the same time. An armored convoy appeared out of a depression in the road. Rising up out of a cloud of sand. He swung the BMW back to his side of the line. An officer stood up in the front of the personnel carrier, leading the convoy. He signalled Halsey to stop.

The BMW came to a halt alongside the personnel carrier. Bayer pulled over fifty yards back. The officer climbed down, dusting off his uniform with a swagger stick. He walked around the BMW, then asked for papers. Halsey produced his passport. He listened for any sounds from the trunk. The officer asked him what he was doing crawling along the middle of the road. Halsey said he was sure he saw a camel and he was afraid there might be an accident. The officer spent some time examining the passport. He called Halsey by name, asking for his car papers.

Halsey said they were in the glove compartment and started moving towards the BMW, hoping the car had papers.

The officer shouted in Arabic.

'I'm checking the glove compartment here.'

The officer reached for his side arm. Halsey moved away from the car, reaching for the sky. He heard a door slam behind him but didn't turn around.

'Why don't you have a look in the car for the papers.' Halsey heard heels clicking along and saw the officer glancing over in the direction of the Toyota. The pistol in his hand swung off into space. Then Bayer called out in Arabic. Halsey craned his neck. He saw Bayer holding out her passport with an envelope inside. Fuck no, she's going to bribe him.

Halsey listened to the conversation in Arabic. The officer examined Bayer's passport. She said something and the officer took out the contents of the envelope. No money, just a letter. He smiled and handed back the letter, together with the passport.

The officer said to Halsey, 'I am sorry to detain you. We must be on guard against terrorists.' Handing back the passport. He saluted and went over to his personnel carrier. A muffled cry, barely audible, came from the trunk.

Halsey travelled to the moon and back inside sixty seconds. The officer walked past him, striking the bodywork with his swagger stick, setting up a round of cursing and shouting. Bayer spoke in Arabic again. As the officer listened a look of amazement appeared on his face. He hit the trunk violently, and then laughed as O'Brien and Wilder began screaming unintelligible threats.

The officer was still laughing as Halsey pulled away down the road. The convoy travelling in the other direction, spewing out sand.

Halsey breathed deeply and evenly. He wondered what Bayer had said and what was in the letter. On the left coming up there were dark shapes against the sky. The place he'd been looking for. He made a turn down a dry wadi. Headlights swept across the graveyard of abandoned cars. He saw the Toyota in the rear view mirror. There was a space on the right beside an old Cadillac Eldorado, a burnt out hulk. The place to park.

Bayer left the engine running. Halsey threw the BMW ignition keys as far as he could into the tangled rusting wrecks and strolled over to meet Bayer.

'I lost my virginity in a place like this. My old man wouldn't let me have a car. He had an idea I was going to get myself killed.' Halsey glanced back to the BMW. 'What did you say to the Libyan soldier?'

'I said that we were transporting dangerous CIA spies.'

Halsey said, 'What was in the letter?' He moved over to the Toyota.

'It's a letter from Captain Musa that says I work for him and that I have carte blanche.'

'Useful to have.'

Halsey found a nylon bag and brought out a wind-up alarm clock. He wound it up as he strolled back to the BMW.

'Okay, Jack. I'll be saying goodbye now. I'm leaving you with a little something to remember me by. It's right here on the trunk. Now if you don't move around, it won't go off.'

Halsey released the key and the clock started ticking. He took two pieces of tape from the face and secured the base to the metal. 'Frankly, Jack, I don't see how even James Bond could get out of this one.'

Taking the Luger from the holster he separated the cannon from the butt and sent the two halves in opposite directions.

They crossed the border in the Toyota. Sharing the driving the four hours to Tunis. Just before nine, arriving in Hammamet, they decided to check into a beach hotel and call the airport. From their beach cabin Halsey booked them on a two o'clock flight to Zurich. 'That gives us four hours to kill.' Halsey put the phone down and lay back on the bed next to Bayer.

'There you go again, killing time.'

Sean Connery walked across the field over to the Learjet. He was talking with Cec Linder, the actor playing Felix Leiter, his CIA buddy. Talking in Arabic. Halsey stared at the TV, remembering the conversation. Sean Connery asking why he was invited for lunch at the White House. Cec Linder telling him it's so the President can thank you personally for saving the world's monetary system.

He doesn't have lunch with the President because Goldfinger intervenes. Halsey imagined the President pacing the oval office waiting, pissed off because he wants his lunch.

Halsey wondered what the Arabs watching made of the movie. Under the white and orange silk parachute canopy Sean Connery and Pussy Galore, played by Honor Blackman, are fucking. Because that's the way James Bond films end.

Halsey ran his hand up Bayer's leather skirt, biting her neck. She was wearing laddered stockings. His hand reached her thigh.

Bayer said, 'Listen, I have something to tell you.'

'What? Is it important?'

'Yes.'

'What is it?'

'I have my period.'

'Oh.'

'It's all right. I have some jelly in my bag. You can fuck me in the ass.'

Bayer got out of bed and found her purse. She put the Walther on a side table and searched through the contents, eventually finding a small jar of Vaseline, handing it to Halsey. She threw her purse on the bed and raised the hem of her skirt up to the waist, then bent over the side table. He saw her pink anus, her white ass framed by the black line of her garter belt and stockings. Thinking Christ, I wish I had a camera.

Halsey said, 'This is going to change the whole basis of our relationship.'

'Don't talk, just fuck me.'

What would Sean Connery say now? Maybe: 'Oh, that reminds me to call Francine, tell her where Jack is.' Order a bottle of Dom Perignon '53.

A NOTE ON THE AUTHOR

Mark Wainwright was born in London in 1950.
After a career in film and television production, he is now
a full-time writer.